READER

Daughter of Time: Book 1

ERECSTEBBINS

Twice Pi Press

Only one thing is impossible for God: to find any sense in any copyright law on the planet.
—Mark Twain

This book is a work of fiction. Any references to historical events, real people, or real locales are used fictitiously. Other names, characters, places, and incidents are the product of the author's imagination, and any resemblance to actual events or locales or persons, living or dead, is entirely coincidental.

Published 2013 by Twice Pi Press

TwicePiPress@gmail.com

Cover design by Erec Stebbins. Hans De Ridder for the CAD model used to create the Orb. Images Copyright © 2013 Cardens Design (Kevin Carden), Bruce Rolff, diversepixel (Yvonne Less), and Petrenko Andriy. Images used under license from Shutterstock.com

ISBN: 978-0-615-76385-9

For Ambra:
I did what I could
and enjoyed the company

Time is the fire in which we burn.
—Delmore Schwartz

Point a

A child's life is like a piece of paper on which every person leaves a mark.

Chinese proverb

Chapter 1

$$\nabla^2\mathbf{A} - \frac{1}{c^2}\frac{\partial^2\mathbf{A}}{\partial t^2} = \mu_0 e\psi^\dagger\alpha\psi$$

$$\nabla^2\varphi - \frac{1}{c^2}\frac{\partial^2\varphi}{\partial t^2} = \frac{1}{\varepsilon_0}e\psi^\dagger\psi$$

Who sees the future? I am conscious of being only an individual struggling weakly against the stream of time.

Ludwig Boltzmann

The dream always began well.

It was a moist and warm spring afternoon, and a soft breeze blew over the lush grass of our backyard toward the house, carrying the strong smells of the newly tilled earth. The sun partially blinded me as I ran over the grass toward the edge of our corn fields, stumbling on my short legs, yet not falling, my arms stretched out to embrace a tall shadow in the light before me. I could not have been more than five years old.

The sun darkened as my father's broad frame eclipsed its radiance, and the shadow transitioned instantly into his familiar form. I leapt into his outstretched arms squealing, and his soiled hands caught me tightly and swung me around as I giggled, staring into his bright-blue eyes framed under locks of golden-red hair. Then he tossed me upward. The ground below me, half green from grass, half rich brown from the newly plowed field, receded as the blue sky enveloped me, and I felt the thrilling tug of gravity grab my stomach, and pull me back to Earth. Several times he threw me, and I went farther and laughed harder each time. Higher and higher I soared, until the blue turned black and the Earth below became a mere sphere, dotted with continents and oceans, and above the stars shone through the thinning atmosphere.

For a moment I floated, thrown so high I nearly escaped the bonds of gravity tying us to our home world, and the stars seemed to tug at me as well—beckoning me, luring me with a cold intensity that my child's senses felt as vaguely threatening. My giddiness began to turn to anxiety as I felt something wrong, something impure out there that waited in the diamond-pricked blackness in front of me. Something searching...*for me.*

But then I began to fall again, the air rushing over me, through clouds and air currents, seeing the ground first as a patchwork of squares and rectangles as from an airplane, resolving slowly to the familiar patterns of our neighborhood, and, at last, to that of my own family's farm. Spinning slowly in my downward trajectory, I saw my father from above, patiently waiting for me, arms outstretched with hands held high to catch me. The air whipped my clothes back behind me as I hurtled downward. Wasn't I going too fast, falling without aid from the edges of space? How could he possibly slow my momentum, catch me before I plunged devastatingly like some fiery meteor into the ground?

But he did. With a slight impact, I was caught and safe in his arms, some extra momentum diverted into a swinging motion, once more spinning me in circles until I laughed. Slowly, he came to a stop and set me on the ground, my head a mess and dizzy, my legs wobbly. He smiled down at me, tousled my hair and said, "Only you can go so high, Ambra Dawn. You were meant for more than just this place."

His words were so lovingly spoken, and yet in my heart they echoed ominously. And, as if in answer to my deep fears, his face clouded, and he focused behind me, rising from a partial stoop and gazing across toward our house. My eyes followed him upward, and then my entire body turned to track his gaze.

Standing outside the back door that exited from our kitchen was my mother, her long red hair caught like a sideways waterfall in the breeze. Yet she stood still. *So terribly still.* Her face was frozen in stone: anxiety, fear etched in every line. One arm was raised at ninety degrees to her body, pointing like an arrow in front of the house. She remained pointing, unmoving, like some directional sign indicating the path we must follow.

My awareness sped toward her, stopping in front of her face, then turning and following her arm from the bright light of the day outside and into the dim blackness of the kitchen, through the inside of our house, and then out again from the front door.

Three black cars with tinted windows were parked in front of the house. Out of these cars stepped a troop of tall men in suits and dark sunglasses, several of them very broad and muscular, with earpieces and wires dangling from them. I found myself no longer in a small child's body but now inhabiting that of a preteen of eleven years. They brushed me aside and herded my parents into the house. I followed behind them, feeling ignored and unwanted. A terrible sense of foreboding hung over me, and the darkness of the men's suits seemed deeper than that of the space I had gazed into only moments before.

Short, and yet long separations of time. The way of dreams. For me, the way of life.

They sat around the kitchen table, the smaller men talking to my parents, the larger ones posted like soldiers around the house and out by their cars. My mother was getting very anxious. She spoke with a shrill note in her voice. The small room was so still and quiet after the wind and openness outside.

"I don't understand. We don't know who you are. We can't just turn her over to you without more information, whatever you say."

"Mrs. Dawn," said the smallest man, with a raspy voice that made my skin crawl, "we are a special governmental division, and we have developed unique technologies for the military. One of these is a special type of laser. Army doctors have shown that it can be used to kill cancer cells. We can promise you a full cure, without major side effects. No one else can. But this is top-secret technology. We cannot share this with you or anyone else – not even your doctors. Therefore, her treatment must remain secret."

He took off his dark glasses and stared at my mom, but I was sitting behind him and couldn't see his face. "A doctor in the Omaha unit is a friend of mine. He was direct with me – she won't live past next year with current treatments. We are your only hope."

I saw my mother tear up and my father's jaw become set. "Now you look here. You've got no cause to be speaking like that and upsetting my wife. This is all irregular. Government or not, it ain't my way to trust shadows. If what you're saying is true, we'll work with you. But I've got to know more."

"But Frank, you *heard* him," my mom began.

"Never you mind what he said. I don't like this talk. We ain't shopping for some used car right now."

Just then, I dropped the wooden toy I was holding in my hands. It was a small hand-carved globe, with all the continents embossed on the surface. I can see it now hitting the wooden floor with a thud and rolling out of the kitchen to the living room. My heart constricted. *The Earth! I did not want to lose it!* The man in the dark suit with his back to me turned around, and then I screamed.

I couldn't help it. I was only eleven, and it was too much for me. That demon face – I had seen it before. In another dream. Dreams within dreams. His face was part of a foggy future vision, one I had forgotten and that rushed back through me like nails in my veins. Flashes of future memories whipped through my mind of pain, and fear, and loneliness, and horror – all connected to this face grinning back at me like some fiend from hell.

I ran. I jumped from my seat and ran like I've never run in my life. Behind me I half-heard the shouts of my parents calling my name and the harsh barks of this man to his soldiers. "Get her!" Then the horrible screams of my parents behind. But I could not stop running. That terrible sense in a dream of a monster approaching from behind grew within me, and I could feel its breath and fangs approaching, gaining ground, nearing to grapple at my back and legs.

I ran so hard I thought my chest would explode. Across the manicured green of our backyard, into the high fields of corn that spread out like a sea on all sides, grown thick now near harvest season. The stalks slapped me in the face, on my arms, across my chest as I ran, my breath like deep wheezings from some dying thing. Where was I going? I didn't know. *Away. I had to get away.* "On the other side of the cornfields," something screamed in my mind. There was safety, if I could just get through the fields, to the road, I would find a car, someone to take me to get help and protect me from the monsters following behind. I was close. My panting was like a windstorm in my mind. *So close.*

And then a sharp pain, a bright light like a flash in my eyes, and I was on my back, a dark figure towering over me. Warm liquid trickled down from my nose, and I felt too weak to move.

A second figure stood over me, blocking out the light of the day. In the shadow of his body, I saw that demon face again, smiling, laughing as he stared down at me.

"We've been looking for you for a long time, little girl. Don't think you can escape. Don't *ever* think you can escape from us. We have plans for you."

I couldn't respond: fear, pain, and nausea swept over me, and the world above me shrank to a small point as darkness filled in the sides. In a moment, all was black, and the sky was gone.

The same dream. Experienced countless nights. Memories of the past recreated. But this time it did not end with the darkness.

In that absolute black, I heard voices. *Your* voices. Millions of them, rising like an ocean of sound, a chorus calling to me across the ever-changing fabric of Time. And in that half-asleep state, moments before waking, when inspiration meets the practicality of day, I *knew*.

The answer was clear before my mind.

Chapter 2

$\forall x(F(x) \leftrightarrow x = n)$

In the world's audience hall, the simple blade of grass sits on the same carpet with the sunbeams, and the stars of midnight.

Rabindranath Tagore

Nothing is ever as it seems or is as it might be.

Stay with me for a while, hear my story, and then you'll understand. Understand just how different everything around you is from how you now believe it to be and maybe come to terms with just how important you are to what might someday come to be.

On the cover of this book you're reading is an author's name. He believes this story is full of his ideas, born from his own mind. It's not. *I* am writing it *through* him. In his reality, it's all part of a clever plot he's stitched together, even down to this very sentence that says he *isn't* writing it. Instead, it is the effort of my mind reaching out, back through what you call Time, and inspiring his mind, shaping his thoughts, convincing him of this reality.

Sounds crazy? It is. I know it is. And *I'm* the one doing it. But you should look down, grab the buckle and fasten your seat belt, because it's just going to get worse.

I don't enjoy doing this, playing puppet master with this citizen of your time. But our need is hopelessly desperate. More than you can imagine has been lost. And we are left with nothing but ashes in the cold of space.

I've done worse. This is dangerous, both for his mind and my own. Already, I have failed many times to send my message, and my efforts wrecked the receiving minds, driving them to madness. At other times, what has come out of the author has been a story so distorted, so warped by his own imaginings, that the message is lost, and can't achieve its purpose. Your libraries hold some of these disasters. I can only hope that this, my last effort, will not fail.

There is so much to explain, so much that you need to understand before you can accept the message, and take the step we so desperately need you to take. So many things—strange things, horrible things. Things that can't possibly be true, but are.

You will also need to understand something about Time. This may be the greatest stumbling block. Alone, it's like a monolithic stone, an arrow marching forward like some godlike unstoppable force, rolling through history. What has happened is frozen in the Past, untouchable and unchangeable, and what will happen, the Future, is determined by the Now. But the Universe laughs at such simplistic ideas.

The first thing you need to let go of is the idea that Time *is* alone. *Space* and time go together, and feed off one another, in grand loops and dances that change both. I know this, because this dance plays before my mind's eye like a rainbow in the mist.

Because of this, you must let go of the idea of the Past as set and the Future as something that does not exist. *Space-time* is an ever-existing clay trapped inside the great bubble we call the Cosmos. Like clay, it can be shaped, changing past, present, and future. Always with rules. But not yet with rules any creature has come to fully understand.

Sadly, these are only abstractions, colorless phrases that teach little and distort much of the living experience. I hope that you will understand more as you hear the story.

But it is only because of these truths that I can even reach you now, and only because of them that I need to. You see, as much as the future can reach back into the past, the *past* can reach *forward* into the future. And in our time of need, we need you of our recent past. You have a part to play in righting a terrible wrong, saving billions of lives, and reversing the horrific fate that has descended upon humanity. Somehow in these pages I must convince you of this. May I be forgiven if I can't.

My parents called me Ambra Dawn, and I am a Reader. But this is *our* story.

Chapter 3

$$S = \int \frac{\dot{x}^2}{2} dt$$

Wisdom leads us back to childhood.

Blaise Pascal

I was born in the yellow-green cornfields of Nebraska.

My father was an independent farmer, one of the last not bought up by the great agribusiness corporations of the twenty-first century. When I knew him, he was a tall and lanky man in his mid-forties of Scottish heritage, his fair skin always reddened and hardly tanned in the long summer seasons. He had crisp blue eyes and large hands that could tear open an ear of corn in a single fluid motion. When I was a small child, before I was taken from my parents, he would hold me in those huge hands like a small ear of corn, often tossing me high into the air as in my dream and laughing until a thousand lines creased his face.

He had a real gift for predicting the weather. Not trained in any meteorological sciences, he was a more accurate forecaster than the US Weather Service, which saved more than one harvest. It was one sign of the terrible genetics that would combine to produce me.

My mother was from a Celtic background too—an Irishwoman new to the United States. She *found* my father more than she met him, with a sense of destiny that she helped make come true. She looked like a stereotype out of a book of fables—a classic lady of the Green Isle, pale and redheaded, fiery in spirit and with her tongue. The recessive genes just keep adding up.

Even more than my father, she *forecast*, but she forecast broadly into many areas of life. Maybe four hundred years ago they would have burned her at the stake for witchcraft, but my mother was a devout Catholic and used no spells or prayers to divine the future. Such things just came to her. As I would learn painfully, they came not from the supernatural but from the all too natural, buried deep within her brain, in a soft spot of unusual tissue and blood vessels that any neurosurgeon, had he taken a look, would have dismissed as a small cyst – an unnatural growth of little significance.

Two years after they were married, I was born.

I got my mother's red hair and green eyes. Both parents' skin seemed to combine in me to the palest white possible outside of albinism. The real kicker, though, was a combination of genes that led to a tumor in my brain in the same place that my mother's small psychic cyst lay. We'll get back to that soon, because without that tumor, none of what I am going to tell you would have happened.

In the beginning, I was just a normal farm girl. Well, maybe *normal* isn't the right word. I was *definitely* a farm girl, though. By the time I could walk, I was playing with the animals, rolling in hay, and happier out in the air with the earth under my feet than anywhere else. How cruel is the irony when I think back on what has happened to me. What I would give now to see the sky again, to feel the earth underneath, or to run through my hands the fresh soil after it was plowed. To even know it was still there, that it existed *somewhere*—that would be enough, more than I would ask for after this terrible journey.

But normal, no, I guess I can't say I was ever really normal. Normal means seeing things and reacting to things like most people. Looking like most people. Being treated like most people. One after the other, I lost all these things.

First to go was seeing things like most people. Even early on, I think my mother knew something was different about me. When I got old enough to notice such things, it seemed that she was always looking at me like someone would an artifact from another world. She loved me, but she sensed there was something *other* about me that even a mother's love couldn't get beyond. Maybe it was her own sixth sense. But somehow, she *knew*.

In a way, that was good, because I never had to worry about surprising her or letting her down. I don't think my dad ever really knew, not even when they came to "cure" me. Which was good in its way, since his love never had to get through any walls and always reached me.

But the first time I realized I was a freak was when my dog died.

When I was eight years old, I was already experiencing many wild and strange dreams. After I described a few to friends and my parents, I learned by their reactions that some of my dreams disturbed them and were best left inside my own head. Crucified unicorns, roaches crawling out of my eyes, light beams causing holes to sprout and blood to pour from my arms—that kind of thing. But I had learned by then the difference between reality and dream. Or so I thought.

One night I dreamed that our sheepdog Matt died. Matt had been with us from a few years before I was born. In the dream, he was running around in a thunderstorm, barking like he does at the deep subsonic roll that drives some dogs crazy, and in a flash of lightning, he seized up, just fell over, dead. In the dream, I could see inside him, saw the clot in his heart, watched the life like some light dim in his mind. I woke up shaking and afraid, but I didn't tell anyone. Another dream to keep to myself. One I could slowly forget.

Three weeks later, a storm front rolled in from the west. When relatives would visit from other parts of the country, my dad would always talk about the weather and make his flat joke (as my mom called it): "Well, it's really flat out here this time of year." Nebraska is *really* flat, and you can see the storms coming for hours in the daylight, an express train made out of dark, gray mountains pushing like a tidal wave across the plains. I started shaking again, not because I am afraid of storms, but because I was afraid of *this* storm. Because I had seen it before.

Then the sun darkened, and the rain poured down on us like syrup, and I watched like I might a horror film on TV the replay of my dog barking and running and falling over dead in the grass. This time I couldn't see through him. But I knew. I knew what was inside.

And I knew I was a freak.

It's hard to be normal when you don't see things like other people. In my case, I saw things that no one else could see. Visions in Time. Not intuitions, not a vague sense of doom or excitement – *visions.* They began in dreams but soon came even in the waking day. Not only visions of the future – for a

Reader, it's actually a lot easier to see into the past. Visions of what was and sometimes, what was to be, came more and more frequently, disturbing my days and my nights, pushing me further and further from people, walling me off from the normal world. Believe me, when you have seen your own birth, watched your mother scream in agony as she pushed you into the world like some deformed lump of lasagna, it changes you. When you can't tell anyone around you these things, not even your parents, you are trapped in a prison where you slowly form your own thoughts. *Different* thoughts. Thoughts that shape you inside and out.

And that is when you lose the ability to think like normal people.

By the time I was ten, I was one odd little girl. I couldn't really relate to the kids at school or to any adults. All I had were my own thoughts and, of course, the visions. Like some ghostly companion, they were always with me, playing reels behind my eyes, movies only I could watch. Some boring. Some interesting. Some horrible. Things I knew were somehow real or that I feared would be real someday.

I became ostracized by my peers. My teachers couldn't reach me. My parents became very concerned. Finally, they took me in for evaluation. A few examinations by psychologists, then doctors, and, at last, the neurologists. Brain scans. *Finally*, there was something concrete they could hold onto, something clearly wrong with me, something to explain all the weirdness and problems.

And something that brought me to the attention of those dark forces that really control the fate of our world.

Chapter 4

$e^{i\pi} = -1$

Behind the ostensible government sits enthroned an invisible government owing no allegiance and acknowledging no responsibility to the people.

Theodore Roosevelt

If I could give you any one piece of advice that I think would help you in your time, I would say turn off your TV.

Unplug it, place it on a cart, and roll it into the river. *Never* watch it again. Take your video game console and controllers – build a bonfire. Don't *ever* go online again. I'm completely serious. What I know and what you don't, is that all our digital technology was not the product of our tremendous cleverness like everyone believes. No, it was a gift, *from above*. Or rather, a poison, a drug—electromagnetic narcotics for controlling their human herds. Call them high-tech cattle prods, if you want. To *Them*, you're all just a gene pool with potential, kept docile and reproducing ignorantly while the greatest show on Earth called *human culture* plays out. One giant sham.

Some of you know it. Some of you with half-awake Reader potential. Some of you feel it. Some of you outcasts, those who never fit in and end up on the streets or in the mountains or in institutions—you knew all along much more of the truth than our comfortable and successful herds. You suffered that deep discomfort, afflicting all your thoughts and actions, that sharp sense that something is wrong, deeply wrong with the world and how it is being presented to you. The sense in the back of your mind that things *don't fit.*

Well, they don't. I'll explain more as we go on. Meanwhile, pick up a book, go stare at the stars. *Think.* You're a junkie, strapped into a pleasure tube – a pig ready for the slaughter, or worse. Don't let them control your mind anymore. Advice from a former slave. Take it or leave it.

My journey of bondage was about to begin. The brain scans were very clear. Even at eleven years old I could understand. Also, there were vague visions, like half-glimpsed dreams. In the beginning, Reading the future is like that, more like *remembering the future* than seeing it. The past too is like a memory, slightly out of focus, sometimes wrong, but mostly right. The future, well, that's like a wild dream. Ever woken up from a dream, the details like colors bleeding out from your mind, until several hours later, you can only hold onto the most basic and faded outlines? That's a vision of the future. Most of them, anyway. Sometimes, like a horrid nightmare, the vision will be so strong you remember almost everything. Like a nightmare, these visions, *prophecies* if you want, will shake you out of your normal state of consciousness. It's a psychic slap in the brain. But those are very rare. Mostly, it's half-remembered somethings you can never quite place.

Those were my visions of my own future, of my illness, of the soon-to-be nurtured tumor in the middle of my head. The doctors were amazed I could still see. The mass was the size of a golf ball then – quaint to me now, really. Near the back of my brain, it was lodged, growing, between what neurologists call the occipital and parietal lobes. These are basically big slabs of your brain that do different things. The occipital lobe, at the very *back* of your head, processes visual information from your eyes (which are at the front of your head – God works in mysterious ways, believe me). The parietal lobe does a lot of things, like sensing where you are, navigating, working with numbers, moving objects. No, I'm not a doctor. What I am is a freak with a freaking tumor growing in the middle of all this stuff, so, well, it *matters* to me.

The tumor was mostly growing out towards the occipital lobe like some elliptical golf ball, crashing into all those cells that process information from my eyes. The doctors were amazed I wasn't blind yet. My parents looked sick listening to all of this. I was half-scared, half-remembering some blurry future where all this stuff wasn't nearly the worst that was going to happen to me.

"It appears to be a fast-growing tumor," one of the doctors said. "Many children's tumors are, growing quickly, the cells dividing quickly like the rest of the growing body, but even worse. This is very serious, and very difficult to treat. We recommend you send her to specialists. We can't treat her here."

So began the long search for doctors across the country. Nebraska has some good medical facilities in Omaha, but they still referred me to New York, to Sloan-Kettering Cancer Center. My parents were on the phone for hours and hours to doctors and relatives in the area. By then we'd all seen enough doctors' offices to last a lifetime. And all the time, the brain scans showed the thing inside my head kept getting bigger. We prepared for a long trip to the East Coast.

Then one day, just like in the dream, without a phone call or any kind of warning, three black cars with tinted windows pulled up to our farm. Out of these cars stepped the men of that nightmare that I relive over and over again. They came, they tried to convince my parents to release me into their "care," and when my parents would not, they took me by force.

When I awoke from the blackness, I was being roughly unloaded from the car by one of the burly men in a suit, maybe the very one who knocked me unconscious. He threw me over his shoulder, grunting as he carted me towards a bland building covered in metallic gray like some enormous warehouse. In my foggy vision it seemed so unimportant, so featureless and unreal, yet it would be my home for many years to come. My prison. A place from which, as the man had promised, I would not escape.

Chapter 5

$$\nabla \cdot \mathbf{E} = \frac{\rho}{\varepsilon_0}$$

Madam, I have come from a country where people are hanged if they talk.

Leonhard Euler

While I lived as their prisoner, before I was sold into slavery, I knew in my heart that I had no hope of escaping. I had no hope of living very long. The things they did to me, the conditions of my life convinced me that I had gone to hell, or hell on Earth, and that my time here would be the final years of torture before my death. Because I did not understand anything, had none of the knowledge that I would later slowly piece together, their purposes seemed meaningless, random and obscene – torment without any goal except to drive me mad, to tear all hope from the soul of a young child.

When I lay unconscious on the ground in the cornfields

my dad had planted himself – that was my last day in Nebraska. I never returned. Now, returning is impossible. That day was the last time I would ever see my parents. At the time, I didn't know what had happened to them. You might think that ignorance of their fate would have been a curse. I'm sure it would have. But it is also a curse to know exactly the fate of those you love, when that fate is evil. The past is not hidden from me, especially when it concerns me closely. It wasn't a year before I had experienced a vision showing me their murder, the cruelty of the men who visited my house, how they disposed of their bodies without respect, dignity, or care.

I'll spare you details. But I wasn't spared. And even if I suspected, the visions mercilessly gave me no chance to hope or doubt. By the time I was twelve, I knew I was completely alone and in the hands of monsters.

By then my eyesight had started to go, but I was way beyond expecting my captors to care about that. As you'll see, it was just the opposite; they wanted me blind. And they always got what they wanted. During my first year, as my vision started to fade, I was introduced to my new "home" and my new way of life. I learned for the first time how to live in constant fear. When I displeased them, they beat me or starved me for days. For the first few months, for even the slightest infraction of their strange rules, I was beaten. Again and again, until I became what they wanted – so afraid of pain, so living in fear of their cruel police sticks and electric wires that I became like some caged animal, totally responsive to their commands. A well-trained monkey.

Their rules were both simple and strange to me, at least at first. There were the understandable, if awfully harsh, rules about living – where to stand and sleep and eat, how to behave, how to answer questions and commands. Speak out of turn to another child – yes, there were many of us – and the stick might smash across your mouth. Out of your bed in the middle of the night? Maybe because you needed to stand, or pee, or think, or something? The cameras in the rooms would record it, and the next day you might be plugged into the wires, fire sent inside your nerves. Not enough to damage you. They didn't want to devalue their product. But it was more than enough for their purposes.

The other rules were the scariest, because none of us could understand them in the beginning. There is nothing more frightening than being asked to do something you don't understand and being punished when you fail to meet their expectations.

Many days we would be paraded out of our rooms and forced to march down long corridors that looked like hospital wings toward glass encased laboratories with rows of electronic equipment. They would hook us up to the equipment: large helmets with a hundred wires running from the top into computers. Our eyes would be masked by opaque glass in the helmets and our ears covered by headphones that blocked out all noise except the commands of the experimenters. Then they would ask us to describe what we saw, to find our way through labyrinths our eyes could not see. When we failed, they were displeased.

My heart bleeds now looking back at my twelve-year-old self, sitting utterly alone with a giant electronic helmet on my head, surrounded by people who killed my parents, who beat and tortured me, and who asked me to see the universe in a way I did not understand. I feel even worse for the less gifted children, who day after day stumbled and failed to progress, and who day after day were punished.

In this place, I was both lucky and unlucky. Lucky, because

it soon became clear that I was special. Even before they realized my progress, I *did* begin to see *something* when other stimulus was removed. As that something became more clear, I was able to more and more confidently find my way through the trials they erected for me, even though I did not understand the purpose. Even if I did not understand *what* it was I was doing. As my eyesight began to fail—so that soon the dark glasses did little to take away what was almost gone—I began to develop a conscious new sense. Patterns, substance, *something* was becoming clear to me, and I gained the power to succeed. At that stage, that was all that mattered, some end to the displeasure and cruelty. I was crushed and nearly broken. It didn't matter why, as long as the pain stopped.

Soon, I became all the rage with the men and women in white coats. How they fawned over me and smiled, happy with their little animal that was performing so well. I was isolated even more from the other children. Around that time, the operations began.

It was good that I met Ricky before they started the long series of surgeries. Ricky was the only kid I knew who seemed able to smile in this sterile place of fluorescent lights and metal corridors. Silly and fat, a few years older than me, and an obsessed Red Sox fan who could name every player and team statistic since 1908, Ricky became my only friend. The others were too hurt, too traumatized and too afraid to open up to anyone, and like shocked lab rats, they huddled to themselves. Ricky braved many beatings showing some sort of life, some sort of humanity in this place. And once or twice he even made me smile. Doesn't sound like much, but in this place, a smile was a miracle.

I asked him once how he had the courage to dare the things he did. He laughed over the lunch food. "My fahther," he said, with the full-mouth "ah" of Boston, "beat me worse than this many nights, after he'd been drinking." He leaned close to me, glancing over his shoulders, and back, looking into my eyes, eyes that saw him only as a blur now. "These white-coats, they're mean jerks and all, but they ain't nothing compared to a good drunk."

"Ricky, why are we here? What do they want from us?" It was the first time I had asked anything like that since I arrived.

He shook his head. "They won't tell, and we ain't gonna find out. What's important is not them, but *us*. What *we* want, why *we're* here. If we make it all about them, well…" he pointed around to the other kids, "we'll just end up like them. You got to find your reason, Ambra. And hold on to it. Don't let them be your reason, or take yours away."

I didn't really understand what he meant then, but his words stayed with me, circling in my mind. Months later, when things got worse for me and I nearly lost myself to despair, his words landed somewhere deep inside and planted themselves, growing slowly but steadily into a great oak tree. A tree with deep roots and colossal arms, and ten thousand leaves blowing in the wind of my soul. His words imploring me to find my reason, any reason, saved me.

It wasn't much later that they took Ricky away. He knew it was coming. "I can't make heads or tails of these tests," he told me. "I'm not what they want, Ambra. They won't be keeping me long." He sounded sad but not defeated. I always remember that tone in his voice, when you know that you can't win, that the end is there, but no matter what the powers do to you, you won't ever give in or stop being you.

I don't think I would have made it through the next two years without remembering his inspiring words to me that day. Months and years of having monsters cut on you, carve up your skull and brain, and for such a terrible purpose—I would have given up, my soul would have been broken. But even as they did these things, I found my way. I found my reason.

Deep into the past I retreated, and out of the past I slowly stumbled into my future.

Chapter 6

$\nabla \cdot \mathbf{B} = 0$

True knowledge comes only through suffering.

Elizabeth Barrett Browning

He was younger than the other whitecoats, with a sparse beard and longish black hair. At least that's how I remembered him from the many times he had worked with me. Now, he was a featureless blur, and I knew him by his voice.

The excitement was too much for him. He bubbled over with words that he should not have been speaking to me.

"You're special, Ambra," he said as he took the helmet off my head. "We've never seen a child like you before. You've mastered all the navigation drills, succeeding in ways we don't even understand. And the other things you are doing…what are you doing in there, Ambra?"

When they ask you a question, you have to answer.

"I don't know, Sir."

He stared at me for a long moment. "No. You probably don't." He sighed and turned away from me. "We haven't had a visit in a year. Soon they will come back, and we will lose you." He sounded genuinely distressed. Not for me, to be sure, but for losing his prize guinea pig. Then something brightened his tone.

"But next week a new phase in your training will begin. Next week is your first surgery!" he said excitedly, seeming to expect me to understand the import of the statement. My expression clearly depressed him.

"You know what the surgeries are for, don't you?"

I was still naive enough to think back to the original excuses these criminals had given my parents before they murdered them.

"No. Maybe…for my tumor?"

His voice lit up. "Yes, Ambra. Very good. For your tumor." Talking to me like I was three years old.

"They will take it out, finally? It's getting hard to see."

There was a long pause. I became very afraid. In my small hope I had spoken without being addressed first, and perhaps I had said something wrong. It had been some time since I had been beaten and a long time since they had shocked me. The thought of either made me start to sweat.

Finally, he spoke. His voice was sad. "Yes, we've noticed your visual impairment. It is not unexpected." He set the helmet down with a thud on the counter. "Come, our time is finished here. I won't see you for a few weeks, not until after your recovery. Over the next few months, we'll see how you progress."

That was the first hint of what they were planning for me, and the first sense I had that what was happening was part of something larger than me, or even this place. *Who* would come soon? What was navigation? And why was what I was experiencing and responding to in their tests so important to them?

But I had little time to learn more. The morning came, and I was whisked into a prep room, shaved bald, and had my scalp drawn on with Magic Markers. I was then wheeled into the operating room under bright lights and the gaze of several blurry figures I assumed were the surgeons. A needle was stuck into my arm, and I saw a shape that must have been a bag of some liquid feeding drops into my veins.

The room shrunk to a point. I was on the outside of the universe. Just as suddenly, it was back to full size. I heard myself say "Wow." Again it happened, and I felt farther away from the universe than ever. The third time ended in blackness, broken by a strange awakening of pain and dizziness that blinked out in a moment and a final return to consciousness lying in a bed.

I could tell that my arm still had a tube wired into it, and my head felt twice its normal size. I reached up to touch it, and it was a large swollen thing, wrapped in bandages. Sitting at my side was a blurry shape, the voice recognizable. It was my talkative scientist friend. *Dr. Talkative.*

"You're awake, Ambra. Good. That's *good.* The operation was a success. Aren't you happy?"

My throat hurt, and I could barely gargle out words. "Is the tumor gone? Why can't I see better?"

"No, Ambra. The tumor is still there. It will *always* be there, growing larger and larger. We've created space for it. We've opened space for further growth inside your brain and opened the back and top portion of your skull. It will grow outward now much faster, so much pressure and hindrance removed. You have a temporary new skull of composite material in place with a greater circumference. It will have to be replaced, of course, as the tumor grows further. And that growth will be aided by the new blood supply. The surgeons are very talented. They routed vessels from the occipital lobe over to the tumor. To better nourish it. Of course, this will accelerate the loss of vision, but that cannot be helped at this point. All that matters is the tumor. Your *gifts* come from it, Ambra. It is your space-time eye!" he chirped out, laughing. "God, you are going to be a star!"

He patted me on the arm and stood up, walking out of the room and leaving me feeling like some terribly twisted form of life.

And sure enough, a month later I was totally blind.

Chapter 7

$$ds^2 = \frac{1}{2\omega^2}\left(-(dt+\exp(x)dz)^2 + dx^2 + dy^2 + \frac{1}{2}\exp(2x)dz^2\right)$$

I myself am time inexhaustible, and I the creator whose faces are in all directions. I am death who seizes all, and the source of what is to be.

Bhagavad Gita

My dad used to say every cloud has a silver lining. So what do you get for being stricken with a giant, literally head-splitting tumor that destroys your sight and a fake skull and grafted skin to cover the extra surface area of your head that will never grow a hair that leaves you looking like the cross between a bulbous-headed alien and a middle-aged man? You could say I was given extraordinary powers and a central part to play in a power struggle between good and evil. But I never wanted any of that. At the time, I got Ricky's Red Sox hat.

I don't know how he did it. It shouldn't have been possible with all the security and paranoia of this place, but somehow, he managed to smuggle in his Red Sox hat, keep it hidden from them all that time, and then hide it my room, stuffing it inside the metal tube that served as one of the legs of my bed. I was lucky to find it, or maybe it was inevitable. My sight going quickly, I began to use my hands and feet to feel out everything around me. I had to learn to move about on my own to some degree, and I took the first "steps" toward that in my room, touching everything, feeling the walls, furniture, even the air as it changed directions and taste, telling me if a door was open, or a window, or if some machinery had been switched on. As my sight died, my other senses were growing —including my *other* sense, but I'll get to that later.

In the weeks of recovery following my surgery, after being transferred from the medical wing back to my cage, I had lots of time to do nothing. And it seemed that the cameras didn't care anymore what I did. One day, feeling around, I found the cap, stuffed in the tube, rolled up and mashed so that it would never recover its intended form again. But it was Ricky's hat, all right. I knew that from the smell and his description of the 2084 World Series Champions emblazoned in raised letters on the side, as well as the Ricky Hernandez signature scrawled inside in permanent marker that someone described to me later on. Complete with phone and address in Boston.

I think one of the first steps I took away from the pit of madness I was close to falling into, was putting that cap on, and not giving a damn what they would do to me. My head was already too big for a normal human hat, and this was just operation number one. I unsnapped the back, left it open, and it fit. Kind of. The grafted skin was tender and sore, but I wore the hat anyway, and it covered the new addition to my body, giving me an almost normal appearance again. My hair would grow in over time from the part of the scalp that still had hair, slightly above the cap, so that from a distance, if you didn't look too closely, I might just look like a normal redhead wearing a Red Sox cap.

I took to wearing it all the time. At first, the whitecoats sounded slightly disturbed by it, but then—*a miracle!* Since I was now their budding superstar, I got special privileges, and they let me wear it and stopped commenting. I guess they wanted to keep me happy, keep me performing.

The other thing that saved me was retreating into the past. Not psychologically, where I retreat into *my* past memories to hide (even if there was some hiding going on). I mean *everyone's* past, including my own. As I learned later, a Reader's power grows and matures fastest in puberty, and I was right in the middle of that, my whole body changing. It might even have been something I could have obsessed about—my changing body—if it weren't for all the other stuff that pushed it far to the side. But at the same time that I was impressing them more and more in their little examination room, other things were happening to me, things they didn't know about. One of the first I noticed was my growing power to enter the past. I still had future visions, but what obsessed me, what came out clearly, in high-resolution detail, and what I began to be able to *control*, were my visions of what *had* happened. Or, as I like to think of it now, what might *have had* happened. Like I said, past, future – both are fluid.

In the dark and pointless hours in my cell, I began to have these long and grand adventures. Journeys into events of the recent—and sometimes not so recent—past. As I learned to control my path through time, with greater skill and experience, and with greater concentration, I could direct myself back further and further. During the first few years I was able to do this, I explored things that were emotional touchstones for me. My childhood, my parents' lives, my family, important world events that touched me. It wasn't until much later that the usefulness of Reading the past to the present and future dawned on me. Embarrassing that I didn't think of it earlier, but I was only thirteen. And I was really screwed up.

This ability also allowed me to compensate for something that was depressing me—my lack of schooling. Most children would be glad to be free of school, but let me tell you, when they won't let you learn, and years go by and you realize that there is the entire world of human knowledge denied you, passing you by, you might have a different attitude. I became almost traumatized that my captors had not only made my life this hell but that they had also locked me from all the light of humanity, leaving me ignorant, in the dark, powerless. No books to read or music to listen to or art to see. No new ideas or experiences to grow with. Sometimes I felt like panicking, and I would do math problems in my head or try to remember books I had read.

And that of course is what connected things for me. I realized that in the past, I had access to everything humanity had achieved. So, I went looking for it, spending increasing amounts of time pushing myself through past visions, extending them, improving their clarity. As time went on, I actually became able to sit through visions and learn from them, like a student eaves dropping in the shadows of a lecture. Obvious places to linger were schools and libraries, but really, the entire world was open to me as I came to realize. Did I want to learn about great art? I could study at the Louvre. Learn advanced calculus? I could sit at the feet of Newton (not time well spent, let me tell you). The experiences of explorers as they sailed to the New World—I could be there with them or riding in zero-g above the Earth with astronauts. And as the blackness fell down on top of me in all other aspects of life, the visions continued to bring me sight. Through them, I could still see, see as vividly at times as I ever had with my eyes. I was blind, but in a strange way, I was not.

It wasn't always *easy* to find these visions of the past. When the visions first came, I did not control when or what, even if they tended to involve things close to me. As my skills grew over the years, and as I consciously honed them, I could dance through libraries of visions, flipping through them like pages in some ethereal book, finding those of more interest, and expanding those pages of the past into a landscape. I said I was unlucky and lucky. In this way, I was lucky – I achieved an education no human being had ever experienced. But I would have traded it all in a second to be back on my farm with my parents again.

I became so obsessed with the past that I ended up blocking out nearly all possible future visions. Amazingly stupid, I know, considering how useful future visions might have been. Even worse, I never sought out the history of this place, these people, what and who they were, why they were acting as they did. How much I could have learned, perhaps to help me cope, even escape this terrible place. I don't know how to explain my inability to realize these things except to say that I had nearly fallen into a black hole of hopelessness, and through the exploration of the past I had found beauty, hope, and light. It saved me, carried me through the experiments, the surgeries, the inhumanity of the place. I needed this different world too much. I guess that maybe part of me purposefully ignored things closer at hand, however *useful* they might have been. The other things were more useful. They kept me sane in an insane life.

Chapter 8

$$v = \sqrt{\frac{GM}{r}}$$

I took it up, and held it in my hand. I was a trembling, because I'd got to decide, forever, betwixt two things, and I knowed it. I studied a minute, sort of holding my breath, and then says to myself: "All right, then, I'll go to hell" and tore it up.

Mark Twain

They were all happy, happy voices in the glass room.

The giant helmet came off, and the sounds of the place washed over me once more—the faster flits of motion of the team working with me, their excitement in their motions, breaths, and vocal tones. It was strange – as time went on, as I became better and better at their silly games. It became easier and easier for me, and boredom set in, even as their excitement grew. At first it was such relief to know I was pleasing them so much, and I looked forward to each new session. How quickly it all changed when I think back on it.

It became clear that this device they placed on my head had something to do with stimulating the world of my visions. Strap me in, turn it on, and I could "see" things created in front of me, like some magic laser-disco ball in front of a sighted person. A small child is in awe of the disco ball. In a few years it might seem interesting for a few minutes. If you saw it several times a week as a young teen, well, its secrets were all gone.

Their secrets faded fast. As I approached my fifteenth birthday, it had been almost two years and six surgeries —a surgery almost every four months—and a lot of time growing into my new abilities. By now the tumor was as big as a squashed softball, and my head had expanded at the back and top so that even the Red Sox hat barely fit with the strap totally open, even though I had torn the stitching to make more room. At least my hair could finally grow back in all the way. I vowed to myself never to cut it again—in the dream place where I had such control over my life.

My whitecoat entourage had grown to a team of at least ten, headed by Dr. Talkative. He loved to tell me how big the tumor was, updating me on its slowing growth, its stabilization within my brain. He was bragging, boasting of his pet project that he had guided, boasting of my achievements with their stupid, limited little manipulations as if *he* had achieved them.

I had learned over time that, whatever it was that they were doing, they didn't understand much about it. They could set it up, read the output, and know if I was succeeding or not. But they understood nothing beyond that, like people who use a microwave and have no idea what it's all about inside. They didn't know what I was seeing, how simple it was all becoming, and how I was realizing that there was a much, much greater world to be perceived by this dramatic new sense I was developing. They made me into this freak, but they didn't know what they had made.

As I outgrew their disco ball, I was better able to ace those little tests with it. Soon, it became something I could do in the background, while I thought about other things or even explored the past as had become my obsession. That was the case on the day the bad news came.

Just as the team was bubbling over with joy from my latest *bored out of my mind* performance, Dr. Talkative came into the room like a dark cloud. I could sense it in his voice and movements; I could nearly smell the anxiety in his sweat. Everyone else in the room likely figured it out by seeing his face. I bet it looked bad.

"I have some bad news," he overstated the obvious. He walked over to the computer station and paused a minute. "Fantastic performance today, Ambra." He sighed. "I think you've outgrown us."

He placed his clipboard down with a clack and stepped back into the middle of the room to address his staff. "And like all children when they grow up, you must move on."

I heard several audible groans and the shifting sounds of uncomfortable people. One woman spoke up somewhat shrilly. "They can't come now! She's just showing us her potential! They won't care about what she can do, what she could become. They'll strap her into a navslav ship and she'll waste away her life like the rest of them!"

While it wasn't exactly comforting to hear that I was headed for a lifetime of servitude, her outburst opened my eyes, so to speak. Truly startled me for the first time since I had come to this place. To hear them fall from the top of the food chain – it was priceless! *The fear in their voices.* Who were these mysterious *They* that were coming and over which they had no power? After coming to view the whitecoats as my local non-benevolent deities, it was discombobulating, and liberating, to see them shake.

"That's enough, Katie. It doesn't matter what we think or want." He paused a minute and spoke mordantly. "As you know, we have in our enthusiasm...*tampered* with their property. I believe it was a step in the right direction for science, for the potential that lies within the human race. But *They* may be displeased. I don't have to remind you how serious the punishment can be for infractions." There was complete silence. I could hear my own heart beat.

"Nevertheless, as your group leader, I will take full responsibility for these actions. I pray you will maintain your appropriate demeanor when our visitors arrive tomorrow."

"Tomorrow?" someone called out in disbelief.

"Yes. For some reason, we did not receive their long-range communication. They are entering orbit as we speak. Representatives will arrive in the morning."

Chapter 9

$2^{\mathbb{N}} > \mathbb{N}$

Once upon a time, Zhuangzi was dreaming that he was a butterfly dancing and flying about, joyous and free. He had forgotten that he was Zhuangzi. Then he awoke and felt himself solid and sure. But he didn't know anymore if he was Zhuangzi who had dreamed he was a butterfly, or, a butterfly dreaming that he was Zhuangzi.

Zhuang Zhou

In orbit?

What in the world did this mean? Frankly, in my readings and self-education through the accepted annals of human knowledge, the idea of visitors from outer space was an extremely unlikely and fanciful scenario. Like believing in ghosts. Or little blue elves. Sociology argued that human claims of visitation were the modern extensions of being visited by demons or angels, a "projection of our well-documented, overly active imagination contextualized to the modern mythology," as one lecturer put it. Harvard professor,

I think. And science texts, and respected astronomers and astrobiologists had pointed out many clear problems with extraterrestrial visitation. One of the most basic was the fact that the distances between even the closest stars would require centuries of travel. Hyperspace and warp-speed were inventions of science-fiction authors to make their stories possible. How ironic that my future would be intimately tied to hyperspace travel of a very real sort, helping to guide aliens that couldn't possibly be visiting us. It was a sad case of solid thinking being wrong, even if more admirable, and loony thinking being right. Well, I can tell you—life isn't fair.

It took me a while to fall asleep that night. In the early hours of the morning, I awoke and was washed over deeply with a powerful vision. In the vision, I stood in an enormous chamber carved out of some strange and unearthly material, like some cross between marble and the sand of an anthill. Odd patterns in unusual color mixtures decorated the walls and floors. Huge moss-green pillars that seemed to grow like trees with numerous branches erupted from the ground and climbed toward the dome-like ceiling, supporting it in a hundred places. Rows of these led forward to a throne of some kind, on which sat a monstrous form, humanoid yet not human. I watched a young man led forward, obviously in pain, by similar humanoid creatures, their insect-like forms towering over him. As he was dragged to the throne, which sat raised above the rest of the floor by a set of many steps, I realized in horror that there were human shapes chained to the walls on either side of the throne.

I won't describe to you what had happened to them. You might could imagine terrible things, but this would be worse. The creature on the throne turned a set of three eyestalks on what might have been a head toward the man. An artificial sound filled the room as it spoke in a hideous tone. The language was English, if awkward, and clearly translated by some kind of machine, produced in a *basso profundo* with extensive lower frequencies that made the bone and artificial material in my skull vibrate.

"Human Reader—you have lost the time. If you and we cooperate, you to be able to rescue your people. If you do not, these deaths here only a mild beginning will seem."

The young man was exhausted, yet a fire burned deep in his eyes. I watched him clench his jaw. I knew what he would say; I could not believe it. I wanted to grab him and beg him to stop the pain I saw around that throne and that I felt in those metallic, insectoidal words.

"No!" he cried out. "You can do with me as you wish, but the Other will find her way. She will bring an end to you. You cannot hide—she watches even now!"

The words shook me, and I lost the threads of the vision. The room came into focus. I sat on my bed, cradling my knees. Tears came pouring down my face, and I fell asleep crying like a little child.

I awoke to the sound of my door being opened, and heard the rapid footsteps of someone entering the room.

"Ambra, you must dress now. You must come with me *immediately*."

It was one of the women, an aide on the experimental team. Her voice dripped with fear.

Chapter 10

$$G_{\mu\nu} = 8\pi G(T_{\mu\nu} + \rho_\Lambda g_{\mu\nu})$$

In the ordinary theory of relativity, every line that can describe the motion of a material point, i.e., every line consisting only of time-like elements, is necessarily non-closed. An analogous statement cannot be claimed for the theory developed here. Therefore a priori a point motion is conceivable, for which the four-dimensional path of the point would be an almost closed one. In this case one and the same material point could be present in an arbitrarily small space-time region in several seemingly mutually independent exemplars. This runs counter to my physical imagination most vividly.

Albert Einstein

The room was dank and yellow. Dank because they had raised the humidity to some absurd level so that moisture dripped from anything it could condense on—glass from the windows, metal on the walls, and the dark-green material like none I'd ever seen that made up the bulk of the funky alien spacesuit in front of me. Yellow because the lights in the room were only yellow, emitting few other wavelengths, which I assume was another effort to comfort Squidy as he (she? it??) swam in the sea of whatever liquid was inside the suit—likely water, or why the humidity?

Squidy was definitely an alien, or else some mutant octopus that had grown intelligent and been provided with an earthsuit by the U.S. government. There was something like a head, which was a dark brownish-green, oblong and squishy like an octopus's head, but at the same time very different. One difference was the random-seeming patchwork of what I had to conclude were eyes of some sort. The long whiskers extending from many parts of the head gave Squidy the look of a cactus that had forgotten to shave for a few days. The arms were also very octopusesque, with no suckers but tens of very thin tendrils at the end, all of which were dexterous. These "fingers" could manipulate objects that floated inside the suit as well, positioned by some unknown mechanism, composed of materials completely, well, alien.

You are likely asking yourself, "*How does she know all this? She's blind.*" Amazingly, as I saw these things, it did not surprise me at the time. Something about the stress of the situation shoved my brain into survival mode, and in this mode it learned to integrate my powerful new sense into its general scheme of decoding reality. Only later—much later—when I had time aboard the navships to contemplate, did I piece together what had happened in that session and learn to apply it from that point on, to my great empowerment. It was then that I realized that my highly developed abilities to see into the past had a very practical application to the life of the blind.

So bear with me for now and trust me when I tell you, my descriptions of the event are accurate.

Dr. Talkative was there, too. He looked like he had

Salmonella poisoning. The female aide walked me in and led me to a chair in the middle of the room. This was the scene out of a nightmare or horror movie: a dentist chair that was made out of metal with no cushions or anything to make it comfortable and was, in this case, also dripping wet from all the humidity. It was designed with many restraints for arms, legs, and head. I felt myself sweating in the dampness as she sat me in the chair and clamped the metal restraints over my wrists. My breathing became labored when my ankles were locked in, and I think I actually began to shake when they placed the metal band around my head. As she snapped it in, my neck was jerked backward so that it was like someone was pulling my head back by the hair. But I couldn't move my head. I couldn't move anything. They could do anything to me, and I could not even try to stop them.

"I'm sorry, Ambra," she whispered, her voice shaking with the tones of pity and fear, and I heard her scamper out of the room. The door to the chamber closed with a loud metallic clank.

"Try to relax, Ambra," began Dr. Talkative. "You are property of the Navigation Conglomerate, and a representative of the Sortax is here to examine you. You will speak when spoken to and obey all his requests. Your life and your future depend on his assessment of you today."

Then Squidy took over. There wasn't any doubt that it had been in charge the entire time, of course. The sound that came from it shook me even further, as the artificial voice of a translator, while less heavy in lower frequencies, carried a tone and quality I had heard only hours earlier in my dream. It was the same voice of the insect creatures that had tortured and killed the human beings in their throne room.

"They are that, which they changed?" it croaked and rang out.

I didn't know how to respond.

"He is asking if you are the one that we have worked on. He means our operations with your tumor, Ambra."

"Yes, I guess, I am."

"They are that, which were not authorized." I didn't respond, assuming it was a statement and not a question. Dr. Talkative squirmed in his seat. Squidy only floated about, making little jerky movements every few seconds.

"They will serve in navslav the ships and supervised. They with value, exchanged for with the Dram." A small glowing objected floated into the path of several tendrils inside the suit, and the tentacle holding the device reached out toward me.

My mind exploded.

I screamed in agony. Truly, I had never known pain before. Not the surgeries, not the beatings or electric shocks, nothing prepared me for the fire that was poured inside me. I don't know how to explain to you. You don't have my tumor, my sixth sense. Even with my other senses, I had never known such pain. As a light thousands of times too strong for your eyes flooding all your experience, tied to two red-hot iron knives then driven into your sockets at the same time, my new sense that I had grown into, come to explore and know and integrate into my consciousness became the raw skin over which a new and terrible acid was poured. Every muscle in my body convulsed, and I projectile vomited across the room, coating my visitor and Dr. Talkative in the process.

I could not, of course, process this at the time, but the pain ceased, the world dissolved, and the next thing I knew the sad woman was bent over me calling my name, wiping my face clean, and removing a needle from my arm. She was nearly as pale as me, and sweat beaded on her forehead.

"Ambra, please, talk to me. Are you okay?"

"Mom…I want my mom…" I'm embarrassed now at how weak I became.

The woman had tears in her eyes. "I'm sorry, Ambra. She's not here. Please, you need to wake up, *now. They* need to question you further. *They* can't wait for you to get any better," she said, a suppressed anger in her tone.

She wiped a cold, damp cloth over my face. I tried to focus, to bring my concentration back from the pit of hell that still burned around the edge of my consciousness. Slowly, roughly, it came. The dank room, the two forms in front of me, one horrible, from a nightmare, the other the man who had engineered a series of surgeries on my brain that had left me deformed, different, and, I now knew, terribly vulnerable.

"Ambra," started Dr. Talkative as the woman once again walked out of the room. "We are sorry for that…disruption. You were being scanned with a device that is designed to probe your powers of perception. Only it is calibrated for a normal Reader. You are not normal. The signal was too strong," he said, a tone of shock and pity in his voice. Later, when examined by the doctors of the Resistance, I would learn that I had almost died that day.

"Enough," clanged out the voice translator. "We must again scan."

"No…please…" I begged them. I would have done anything at that moment to prevent them from scanning me again. Given them anything. Promised anything, said anything. It would not have mattered what—jump off a cliff to my death? Sure. A thousand times easier than being scanned.

"Ambra, it's ok. We've lowered the signal strength considerably. It will be safe now. You must be conscious for the examination. Please let us know if you are in pain."

"The pain do not constitute," it injected.

"She may be valuable to the Dram," Dr. Talkative noted.

"They may be," it concluded.

It raised the device toward me again. Instinctively I tensed, and while the experience was painful, it was tolerable. If it had not been for the first injury, this scan may have been only uncomfortable, and not painful. Sunlight on a burn hurts, *it burns*, though it does not burn healthy skin. But even as it hurt, it was interesting to some abstract part of my mind. This was the advanced version of the disco ball. Disco-ball 2.0. *The patterns!* The structure and substructure—it was like nothing I had experienced from these artificial devices. When it ended, after images of dancing shapes in multiple dimensions filled my mind, and stayed with me for days.

"Not authorized. They are for the navships," it sounded out as the visions faded.

"No! She is more than that! You can't fry her mind like that and then expect to get a meaningful scan!"

The creature turned its earthsuit-encased form toward Dr. Talkative, who shrank like a shadow when the sun rises. "Not authorized," it spit out as it turned around and lumbered awkwardly toward a door at the other end of the room.

As it left me and the doctor alone, I felt a kind of relief. A relief even in the presence of a man who had made me into the freak I was. Relief because, however traumatized we both were, whatever he had done to me and whatever had been done to him over the years, we were both human. Until you are in the presence of the alien, the truly alien and not simply strange, you can never know the deep meaning of the presence of another human being. Even your tormenter.

I sat there, wet and stinking in my stained clothes, still strapped into the metal chair and unable to move. My entire body hurt.

He looked at me and closed his eyes. His hand reached out and pressed a button on a controller hanging from a string around his neck. Several seconds passed, and then the door behind me opened, and I heard the sound of footsteps.

"You'll leave tonight with the other children."

Chapter 11

$$-2\exp(-x)\partial_t + z\partial_x + \left(\exp(-2x) - z^2/2\right)\partial_z$$

Time is no specific character of being. In relativity theory the temporal relation is like far and near in space. I do not believe in the objectivity of time. The concept of Now never occurs in science itself, and science is supposed to be concerned with the objective.

Kurt Gödel

I'm sure it must be frightening and exciting for kids to leave home for camp, being away from their parents who have always cared for them, living with many strangers, new rules, new dangers and opportunities. Or going off to college, really stepping out for the first time as an adult, even if you have a safety net most of the time to fall back on. *Adventure!*

To hell with adventure. I was scared. Terrified, actually. Just a few years before I had lost a beautiful life —a nice home with parents I loved and who loved and cared for me. I eavesdropped on the past and saw them murdered. I was deformed and tortured by the disciples of the organization that had destroyed my family. Now this terrible place seemed like a haven, a refuge compared to the infinite dark and alien that awaited above. Soon these creatures would take me and some untold number of kids with them like trained animals, take us away from our home planet and away from any sense of security or the familiar.

I didn't know how I would make it. In the coming year I would see many an Earth child *not* make it, grow physically or mentally sick, wasting away or exploding in madness. And the sick were removed efficiently.

For the time being, I sat in my room, wearing the long and featureless robe I had been instructed to put on, my hands in my lap, cold, curled tightly into one another. I had no belongings—no books to read (even if I could read them anymore), no music, no mementos of family, no toys, no evidence of a life of any kind. Only my Red Sox hat, perched on my big head, and I didn't know if it would survive what was coming. I looked out unseeing over my bare room as the minutes dripped slowly by, one unit of time after the other. Waiting.

The door swung open and I jumped. It was Dr. Talkative, which was unusual, as he had never visited my room. He was alone, which was also unusual, since his staff and team nearly always followed him or lurked nearby. The door closed with a click, and I heard the sound of a metal chair being dragged across the stone floor and placed in front of me. With a sigh and disturbance in the air, Dr. Talkative sat down.

"Ambra, we don't have much time. *They* will call soon for the children, and we must deliver you to the docking chamber." His clothes rustled as he shifted his weight, a short silence ensuing as I waited for him to say whatever he was there to say.

"Ambra, it is unfortunate what happened during your

examination. Years of work destroyed because that clumsy Sortax representative would not listen to me. I *know* you are capable of so much more."

Tears started flowing down my cheeks. After everything, after all they had done to me, even after the sense of strength and rebellion the last few years that I had found as I mastered their system, it all evaporated. I crumbled into a small ball and could feel only the desperate guilt of a wayward child.

"I'm sorry!" I sobbed uncontrollably. "I really tried." Sobs shook my shoulders, and my breath came in gasps.

Then the strangest thing happened. He rose and sat next to me and placed his arm around my shoulders.

"Ambra, listen to me," he said, and I slowly stifled my sobs. "Humanity is in a terrible place. There is so much you don't know. Cattle, Ambra. We are nothing more than bipedal cattle to these aliens that rule space, that rule us to the ignorance of most of our kind. I'm sorry for what I have done to you. Years ago, before *They* took me, I would have been ashamed of it. Perhaps I am inside, still. But I became a slave. To succeed within the system I found myself in—that was all that mattered. *Don't you make this mistake*. Please, Ambra, because I am going to tell you something only I know, something that is important, I believe, for the human race. Something I have buried inside me, denied, rationalized away for years."

I didn't know what to say. Nothing made sense anymore. Nothing was sane.

"Please, just listen and remember. You can't process it all now, but you will later." He paused and then spoke in a whisper, his sentences strangely inflected. It was like hearing scripture.

"Many years ago, when I first came to this place, still working as a staff member with the young children being brought into the facility, a young boy, not much older than you are now, was preparing to ship out, just as you are tonight. I had given him his last series of shots like you got earlier, and was about to send him off, when he spoke to me. He was a very gifted child, second only to you, Ambra, in what he could do with the space-time matrices. He stared at me with his deep-brown eyes —I'll never forget them or the words that came out of his mouth.

'Doctor, a woman will come, a young girl. She is the Sunrise, she will see with Truth into the darkest night. She is our hope. She will be the savior of this world in its time of need. You will know her by her sign, and you will understand after you have wronged her. Before the end, you must repeat this to her: Daughter of Time, you must wake, and not fear to gaze forward and walk the path set before you. We are waiting.' "

He paused and cleared his throat, his voice cracking. "These were his last words before I shipped him off to a life of slavery. I paid them no heed, thought them mad ravings, and pushed them out of my mind. When you came, and my ambition blinded me to everything except your terrible gift, I did not hear his voice, or *would* not hear it. Even as they returned this last year to haunt my dreams." He paused a moment in silence. "Now, I can't stop hearing them."

He cupped my head in his hands: I assume he was also staring into my eyes that could not return the gaze. "I want to say those words again: *Daughter of Time, you must wake, and not fear to gaze forward and walk the path set before you.* Ambra, he meant *you.* He was a powerful Reader, and he forecast your coming. He *saw* you in the fields of Time. Listen to him. He was speaking of you, that you have a part to play for all of us in a possible future. I can't undo what I have done, but I can try to play my part rightly for the first time. Don't be afraid,

Ambra. *Survive.* You are important beyond the dreams of men."

He stopped and exhaled, and then stood up and walked to the door. "My actions have doomed me, Ambra. They will make an example of my tampering. My last hours, my last minutes, I have spent giving this message to you." The sounds of scurrying feet and raised voices grew from the hallway, and I heard intermixed with it the chilling echoes of the voice translators. It was beginning. *They* were coming for us.

"You've never even been given the courtesy to know my name—I who have made you what you are. I'm sorry we have been so inhuman. My name is Frank, Ambra. Frank Fields. Forgive what I have done and remember his words."

The door opened and then closed quickly, the air pressure blowing against my face, the swelling sounds outside spiking in intensity and then dropping to a muffled drone.

I felt I was going mad.

Chapter 12

$\forall n \in^{*} \mathbb{N}, ^{*}\sin n\pi = 0$

A journey of a thousand miles started with a first step.

老子 Lǎozǐ (Lao Tzu)

When you first begin to *see* as a Reader, you have no experience, nothing to connect the new sensations to, and your brain works the new information into all its preexisting patterns— images, ideas, emotions. Dreams play things out as your brain tries to process it all. Then, it begins to leak into your days. Visions that are the product of this confusion. That's as far as most have ever gotten in human history – seers, prophets, madmen. A new sense organ in a minority of the population, hardly developed. Granting visions, often loss of sanity.

An irony is that in all other things, we humans are the idiots of the galaxy, the least evolved intelligence, life-forms considered backward, primitive, and enabled in their technology only by the aid of more advanced life.

In this galaxy where we have so little to offer, our only value is in prescience, this poorly developed sense organ, that rivals, and often exceeds, that found in species far more developed in every other way. An accident of evolution that made us the idiot-savants of space-time.

They harvested us through human farmers, picked those with real potential, took some of us to God knows where across the galaxy for breeding programs, cloning attempts, and, of course, for the navships. Scattered about star systems and nebulae, entombed in oppressive and harsh prisons, humans serve the space-faring needs of many creatures that are otherwise disrespectful, even contemptuous, of our very existence and presence among them. We are a necessary evil.

With me, the humans they empowered got carried away, and before they realized, my captors had created a monster. *Me.* A monster for all involved, human and *other*. Because, while I am certainly monstrous to my fellow earthlings, my gift is a terrible threat to the galactic hegemony of the Dram – of them, you will hear much more soon. In me, the organ is beyond developed. It has become my dominant sense, unfathomable even to the most powerful Readers of any species. I no longer can see the light of day, but I can see the energy of tomorrow and yesterday. Even though I can't tell you what it looks like exactly, I can say that it isn't much different in spirit from what I saw with eyes: beauty, horror, and everywhere, *existence*.

As the ship raced through the Earth's atmosphere, taking me for the first time beyond my home planet, I was still, as far as my potential, very much asleep. A sleep that was, as I tried to explain, more emotional than anything else. I wasn't ready to accept what I was becoming or to grasp the power my unique insight offered to me. I had to adapt slowly. But the time was coming, and soon the first real steps would be taken. Frank Field's last words lodged in my mind, buried like lily bulbs waiting for spring.

I suppose a trip into space should be described with lots of vivid images of breaking through the atmosphere, seeing the first blackness and stars, and the sunrise over the edge of the Earth. For me and the fifty or so children onboard, the only thing to describe was the tiny space we were crammed into, turbulence, and the feeling that we were going to asphyxiate.

From the facility on Earth, we were marched in line down a long corridor into a large hangar that opened up to the night sky. The chamber was very large, football field-sized, and in the middle was a spaceship. Now that I know more about these things, it was a surface transport, designed to ferry cargo planet-side from a starship. But at that moment, it was the first time I had seen anything like it, and it was overwhelming. As big as a tanker, shaped like a cross between a flying saucer and the space shuttle, it was ringed with earthsuited Sortax. By the time the chamber was entered, there were no more humans around us. We were alone with monsters from space who were putting us into their ship to take us away.

We all walked quietly in our thin robes, cold and afraid. Several kids could be heard sobbing, and one or two broke down and refused to enter. The response from the Sortax was rapid and harsh. They would extend a dark rod towards the child who would then scream in pain and collapse. The Sortax would command the child to move forward in line, and, after that pain, each did.

Inside, it became clear how alien we actually were. The ship was designed, of course, for its crew, these sea-dwelling Sortax with their many arms and liquid-filled suits. The ship inside was designed with liquid filling nearly all the chambers, and I marvel now at the compensation the Sortax must have used to offset all that extra weight. There were "airlocks" of a kind for the natives (*Them*), that we bypassed without engaging. A short tunnel led to our holding pen, which, once all the children had entered, was sealed off from the rest of the ship.

Sealed off from the rest of the ship. That essentially describes all the interactions of humans with any of the diverse alien species in the galaxy, as compatible environments rarely existed. Some needed liquid medium like the Sortax, others required some kind of gaseous environment. Often these gases were toxic or otherwise incompatible with our survival. One ironic exception turned out to be the Dram, the Romans themselves. who ruled over all the other species and who required a very similar oxygen and nitrogen content to that on Earth, even if their Earthlike planet was on the other side of the Milky Way. The other were the Xix, who needed only a small modification to an Earthlike atmosphere, which they achieved through a device worn around their necks in our presence, if you could describe the Xix as having necks.

So, in nearly every ship I was on, humans were walled off from the host species in our own climate-controlled cells. *Controlled* was always a loose term, as many ships provided air and temperature that was just slightly better than unsuitable for human life. That was my impression when we entered our chamber on the Sortax ship, although now I know that their efforts were slightly better than average.

At the time, once the doors closed and we were at the mercy of their climate system, it was oppressive. The air was acidic, burning our throats and eyes. It stank in a manner that to the human senses was unidentifiable— alien, and it was sickening. With no instructions or warning, we were provided makeshift seats and straps, and soon the ship blasted off into the sky; several children who were not prepared were sent flying to their deaths or suffered serious injury. It made no sense. If they wanted us, why treat us like this and risk our lives? Some sort of demented natural selection for the best slaves?

The ride to the starship was short, and soon after a jarring docking (I bet such dockings weren't so bad for Sortax floating in water) and a long wait (likely for the Sortax to leave the ship and to pump out the water for our exit), our hatch-like door opened and we all looked out to see what awaited us.

Amazingly, standing in the doorway were two human beings. They were dressed in robes not too different from our own—thicker, more worn, with strange markings across the back. They were likely in their twenties, although they looked older. As I was to learn, life for humans in space under alien care was shorter than on Earth, full of many more health problems and complications. Most of us did not live beyond forty years, and by the time we hit our thirties, we looked sixty.

A moment of hope and relief swept through the group of children. It was quickly dashed as the men spoke.

"No words," one barked. "You will do as you are told and prepare to serve the Sortax. This is a training vessel, and you will be instructed in guiding the navships to the Orb portals. Nothing else matters to your existence. If you cannot perform, you will be discarded. You are to report to us or other Human Shepherds. Under no circumstances are you to attempt any contact with non-human residents of any ship. Follow us to your quarters."

They turned, and marched from the door, leaving us stunned and empty. One by one, we stood up, stretched our sore bodies bounced by the trip through Earth's atmosphere, and walked through the door to our new life.

Point τ

I am become Time, the destroyer of worlds.

Bhagavad Gita

Chapter 13

$V - E + F = 2$

To delve into the deepest mysteries of nature and discover the underlying truth has been denied us, but with the right imagination, a hypothesis may explain many phenomena.

Leonhard Euler

So my new life began – a life of military constraints, claustrophobic imprisonment, long training sessions, and a horrible sense of separation from all that I was. In space, without night or day, without clocks or anything to mark the passage of time, it was hard to know how long we had been there, how long the sessions lasted, so that the orderliness we took for granted and depended on vanished, and soon, all sense of normalcy was lost. For many it became too much. As they lost their connection with Earth, its rhythms, its air, its life, they lost their bearings internally, and their minds with them. These were efficiently removed and never seen again. There doesn't need to be much guessing as to what happened to them.

It might have been the same with me, because my being is very tied to the Earth, and even in the harsh metallic and sterile center I had been trapped in before transfer to space, I had suffered for the disconnect from the land. You should remember, I am a farmer's daughter.

In space, it was so much more terrible. I saved myself again by exploring the past, finding some powerful echo of Earth in the lives that had lived before me. When the complete separation in this alien environment would descend on me, I could find some solace in Earth's past.

For the time being, for all of us who could adapt, in whatever ways we found, we kept very busy learning how to eat the terrible material they gave to us as food, learning how to function in the toxic air, sleep on the metal shelves allotted to each of us, disregard our privacy and cleanliness in an environment not designed to comfort human sensibilities. And, above all, learning to pilot along the Strings that spread from the Orbs.

It finally became clear what we had all been gathered for, the reason our Earth masters had taken us from our homes, trained us, evaluated us, sought to hone our other sense for a specific purpose. For such a crude purpose our gift was channeled, but it served a practical need. Amazingly, our unique talent was the backbone of the entire galactic civilization. We were treated, bred, and trained as beasts of burden, but on our backs thousands of worlds depended. Without us, interstellar travel would grind to a halt.

It was initially a shock for many who had been brought on board to have a new kind of helmet set on their head and to see the world as they had never experienced it. For me, it was like walking for the first time into a bright, sunlit city having only seen by moonlight. Whatever these new helmets did, they channeled the "stuff" of my vision, brightened it with great contrast, yet only in a certain color, so to speak, in a single dimension. It was beautiful in its way, and yet only a tiny part of the whole. But within this part was a skill we were required to learn.

In the beginning, we were subjected to simulations. Always, it was the same. From a disembodied point of view, I would see myself approaching a sphere of light of great complexity. To call a real Orb a sphere is a distortion, as the word suffers from the biased view of humans and aliens who cannot see it as I do—the substructure, layers upon layers not unlike an onion, but casting out in independent dimensions beyond the three we perceive with our eyes. My mind's other sense could see in these directions, and the Orbs were more like infinite webs whose projection in three-space was a humble sphere.

The simulations captured only a faint aspect of this— only when we approached a true Orb did its beauty become apparent to me. Our training sims were not focused on the Orbs, however, but on the tendrils, the glowing Strings that spread from them. The Strings extending from a true Orb traveled in many dimensions, but the sims captured only those that were in the visual three dimensions, and it was along these lines that we were to direct the point of view, the ship in reality, when the time came to navigate in earnest.

We would spend hours guiding little simulated spaceships onto the tendrils, one after another after another. What I would find out later is that the galactic hegemony of the Dram was established through using the tendrils to travel through space-time. The Strings could be used as tunnels, shortcuts between any two Orbs, cutting the travel time between stars and planetary systems from eons into days. I did not understand how this happened or why these Orbs had been placed where they had. For the present, all that mattered was mastering the ability to help the ships navigate.

The ships themselves had the technology to exploit the Strings but not the ability to peer into the space-time matrix and navigate. The starships required Readers for this, some from many of the worlds connected by the Orbs or, increasingly, from the relatively cheap and primitive world of Earth that was enriched in Reader potential and powerless to defend itself from the superior technological development of the aliens that needed our singular talent.

I quickly adapted to the tasks, my unique organ giving me advantages no other human or alien possessed, and which I had not even come to fully appreciate. I was surprised to find that, unlike on Earth, my mastery did not bring me advancement or attention. It was not noticed. It became clear to me after a time that it was not individual humans guiding the navships but the collective, that our overall average effort was being used by the aliens to direct the craft to the appropriate String. In a way it made sense, as individually, not even humans had the skills to perfectly navigate—each person would make too many random errors. But averaged over the whole, the outliers, the mistakes, were smoothed out, and the overall direction was true.

True, but slow, inefficient. I became frustrated as I participated, always sure how to direct the craft, but the overall movement was slow, effective, but not the quickest route through space-time. I was only one of a horde, and no one understood what my potential was.

Increasingly, I was drawn to the Orbs. With them lay much more complexity, something far more interesting and inspiring than hitching rides on Strings. While the sim Orbs displayed little of this, as we progressed in our training we made more frequent approaches to the Orb that lay in orbit between the asteroid belt and Jupiter. It was resplendent, *incandescent* compared to the other objects around us in space. Our bright sun, a ball of radiating energy in the electromagnetic spectrum, was a fairly dim and dull object to me. But the Orb, no larger than a major Earth city in diameter, shrouded a terrible beauty. Within it seemed locked a cosmic potential that called to be reached, explored, tapped.

Soon, in my training sessions, I began to focus more on the Orbs than the purpose they had set for us. I saw these close approaches as a chance to study the Orbs, to engage myself when all else of meaning had been stripped from me. In the Orbs I began to see what seemed to be pathways, like trails in the woods, locked off by iron gates. Roads to the past, the future, *elsewhere*. Was there a latch on the gate? I looked; more and more I looked.

Until one of the group leaders called me aside one day.

"Your scores have dropped. You must raise them or be eliminated."

It seemed that they monitored the individual performances in the horde.

"What are the Orbs?" I dared to ask.

"The Orbs are a mystery. We do not approach them. We use the space-time distortions they leave to travel through hyperspace between Orbs. Stick to your lessons, or you will face elimination."

He walked off like a robot, and I knew he meant what he said. As hard as it was, I tore my attention away from the Orbs and back to the assigned task. Soon, our initial group of nearly one hundred was whittled down to less than twenty, as attrition from madness, illness, and poor performance took its toll. Our group was now as optimized as it would get, as I judged from the performances. It seemed the aliens were happy with our progress. Soon we approached the Earth-Orb for the last time and were instructed to guide to a particular String. As we did so, a power surge went through the ship. We maintained our course and approached the String until the spacecraft lay directly in its flow.

What this looked like to the human eye, with its limited sense of a narrow band of electromagnetic radiation, I don't know. I can guess it was fairly unremarkable. The Orb and Strings would be invisible, and only the slow movement of the starship in the vastness of space would be seen. Then, the ship would accelerate dramatically, vanishing in seconds to a small point as it exited the dimensions we can perceive.

To my "eyes" it was an utterly different experience. In the bright and glowing stream of the String, there was radiance passing through the ship, through me and all around me like a churning stream growing to a broad river. As I began to be mesmerized by this vision, there was a whirl of equipment being engaged, a strange tug deep inside me, and then, while my body felt as if it were being turned inside out, my mind drowning in showers of infinitely complex patterns of light and dark that erupted and flowed around me, the ship plunged through hyperspace toward a distant world.

Chapter 14

$$\ell_P = \sqrt{\frac{\hbar G}{c^3}}$$

Execrable son! so to aspire
Above his brethren, to himself assuming
Authority usurp'd, from God not given.
He gave us only over beast, fish, fowl,
Dominion absolute; that right we hold
By his donation; but man over men
He made not lord; such title to himself
Reserving, human left from human free.

John Milton

I should explain how it was I became able to "see" the events around me. The descriptions of the events to come all depend on this ability I first tapped into on Earth during my first meeting with the Sortax. It was in visiting their home world during our first real navigation that this skill blossomed within me so that I could recognize what I was doing and control it at will. Perhaps being among them again, in the presence of so much that was alien, helped to trigger it. This skill has allowed me to compensate for my blindness.

The power to visit the past, which had not only provided me with an education but also a refuge in which to hide from the painful realities of my life, offered something immediate and practical: the power to form images of things around me. It was as if my mind could weave a tapestry from memories so that my new, strange sense could wrap its impressions in the visual metaphors of my lost sight. These are what *visions* are for a Reader, the blending of our sixth sense with the efforts of our mind and imagination. It is a painting of the impressions of this sense in a manner we can understand. Perhaps if we had developed the ability to Read as infants, we would not need to do this: we would "see" in this new way just as we see with our eyes and smell with our noses without needing to frame the experience with another sense. But our abilities begin near puberty, when the rest of our brain has already been shaped and is far less plastic than it once was.

In the beginning, I had used this sense to learn of things I could not have known any other way. The further from my own personal experience, the harder it was to "see," as if such things were at a greater distance. Naturally, many of those things I was most interested in were very far away and required great concentration, and I had to practice my skill to perceive things in any useful manner. The significance of things very, very close, those things that were very easy to perceive, I had initially failed to comprehend. I had ignored them— things that were obvious to me for many other reasons, and that were also part of the world I was seeking to escape emotionally.

Then the Sortax came to Earth, and in the panic, the fear of being near the truly alien, my survival instincts focused my awareness, focused it tightly to Read moments, milliseconds that were only recently past and that were very close to me. If you Read so close to the present, it is very little different from *seeing* the present, except that you have the power to see not only what you might have seen with eyes, but also beyond that, to all the events you chose to explore through space-time. And so it was and became again as we descended through the turbulent atmosphere of the Sortax home world. My mind focused, and this time I understood what I was doing. This ability served me tremendously from that point on in my life. It was also the starting point for the next obvious step – the exploration of events not only moments past but also short times in the future, and from that, the much harder and powerful deliberate search into the future of events to come.

Once through the clouds, the vastness of the planet became clear. Perhaps three times the size of Earth, the entire surface was covered with purple water, and through a descending orbit that traversed nearly two-thirds of the circumference of the world, no sign of land, not even a small island, was present. It became obvious that there would be nothing to "land" on, and that these creatures lived beneath the waves, and under them we would be going.

The ship soon arced sharply over the sea and then made a swift dive down toward the violet water, shuddering as impact was made. The howling sounds from streaming across the atmosphere were replaced with the churning flow of liquid outside the walls of the ship, and quickly the sounds of pressure on the walls could be heard as a soft groaning as we plunged deeper and deeper into the ocean. The Sortax must have lived terribly deep in these waters, and I wondered how creatures like us of fragile flesh, bone, and air could survive at the depth and pressures of their underwater cities.

After what seemed like hours, the ship, now more a submarine, stopped descending, and the metal-on-metal clunk of our docking rang throughout our small room. Then there were several moments of silence as the terrified breathing of those around me punctured the air. Once again we were placed into the alien and unknown: alone and powerless. This time I was less afraid, assuming that there could hardly be anything worse than what had happened to us so far.

I could not have been more wrong.

The door to our chamber opened, and our human Shepherds instructed us to follow them out. The Sortax must have exited through another location this time, likely one designed for their underwater lifestyle. Our exit was under atmosphere, and we were not given any suits to put on. Instead, the ship had docked with a corridor that led deep into the recesses of our new submerged city, or a small air bubble within it. As we walked down the tunnel and then into the many chambers that were maintained in these Earthlike conditions, I was amazed that these aliens had gone to so much trouble for our survival. I was soon to learn, however, how wrong I was to think this was all for us.

"Into the examination room," barked one of the Shepherds, as he pointed to a large chamber to our right. The architecture was disturbingly unlike anything a human mind could have designed. The walls and supports undulated as they curved toward the domed ceilings; the material was some type of metal never seen on Earth, a pale green that seemed almost to give off the slightest glow. Illumination came from what seemed to be a moss-like substance embedded in the metallic walls themselves. The floor was of a similar metal, but more brown, and it was incredibly slippery so that several children had fallen already.

As we entered the chamber, we had our introduction to the Dram. Tall, insectoidal soldiers that were right from out of my earlier vision. Several stood at what seemed like attention beside large pieces of equipment, carrying long objects that even in their alien form could only be weapons. Smaller Dram, marked with symbols on their thorax regions that I could not decipher, crouched down, adjusting elements of the machines.

One by one, we were led to these clusters, were stripped, forcibly placed onto a square region in the center of the machinery, completely restrained, poked and prodded in every orifice. Skin, hair, blood, saliva, and mucus samples were torn from our bodies, devices run over different parts of our anatomy, and all the while we lay helpless and terrified as these enormous insects appeared ready to dissect us on the spot. As they removed my clothes, I did not resist them, but I held on to the one thing that mattered to me—the Red Sox hat given to me by Ricky. I balled it in my fists, clenching them tightly, willing to suffer whatever might come if they tried to take it away. Lucky for me, they didn't seem to focus, or perhaps didn't care, about the crushed baseball hat in my palm. They were too busy removing all possible dignity from the rest of me.

In all that turmoil, I was unable to recognize the startling fact that the Dram were breathing the same air we were, were living at our pressures and temperatures. If I had noticed, I would have pieced together that these chambers were not for us but had been made long before to comfort the Dram, whose control of all planets in the sphere of the Orbs was near absolute. They ruled with such power over the galaxy that the Sortax had allowed this giant air bubble to be lodged so deep within their undersea civilization.

As they finished with me, a probe came out from the side of the examination equipment. A Dram worker rolled me so that my back faced the probe, and instantly I felt a searing burn across my skin. I cried out, as so many others had, but could not move as the sharp ends of the Dram worker's many arms held me in place. A small chip had been inserted into my skin that held all the relevant data for those who would be in the market for human Readers: my training certification, physiological profile, estimated age, and expiration date.

Then we were marched off into a second chamber that I can only describe as a human market. One by one, we were placed on a small stage and displayed in complete humiliation: alone, naked, cold, and afraid. Small devices that resembled odd cameras whirled about us. A device would also scan the chip in our backs, all the information presumably transmitted to the bidding aliens who needed Reader services. What I didn't know was that, based on a weighted formula of many of our traits, we were each given a score. Those with the highest scores would likely serve in pleasure craft of the rich governmental ships or military vessels. Lower scores meant passenger freighters or, worse, the wild and cheap auction market that attracted any of a number of despicable space travelers. My blindness and deformity lowered my score greatly, and as yet they had no inkling of my gifts, no means by which to assess them.

Afterward, I was led by a robotic drone down several corridors and into the storage room, where we were placed into small, coffin-like containers and packaged for delivery to our new owners. I was doomed to land in the hands of some of the vilest criminals of the space-faring races, of a form I never even saw but whose monstrous cruelty almost killed me. Worse still, through all that they did to us, my spirit was nearly shattered. This is the hardest part to tell you. Even now, I become faint and sick just thinking about it.

I began to shiver. My breath came out fogged, and a gel-like foam spread over my body, injected from the sides of the pod. It was incredibly heavy, and I could not move it, even as I struggled. And it was *cold.* Ice-cold and burning. I started to shiver, but slowly my panic faded. My shivering stopped. I could hardly keep my eyes open. I yawned. Sleep—heavy, deep sleep descended on me like an enormous blanket, blocking out the pod I was in and my fear. I forgot where I was. All light faded as I tightly squeezed the crumpled baseball cap in my numbing right hand.

Chapter 15

$$\frac{\dot{a}^2 + kc^2}{a^2} = \frac{8\pi G\rho + \Lambda c^2}{3}$$

The whole visible world is only an imperceptible atom in the ample bosom of nature. It is an infinite sphere, the center of which is everywhere, the circumference nowhere.

Blaise Pascal

Somehow in that artificial sleep, I dreamed.

I was floating in space. Not in a ship or spacesuit, but floating freely like some child in water, an impossible wind blowing over me from molecules of air that could not exist in this emptiness. I felt no cold despite the fact that it should have been absolute zero around me. The air in my lungs did not rush out into the vacuum and the saliva in my mouth didn't boil. Nitrogen gas didn't bubble in my blood giving me the bends, nor did my eardrums rupture. Despite the lack of oxygen, I didn't get light-headed or pass out. In fact, I felt comfortable. Free. *Was I dead? Was this my spirit?*

I looked around. A yellow star shone at a distance, but

even though I stared at it without the filtering of atmosphere or protective glasses, my eyes were unhurt, and the intense ultraviolet radiation had no effect on my china-white skin.

Our sun. Our home star. It was then that I marveled that I could see.

In front of me was a small point of light. Like a magnet it pulled at me, and I felt my body accelerate, slowly at first, and then faster and faster. Slowly the object grew in my field of vision, a small white coin, then a plate, and finally the pocked surface came into focus. *The Moon*. My rate of approach slowed as the white disk began to fill my range of sight.

An unease grew in my stomach. A sense of foreboding, of danger, even of evil lurking on the other side of the disk. Something wrong, something monstrous was hiding behind our Moon, something deadly and murderous. And I felt it, I felt it searching, seeking, trying to peer around the dead ball of rock. *Searching for me.*

I knew it was close, but I could hear voices on the other side. Voices calling out in fear, terrible fear and pain. Voices crying out together, like some nightmare chorus, rising in crescendo and sweeping over me like a tempestuous sea, and then, in one terrible instant, silenced.

What had it done? What had the monster done? Concern for the voices that cried and anger at the monster overcame my fear. I began to gain speed, to drift toward the other side of the Moon. The lunar surface swept past, and my eyes became focused on the horizon, on the edge where I would see the bright-blue of Earthrise. Soon, any moment now, I would see home and find my way to the cries for help. I could hear them echoing in my mind.

They were calling out my name.

Chapter 16

$$Q = 2 - \frac{4}{p}\sin p + \frac{4}{p^2}(1 - \cos p)$$

When I look up at the sky, I somehow feel that this cruelty too shall end, that peace and tranquility will return once more.

Anne Frank

When I awoke from the hibernation the transport pod had induced, the first thing to hit me were the smells. Human odors, not alien odors. Odors of human waste and decay, of sickness and death, of filth from a hundred bodies malnourished, unwashed, and weakened with illness and despair. Right after this stomach-churning stink, small robots grabbed us from the pods and herded us through the entry port into a larger chamber. The simultaneous visual assault of what was left of the human beings on this death boat combined with the smell nearly cause me to vomit—an addition to the room that would hardly be noticed. It took a few moments after that initial revulsion for me to finally look into the deep and hollow sockets of the people in the room, and feel the bone-chilling fear of staring death in the face.

They made no sounds. Standing idly or sitting listlessly, voiceless, bent as with great age, these zombies seemed like cattle in pens, dumb eyes staring yet seeing nothing, hair matted, filthy, even falling out. Sores festered on their legs and buttocks, all too visible through the torn and frayed cloth or, in many cases, the lack of any covering at all. These were people who had lost all sense of personal dignity or sense of self. They were emptied of those things that made them once human, or even animal—they were broken and dying.

I had never seen anything like it in my life, even at the worst of the treatments I had received. There were so many of them staring at us. My entire body shuddered. My soul wanted to scream. What could have done this to them? I took the Red Sox cap and placed it over my bulging head, pulling the bill down over my eyes to shield me from these stumbling horrors. It was a pointless attempt to hide from them.

I had no idea where I was now. After I had been sorted at the Sortax home world, and packaged in the pod, I had been made to sleep. *For how long?* It could have been days or years—there was no way for me to tell. Where had they sent me after that? Who had purchased me? Why? There were questions, but in this place, there were no answers to be found.

Like shepherd dogs, the small robots herded us to the far metallic wall. Small depressions in the floor indicated places to stand, and if we didn't understand, the metallic hounds pushed us around and into place. A loud crash above our heads startled me, and as I glanced upward, a panel slid open to reveal a metal claw with three fingers snaking down toward me. Several people near me screamed, and some tried to run. The robots, merely annoying up to that point, showed that they had a bite along with their bark. They swooped in quickly, zapping anyone out of place with a painful jolt of blue electricity, repeating until we were all back in place. Meanwhile, the claw had descended and clamped around those of us who had not moved, the metal fingers with one hundred joints seemed to morph into a boa constrictor. We were held tightly in its grip.

Once we were all loaded in the claws, they raised us upward into the tube above. Like some part in an assembly line, we were sped along several tubes by the robotic arm, up, sideways, down, and then fitted into place. I was dropped into a hard, wet seat, restraints fixed around my legs and arms, rows of others to my right and left in a similar position. A syringe with a large needle emerged from a small panel to my right, and before I could even react, it had pierced my thigh and injected its contents. To this day, I don't know what was in it, but I assume it was a combination of antibiotics, vitamins, and steroids—something to keep us alive and healthy as long as possible in the conditions I would soon come to know all too well.

Beneath me, the smell of urine and feces. I noticed that the seat I had been strapped to had a hole in the middle. You can guess what that was for, and what the wetness I felt seeping over my skin where I sat must have been. We worked twelve-hour shifts before the claw brought us back to the holding pens where we tried to sleep; nature would call. We were also fed at our stations. Running the length of our row in front of us was a trough that would periodically fill with a green sludge for our consumption. We had to bend forward and slurp the stuff up with our mouths. At first the rancid smell of it prevented me from eating. But after two days, even that nastiness tasted heavenly to a starving body.

After the needle had withdrawn and several of us had screamed or wept or cried out in other ways, the navigation helmets descended and plugged us into the system. It was like the training sessions, almost the same interface for our minds. At first, we were led through a series of drills, clearly not real, as there was no sensation of travel through hyperspace. The crew was not going to take chances on us guiding them through a star or asteroid field. They had lessons to teach as well, harsh ones. For anyone who did not match the correct trajectories, there was an electric shock, a longer punishment than the robots gave, dispensed from the seat. A few in our group screamed on the first run, the pain so terrible that I saw tears in the eyes of a girl next to me. Mentally, a projection of the correct path was emphasized by the machinery from the helmets, and from that all were supposed to learn. Very soon, all in my group had learned, and the shocks and screams stopped. These lessons never ended. Anyone performing poorly could be shocked at any time. Later on, as our physical and mental state deteriorated in this nightmare, our performance dropped. Some lost all ability, and when shocks did not work, the claw descended and removed the offender. We never saw them again.

After those initial test runs and the harsh punishments, the crew brought us online for the first hyperjump. Again, the beautiful Orb came into view, that increasingly seemed to me like some pure thing in a dirty universe. The indicated paths were shown, and we directed the ship to the set course, and then the tug and inversion feeling of the jump passed through me.

Repeat this endlessly, and you have a good idea of our quality of life.

Our time became a drudging monotony. We never saw any

of our destinations. We would guide the jumps, wait in position for docking, hear and feel the loud noises of cargo transfer, and then we were back out and headed to the next jump. This would happen perhaps every hour, giving us ten or twelve jumps per shift. For many it was exhausting concentrating under the pressure of pain to guide the ships correctly. At first for me it was quite simple. As my body began to fall apart over the coming months, it became a challenge even for me to focus on the tasks. By then most of those in the group who had come on board with me had disappeared, having ceased to be able to function adequately. They were quickly replaced.

Much later I would learn from the Xix that this had been a smuggler ship, part of an underground black market of traders that often employed human Readers as disposable slaves. These smugglers ran nearly ceaselessly, maximizing transfers, minimizing downtime, and mercilessly running through humans like some obscene form of organic fuel to drive and guide their ships. It was all illegal but tolerated up to a point by most local authorities. We were considered a low form of life, with poor self-awareness, unable to suffer like the more advanced life-forms. Our exploitation and pain was rationalized away. Laws were often ignored, especially when there was wealth to be had.

I still cannot fully reconcile these two perspectives: one, this galaxy presented academically by the Xix and others, an economic truth of an unfortunate nature; and two, the minute-to-minute torture of the hell I lived through. Those things could not possibly be the same. They were from two different universes. In my current life, I choose not to think of it, because I feel madness lurking in trying to reconcile those incongruent truths. Telling you now is harder than you can imagine. But it must be done. It's part of the big picture, understanding the truth about reality that you have been made ignorant of until now.

After our long shift, the claw descended and carried us like used baggage to one of several large and crowded rooms. These holding pens consisted of cold, hard walls and floors—no comforts, no divisions for privacy, no separated areas to take care of bodily functions, no space for a human being to have any sense except for a festering claustrophobia. We packed ourselves together, cold, choking on the poorly conditioned air that made our throats and eyes raw, lying in our own excrement, trying to find some short period of sleep before the next shift. During this time we went without food. Anyone acting out was quickly targeted by robots. As you can imagine, there were many who could not adapt. Some turned violent, some became catatonic. Either way both were removed, never to be seen again.

It all sounds so bland as I read what I have written. I don't have the words to make you smell the stench, feel the oppression of senses, the fear of smothering in others' awful bodies or of the unclean conditions in which we lay. I know of no way to tell you how this state of existence began to rob me of my sense of self, my ability to think or feel or remember what life on our beautiful planet had ever been like. It was as if all that was real was the horror around me, and anything else was only some faded and remote dream of fresh air, green grass, blue skies, and smiling faces. And hope.

But there was no hope in this place. The dream became ever more remote, seeming a cruel delusion to torment me with beauty and kindness and freedom I could never have. Reality was nightmare, a plane of Hades, and we were the tortured souls never again to know decency.

Every few days the room was flooded with a harsh blast of

cold water at high pressure. It left abrasions on our skin, but for a short while it washed the filth out of the way. The water tasted awful and smelled of toxic chemicals, no doubt to further disinfect the room. Our owners used these coarse methods to keep us healthy—sanitizing washes, injections of antibiotics—as long as was possible. But they would not care for us individually, and even these efforts left us, one after the other, depending on our constitution and luck, succumbing to infections we had brought with us from Earth. Our weakened immune systems could not keep up. Skin sores and boils, respiratory diseases, and the ever-present diarrhea brought us down. Some labored on, seeming to have infinite willpower, dragging their skeletal forms forward, coughing blood, *trying*. Others seemed to reach a point at which life seemed not to matter, and they just lay down and refused to do more, and were removed.

"Nights" were the worst part of it, if you can identify a period as day or night in a place with no sun, no changing lights. Like fish in a can, squashed together in filth, hearing the moans of the sick, the weeping of the broken. Their hopelessness was more infectious than anything else. There was no peace, no rest. I almost looked forward to the navigation hours.

And so it went, hour after hour, day after day, for weeks that blurred in my mind until I could no longer keep any kind of count of time. My body began to waste away. I spent several painful sessions with intestinal illnesses that made me wish to die. Soon, I had lost so much weight that my ribs were like an anatomy chart, my pelvic bones jutting sharply from my sides. My clothes were an unwashed, raggedy set of strips that hardly covered anything I normally would have cared to cover. Ricky's hat was still on my head, but it had been soiled, partly torn, stained beyond ever being clean in this awful place. By this point, I didn't care. I can only assume my eyes had begun to take on the hollow look of the creatures I had seen when I first entered the spaceship. Creatures for whom death is a mercy to be welcomed.

Through all this time, I had lost the ability, even the desire, to travel into the past and had forgotten anything to do with the future. I was a zombie stumbling forward, knowing only to perform in the seats or face pain, to eat as much of the green sludge as I could before feeling sick, and dreading the feverish nights in the holding pens.

It was at this point that I discovered a thing that would have quickly led to my death, or to the breaking of my spirit before my death.

As I leaned over one navigation session to slurp up the food from the trough, a woman next to me was crying. I would have ignored her. Most of us who had been there more than a few weeks began to withdraw from emotional and social bonds. We became zombies, numb to everything around us except immediate and sharp concerns. The woman was staring at me, crying, then she began yelling. She called me a monster. Finally, I looked over at her. She was a recent addition, acquired at one of the last stops. She was fat, her clothes intact. Her emotional outburst indicated that she would not last long. This place would break her quickly.

"How can you? How can you eat that? What have they done to you?" she screamed at me as green porridge leaked down the sides of my chin. "Look! Look at what they make it from!"

Slowly, I turned my head and stared at what she was pointing toward. Even more slowly, the blur of green food cleared, and there, in the midst of the awful glop, was a severed human finger. It had the same greenish hue, partially ground up, but it was a finger nonetheless, clear as it could be. Amazingly, I looked back at her, not yet able to process what my eyes had seen.

"Don't you care?" she moaned. "Oh, God, you're eating each other!"

Finally, understanding spread inside me. It was a terrible revelation. In all that had happened, in all the things that had been done to me or that I had seen, I had at least felt detached, a tortured innocent caught in the monstrosity of others. Now, tasting that food in my mouth, understanding what I was eating, I became the monster. For the first time in my life, I felt tainted. I felt evil. I felt as if the devil had transfused my blood with that of a hundred murdered infants. I was eating my own kind.

I threw up. I vomited over the trough, and for the first time since I had come to this place, I wept. I felt my insides melt, felt my sense of myself as a person dissolve. I had become a disease. I spoke nonsense to the woman.

"I'm sorry," I cried hysterically. "I didn't mean to. I'm sorry, I'm sorry, I'm so sorry!"

But she only cursed at me more, and at everyone in the row. She condemned us to hell for our actions. I stopped crying. It was all so clear. The poor woman, she was so lost. Didn't she know that we were in hell? And we were corrupted by it to the uttermost evil?

I stopped eating. I could not clean myself of this stain, but I could at least not continue to debase myself now that I knew. Let me tell you, though, it was the most difficult thing I've ever done in my life. All that I went through, and all that I would go through—tortures, cruelties, sacrifices—none of them compared to the trial of simply not eating that inhuman,

human sludge. If you have never starved, you cannot understand. I would lean toward that porridge, weeping, wanting to bring it to my mouth, my body screaming at me, my saliva dripping. Somehow, I stopped myself. Somehow, *a madness*, I forced myself to starve more and more, until my body became a thing almost separate from me, and my thoughts like some mind floating above it, guiding the actions.

But it was not a triumph. Don't ever believe that it was. Because I *wanted* that food. I wanted that food more than anything I had wanted in my life or that I have wanted since. You don't know what it is to starve. I only managed because of my own terrible, terrible need to find my humanity, whatever was left of it. Like some dishonored Samurai plunging a blade into his abdomen, I tortured myself for that. But even now I can feel the terrible hunger I had for that food, and it still dirties me to remember it.

My time was now very limited. Quickly, each hour, I grew much weaker. After three days of not eating, I could barely focus on the navigation and slept little at night for the pangs of hunger in my belly. I am sure that I would have failed the fourth day, been punished several times by the chair, and then been removed, to be sent and processed myself into the green slop.

But on the fourth day, the Xix came.

Chapter 17

$$\hat{\mathbf{L}}_{\mathrm{GR}} = p^{\alpha}\frac{\partial}{\partial x^{\alpha}} - \Gamma^{\alpha}{}_{\beta\gamma}p^{\beta}p^{\gamma}\frac{\partial}{\partial p^{\alpha}}$$

The greatness of a nation and its moral progress can be judged by the way its animals are treated.

attributed to Gandhi

If you were to cross an iridescent and elongated Smurf with a spindly-armed alien from early science fiction films, add sixfold radial body symmetry, and throw in a large dose of ballerina-like elegance of motion, you might get something close to the impression a typical Xixian specimen would give. But you would still be missing the heart of these noble aliens, something that I hope I can show you in my own words in the next few chapters.

When I first encountered the Xix, you must imagine me to be hardly human anymore. I was a dying and wasted thing, starving, skeletal, my gums bleeding, sores all over my body. I no longer cared to live and could barely process the reality around me.

The demon-ship that held us in torment had docked, and the usual sounds of unloading and loading could be heard. In the midst of this routine, an unusual racket erupted over the expected sounds. Perhaps I heard explosions, although my mind was not in the best state to process anything. Then a deep silence fell over the entire ship. Distant at first, and then growing louder, footsteps could be heard outside our entry port. Equipment was placed outside the door, and then with a loud crash, the seal was broken and the door pulled aside.

The long and tall Xixians walked in, carrying devices of some kind in one of their four arms. They were uniformed in unusual garb that resembled robes stitched together at several points along the often highly angular contours of their bodies. The clothes were dark blue, with alien insignia and characters I could not decipher, and their porcelain and faintly iridescent skin contrasted sharply with the dark hues.

Of all the aliens I was actually to observe before I returned to Earth orbit, the Xix were the most humanoid, even more so than the insectoidal Dram. To begin with, they were bipedal: two legs, even if strangely proportioned for the Earth-raised, with six-pointed feet harboring not toes exactly, but protrusions that would have to be compared with toes. The legs were multi-jointed, clearly supported by some kind of muscle and structural elements utterly foreign to Earth physiology. Were an Earth creature's legs to bend in several directions simultaneously, attempting to support weight at those absurd and dangerous-looking angles, the bones would snap, the ligaments tear. Instead, the Xix tolerated those ridiculous bends and just danced to a strange rhythm in their gait. Two very long arms near the midsection of their bodies, as long as yet thinner than the legs, also adopted the multi-jointed angles of their lower body. These arms ended in six-toed "hands" very similar to the protrusions on the feet. Nearer their heads, pulled slightly inward, were another two arms, much shorter and thinner, consisting of only two joints and ending in a set of very different hands. These much finer and smaller hands were also radially symmetric but with twelve elongated fingers of six joints each, so bendable, yet strong, that when they moved they almost appeared as tentacles. These hands held the odd spherical devices, like a weapon.

The top of the torso, fused together like a cone, erupted outward with three sets of six eyestalks. This was what I thought of as the "head." Each set of eyes was also positioned with radial symmetry around an axis running through the middle of the body from top to bottom, so that the Xixians could see very well from all directions. Membranous fibers seemed to span the area between the thick and highly mobile eyestalks, but there was too little mass for any kind of a brain-like organ, which, I was to learn later, was positioned in the center of their large barrel chests.

These quasi-humanoid creatures stormed into the holding pen where I lay dying. After scanning the area carefully, they drew back their weapons and spoke into small communicators around their smaller upper hands. All of us drew back instinctively from these creatures, truly monsters for the human psyche. Within several moments, two Xixians in slightly different uniforms – lighter blue, with different insignias – entered through the door. They appeared to have a highly modified form of the "universal translator" worn by other aliens like the Dram or used by the Sortax from their tanks. It was much sleeker in appearance, also functioning as a kind of gas mask to alter the composition of the air brought into their bodies. Once words began to pour through the devices, it became clear that they were of a far superior and significantly more advanced design to those any other aliens used.

The first sounds from the device worn by the two new Xix sounded suspiciously like Chinese to me, and indeed, several Asian men and women in our room glanced up at the sounds as if they understood them. After an initial burst of Chinese, I heard other languages spoken, foreign, but clearly not alien. Even when unintelligible, they were sounds that touched my heart. Sounds of Earth. Finally, the words were spoken in English.

"Please be calm. We are here to help you, to remove you from the illegal confinement and abuse in this criminal vessel. We are representatives of the Xixian Federation, charged with Life Rights for creatures in this parsec. We will take you to better quarters and provide you with medical assistance. When you are healed, we will help you find appropriate and safe work within the Hegemony. Again, please do not be afraid. We are here to help you. We are a rescue party."

No one moved. We were all beyond the ability to believe or process much intellectually. As we stared forward stupidly at our saviors, several teams of Xix in green uniforms—the medical crew, as I came to think of them—rushed in through the door and began to attend to the worst of us. Others were approached by more light-blue-uniformed nightmares, who spoke soothingly and tried to gather humans together and lead them through to the outside. *How gentle they were!* If there was anything to map between human empathy and the alien psychology, it seemed to me that the Xix *felt our pain*, and genuinely cared for us. My long association with them has taught me only how amazingly true this is.

At the time, however, I could no longer stand. I felt the many-fingered yet delicate hands of two Xixian medics lift me onto a hovering stretcher of some kind. Bobbing up and down in a crazed dream, I saw the snaking eyestalk head of one of them bend over and look at me, passing a strange glowing device over my body. A warmth spread through me, and my pain lessened, and slowly, but irresistibly, I fell down into a deep, deep well of darkness and into a peaceful sleep.

Chapter 18

$$\nabla \times \mathbf{B} = \mu_0 \mathbf{J} + \mu_0 \varepsilon_0 \frac{\partial \mathbf{E}}{\partial t}$$

For after all what is man in nature? A nothing in relation to infinity, all in relation to nothing, a central point between nothing and all and infinitely far from understanding either. The ends of things and their beginnings are impregnably concealed from him in an impenetrable secret.

Blaise Pascal

Again, I dreamed.

I floated through the black of spacc, a small point of light growing in the distance. Larger and larger, it took on the dimensions of a disk, a great pocked disk of rock rushing toward my disembodied perspective. *The Moon.* I did not recognize the surface patterns. It was the moon, but not the Moon I knew; craters and lines of patterns were unknown. As the Moon rushed past me to the right, now covering most of my vision, the bright blue and white of the Earth peered over the edge of its satellite, and the Moon slowed to a stop to reveal nearly half of the glorious marble set in the black of space.

Home. I felt myself weep, but there was no body to respond, no tears to fall. Slowly, I felt my perspective gain momentum, revolving around the Moon toward the right, the Earth dipping below the disk. *Earthset.* I longed to see it again, and as I spun around toward the other side of the moon, I felt myself straining to catch a glimpse of the edge of the blue disk breaking out over the lifeless surface of the moon. *Earthrise.*

I traveled over the surface, the dark side of the Moon giving way to the patterns I knew. Continuing, flying in orbit across the surface, and still the Earth did not break over the horizon. *Where was it?* How far around did I have to go to see the Earth? I wanted to go home.

Around and around, peering, straining. A cold chill passed through me, and again I felt the presence of something terrible and wrong. The monster was near. *I had to find the Earth!* I cast my vision across space, straining for a glimpse of anything besides the Moon and this blackness.

A terrible laughter echoed around me. Long and cruel, it pierced my spirit like a poisoned sleet storm, echoing, echoing in the infinite darkness. And I *knew.* I felt it like a knife in my gut. It was gone. *Earth was gone.*

I felt myself scream in silence, my rush around the Moon increasing, spinning faster and faster, seeing remembered patterns of the surface, then back again to the unremembered, around and around, yet everywhere, only darkness. *Only the Moon.* Panic welled inside, I felt as if I were to strain and stretch until I snapped. Around and around until the surface became a blur.

The Earth was gone!

Chapter 19

T proves that if T proves that $(P \to Q)$
and T proves P then T proves Q.
In other words, T proves that $ProvA(\#(P \to Q))$
and $ProvA(\#(P))$ imply $ProvA(\#(Q))$.

Only the shallow know themselves.

Oscar Wilde

I awoke in a soft bed, feeling stiff, as if I had slept for a time uncounted. At first, all was dark, as in my dream, and fear gripped me before I remembered: *I am blind.* Calming myself, I made an effort and scanned the immediate past. From the nothing of darkness, the dream of my past reading became visions of the recent Now, and my location was painted within my mind.

It seemed I was in a small room. A warm light like an early spring morning shone on my face from a kind of lamp overhead, casting earthlike tones to the objects around me. I lay on a small bed, blankets of some strange material draped over me. Next to my head was a blue and red artifact with a stretched and sewn strap in the back, a stained bill and top, stitched lettering across the front—Ricky's hat. It looked like someone had even attempted to clean it. Two broad and strange chairs were in front of my bed. In each chair sat a monstrosity. As my mind cleared, my memory returned, and the months on the death-ship flooded back. At the last, when my strength had failed, I remembered the entrance of the strange aliens: the Xix, *our salvation.* Little glimpses, like half-recalled dreams told me I had awakened several times to lose consciousness, that I had been in several places, attended to by these creatures, but no details emerged.

Where am I?

Two tall Xixians, green robes covering their unusual bodies, sat in front of me, their snaking eyestalks and fingers squirming as the rest of their body remained still in their seats. The fear of them had begun to leave me. Somehow, I knew that these creatures had purposefully taken what was left of us off that ship, and that they had cared for me. Why, I did not know. Fear still remained for what they might want with me.

"Welcome back, Ambra Dawn," said one of them before I could muster any courage for interaction. Its translator was strung about its strange head like a necklace, lights flashing across the surface as words were spoken. "Please, do not be afraid. We are medics of the Xix. We have tended you since our forces retrieved you from the smugglers."

"Smugglers?" I managed to croak out. My throat was very sore.

"Barbarians," spoke the other in an identical pitch, identical accent, although a different personality came through the cadenced inflection of the words.

"You were nearly beyond our aid. Many of your companions already were," continued the first one.

"Where are they all?" I asked, afraid to hear the answer.

"Those that survived are well cared for at a rehabilitation facility."

"Rehabilitation?"

"Yes. We are a division of Xixian forces devoted to identifying groups that violate the laws in place ensuring the proper treatment of underdeveloped creatures. Too often more advanced species abuse their power and resort to treating humans in unconscionable ways, simply to maximize profit. Too many do not believe in your ability to suffer, or do not care. Our job is to police such abuses. Your shipmates will be healed as much as we are able to heal them, and then reassigned to more, shall we say, humane, employments."

My mind attached a soft smile to the words. Of course, the Xix had no teeth or mouths that I ever saw. They never dined with us and it was always my theory that they absorbed their food through their rough skin. I'm clueless about how they interfaced with the translators.

"Why am I here?"

The eyestalks swiveled around and settled on me. "Because you are special, Ambra."

"How do you know my name?"

"You have spoken much in your delirium. We have been careful to record and study everything about you once we understood your value. Shortly after we brought you to medical services, our scans of your body identified items of interest beyond the illnesses and damage to your body that we sought to repair."

"My tumor."

"Yes, Ambra. But I don't think you fully appreciate your condition."

"I hate it."

"Yes, that is understandable. But we often hate things we do not understand."

The second one spoke, its many eyes focusing on both me and the other Xix. "Ambra, who modified you? Was it Earthlings? Or others?"

"Modified me? Oh. You mean the surgeries." I turned away from them. For some reason, I felt ashamed. "Humans did it. They wanted the tumor to grow. I think my Reader powers come from it."

"Yes, Ambra, they do. Did you know that many humans have such tumors?"

I turned back around. "They do?"

"They are much smaller. All humans with Reader powers have this growth in the brain. It is a recent alteration of your neural physiology, within the last fifty thousand of your Earth years. In most it is no larger than the tip of your finger."

"But in me?"

"Your genetics combined to create a benign tumor in this tissue, accelerated in growth by hormones at puberty. The surgeries modified your brain tissue, your skull, vasculature – all to allow the tumor to grow uninhibited. It gives you special abilities."

"I don't want to be special."

"But you are, Ambra." I turned away again. Several seconds passed in silence until the first one continued the conversation.

"We know you are blind."

"Yes."

"The scans revealed the damage from the growth to your brain tissues involved in processing visual information. And yet, Ambra, you see."

I remained silent, turned away from them. I didn't know

what to say. Most of the conversation had been from the first one that had spoken. The second leaned forward.

"Ambra, I too am a Reader. Readers exist in many of the alien species in the Dram Hegemony. But our talents are weak compared to human Readers. And compared to you – there has never been a Reader like you, Ambra."

"The man who did this to me said there was. He said there was one who predicted me."

There was a long pause. The Xixian Reader then continued. "We will not speak of this right now. But what you say is true. But you have the potential to surpass everything that he has done."

My head was swimming. Already fatigue was catching up to me again. *What did they want with me?*

The first one spoke again. "Ambra, how is it that you are blind and yet you see?"

I shook my head. How was I going to explain all this? I couldn't really even explain it to myself. My trips to the past – where they real? Was I mad? Did I really *see* or did I imagine? After everything that had happened to me – kidnapped, my parents killed, the surgeries, the aliens, being sold, nearly driven to death, and now this – how did I know I wasn't mad? And if I wasn't, did I even have words to make sense of it all?

"I…I look at things that were…*before*. I can look and see things, many things, that have happened. It's like a web or weaving dancing in my mind…no, I don't know, I don't know how to explain it. Things far and close. If I look close, and at those things near me, I can see what was moments before, which is like seeing what is now. Almost. That's what it is for me."

The two were silent, and their eyestalks darted back and forth between each other. I guess it's what I would call a "knowing look" for these creatures. Something passed between them. The Reader spoke.

"Ambra, you may call me Thel. I have been assigned to you. There are many things we would like to know. We need to know what you can see."

Finally, it was enough for me. The fatigue, the questions, the strangeness of everything around me. I nearly shouted. "Why?! What do you want with me? I just want to be left alone. I don't want this anymore. *Please*...please. Can't you just take me home?"

Thel spoke softly. "No, Ambra. We can't."

I began to cry.

"For your pain, we would. But there is so much you do not understand."

"What? What don't I understand?" I sobbed out between breaths.

"Earth is not safe for you, Ambra. Earth is not what you think it is. You seem to have explored the past, but not thoroughly, or you would have seen that several hundred years ago, Earth was infiltrated by agents of the Dram. In humans, they found a gold mine, herds of humans with powerful Reader potential. They quickly subverted your cultures, your nations, and guided the development of your civilization with the sole goal of breeding, identifying, and selecting humans of the greatest Reader powers. There is no place on Earth where their influence does not extend. Should you return to Earth, very soon you would be back in their hands."

"Like I'm in *your* hands?"

"We believe we are different, Ambra."

"Prove it. Let me go. Take me back!"

"Ambra, we do not wish to use you as the Dram would use you, only for selfish gain. But we need you. Not only the Xix, but many alien species need you. And your own race needs you, too. Quite desperately."

"What can you need me for?"

"The Hegemony of the Dram has ruled our galaxy for too long. There are those underneath their rule that seek what you would call liberation. This Resistance needs you. Only when the Dram are defeated can they be removed from Earth, and your own planet be freed. Nothing on Earth is as it seems. You are not in control of your destiny. You are puppets on strings. Cattle that are bred, raised, and taken for one purpose: slavery."

I was still for several moments. Have you ever had a sudden sense of truth, of something that was hanging over you, but until that moment, you couldn't see it? Right then, hearing those words, a thousand things came together – the searches in the past, my life experience, their words. And like some landscape becoming clear in a fog, I *knew*. I knew it was true. I had felt it all my life, this *wrongness* of our life on Earth. The sense that things were not making sense, were not as they seemed, and that something – something darker – lay behind it, blotting out the real sun.

"Revolution?" The word sounded electric in my ears.

"This is not the time to speak of it, but yes. There is so much for you to learn. But your powers offer a key to unlocking the shackles the Dram have placed on so many."

"Why don't *you* fight them?"

"As Xix, we are poorly suited to this task."

"Why?"

"It is an irony for many in the Resistance. The Xix have surpassed all others in knowledge and technology, yet we are unable to seek the destruction of others, even for the greater good. We of Xix excel in the making of things, in the healing of hurts, in the explaining of what little of the universal mysteries that we can. Violence, the infliction of pain – these are things we recoil from. It is beyond mere morality. It is wired into our tissues."

"You had weapons when you came. I saw them. And there were explosions."

Thel answered. "The explosions were attacks from the smugglers on our forces. Many Xix perished. The objects our forces held that you call weapons can stun attackers, but they cannot kill them. That is as violent as we can be. And only some of us are able to undertake such training."

The other Xixian followed up on those words. "We know this weakness in ourselves yet we cannot alter it. So, we seek other means or the means to empower others to resist. Ambra, we suspect that you may be that means, what our Resistance has been seeking for a long time. Something to turn the tide. The Dram are ruthless, powered by terrible weapons and technology we of Xix shudder to even imagine. They were the first to probe the Orbs to manipulate them, because they wanted the power. All of the Orbs connect, Ambra, and they are all found near the planets of intelligent life. This led the Dram to many worlds, worlds that mostly were not prepared to resist such an aggressive and merciless foe. Galactic wars followed, but soon the Dram overpowered all. Now, the galaxy rots under the tyranny of the Dram. It must end."

The Xixians did that thing again with their eyestalks and then spoke once more to me.

"We see that you are tired. We have said as much or more than we should have. We will let you rest. You have the means to examine the truth of our words. Use it. Come to see that we do not deceive you. Soon, we will return to speak more, and, if you will consent, to begin to try to understand your real potential. For now, we travel toward the next step in your journey."

"Where will we go?"

"Someplace safe. A secret place where you will learn the depth of what awaits you." The two Xixians stood, legs moving at impossible angles, yet the motion was fluid. They strode to the door at the far wall.

"Rest now, Ambra Dawn, *Reader*. There is much yet that you must do."

The door opened and within seconds closed, leaving me alone in the room. Alone with too many thoughts for my exhausted mind to hope to consider.

Chapter 20

$$zz^* = (x + yj)(x - yj) = x^2 - y^2$$

The mind is not a vessel to be filled, but a fire to be kindled.

Plutarch

The next few weeks found my body healing, and my sense of self returning to me once again. I was still thinner than I ever had been, and the sight of food always made me sick to my stomach. Memories of that horror still are with me. I forced myself to eat, because whatever had happened, whatever my life meant anymore from my old perspectives, the words I had heard after waking on the Xixian ship had struck a deep chord. I didn't know who or what I was anymore, nor did I know what I could possibly want from this existence, but if I could make a difference, if I could help *turn the tide* in a universe I felt had indeed gone very wrong, then that is what I wanted to do. Perhaps in that I might find something for myself. But even if I didn't, I had to live and see what my role might be.

Most of the other humans who had been on the smuggler death-ship with me had been removed to another place, off-ship. Only a few remained, I think chosen by the Xix for their Reader powers, as well as to keep me, their prized hope, from being isolated from my own kind. I became more and more grateful for this as time went on. While the Xix were gentle and kind, if always sharp with their probing, they were fundamentally alien. Even their smells offended some deep part of my primitive instincts. To have other humans around in this alien environment helped keep me sane.

We all worked together with the Xix. First, we were used to help pilot this craft. The Xixian ship was so different than those of the smugglers or the Sortax. Their architectural lines were so elegant, flowing, yet not wasteful. The other ships seemed thrown together by comparison, walls, floors, doors thoughtlessly and crudely assembled, showing signs of decay and impermanence. The Xixian ship seemed ageless, as if it had been made yesterday and would never show sign of wear.

Xixian navigators were onboard, but when we were brought to the navigation pods—small, womb-like boxes as unlike the stalls on the smuggler ship as I could imagine—the native navigators gave way for the humans. We were instructed to help pilot the ship on a strange and roundabout course. Thel, who was ever at my side during my time on the ship, explained that they sought unpredictable and less-traveled paths through the Orb String Tree, as they called the many branching and reconnecting paths of the hyperspace portals. Planets rarely visited by the Dram. Places where their ship would not be searched.

I wondered at this, as I could find no reason why the Dram should be after us. After all, it was only the Xix that had thought me of any value in this alien universe. The Dram had examined me, branded me, and auctioned me off to the lowest of extraterrestrial life. As time went on, I came to understand that it was because of the Resistance. Some of the high-ranking members had to be onboard this ship. That's why they needed such secrecy. Well, the last place I wanted to be was with the Dram again, so I did all I could to help steer us as the Xix wished. And for several months, we never saw signs of any other vessel. The transit times were on the order of several days per hyperspace jump. Unlike the smugglers, we took our time, and the Xix planned each step carefully. They also did not wish to tire us too greatly by using us as navigators, although the work was hardly much compared to what I had known. Instead, they wished us to focus our energies on the training and tests they lined up for us day after day.

Unlike the tests on Earth, or in the Sortax training ship, the Xix tests were much deeper, more challenging, and, as I came to understand, much more instructional in nature. Very soon, I had gone so far beyond the other human Readers that I got my own time, private lessons if you will, with Thel and some of the other Xix Readers and scientists. While I was clearly the subject of their tests, I never felt like a lab rat in their cages. Instead, it felt more like they were my teachers and I their student. I mentioned this to Thel, who seemed surprised that I was confused about something that seemed so obvious to them.

"Ambra, what good will you be to yourself, or us, or others, if you are not nurtured to become truly yourself? We of Xix cannot see an object only as a means to an end, but instead as a seed that must be nourished to become."

"To become what?"

"What it was meant to be."

Sounds cheesy, I admit, but these bizarre-looking things really meant what they said.

For the first time in my life, someone began to try to explain what it was that I was doing, what I was *seeing*, in the way all Readers *saw*. I was constantly amazed at the Xixian translators, which somehow pulled out of thin air the simple human words for ideas in math and physics I knew must be much more complicated in Xixian thought. Thel confirmed this for me.

"I will try to explain, Ambra, but you must remember that human language, even human thought, is far more primitive than Xixian. I don't say this to insult you, but to let you know that the words you hear are simplifications, and because so, distortions of the truth. But it is the best we have at our disposal."

I nodded, sitting patiently in the place I called the Practice Room, where every day, twice a day for several hours, I had my private lessons.

"I was trying yesterday to explain your Reader vision. Calling it *vision* is a good analogy, because like vision, or smell, or hearing, or taste, it is a sense. It is a part of your body interacting with the world around you in a way that gives you information. But it is also a poor word, tying you to a concept that distorts the information you are receiving, just like explaining sight in terms of hearing would be. When you *Read*, Ambra, your neural organ, that growth you call a tumor, is sensitive to particles like your eyes. Not photons, but particles that carry information about space and time. We might call them something like what your physicists call gravitons, if those were real particles that described the physics of our universe. But the gravitons you detect are of a different nature than Earth physics comprehends at present, yet they carry information of the fields of space and time just as photons do of the electromagnetic world."

Physics. I wished I had explored it much more carefully in my searches of the past.

"What is important to understand is that space and time are always changing, in flux, like electricity and magnetism. Your ideas about them are very primitive ones, and your recent physics of the last two hundred years on Earth has only barely scratched the surface of their complexity. But like you once could see the world, what had happened, and what would happen, with your eyes, so you can see such things with your tumor. More directly."

"It doesn't feel like that."

"No, just like it doesn't *feel* like that to *see*. Seeing gravitons isn't like some abstract particle physics diagram. When you were sighted, nearly every moment of your waking day, you were detecting photons, bundles of electromagnetic energy, quanta, wave-particles dualities—light. You didn't see the physics. You *were* the physics, and your mind experienced the powerful green of an Earth plant, the churning froth of flowing water, the diamond pinpricks of stars in the night blackness. These are experiences that shaped your emotions, your thoughts, your actions. Photons. That is something like the way a Reader can *see* gravitons, and yet as different from sight as sight is from smell. But no different in that it is experienced, extending into all areas of our awareness, our creativity, our dreams. We have a sense others don't have and can't really imagine. It's like explaining sight to a person blind from birth."

"Why can't I see the future like I can the past?"

"You can. That is how you navigate the ships, seeing the lines of possible connection."

"But I *can't* see the future like the past! The past I can see in detail. The future—when I do, it's like a dream. So many dreams. I don't even know if they are real."

"And you know the past is real?"

"I learn things that I find out are true."

"And so you will with your future dreams. You must begin to tell us of your dreams, Ambra. They may be very important."

"But I can choose to see into the past, search it, grab details, go where I want."

"We believe that soon you will learn to do this with the future as well."

When they weren't trying to explain what it was about, they were training me to see farther, faster, and with more detail. Most of that work focused on the future. Already, I pretty much could ace anything that they threw at me for reading the past. In fact, I know I could see things that their test couldn't pick up. But I was clumsy with the future, always going forward and then falling back. I was frustrated, and uneasy. As before, it was Thel who helped me understand why.

"You stumble not because you cannot, but because you *will* not."

"I will not what?"

"Ambra, you are afraid."

I sat quietly with this. The truth of it sunk in deep. I knew Thel was right. Always, when I began to peer over the edge of the Now and began to glimpse that giant landscape of what was to come, shimmering like a city at night, I could see the shapes of things I knew, and many I did not. Out there, in the middle of it, were forms of me. Whenever I began to sense them, I felt the landscape snap back and away, my vision darken, and I would lose focus.

"Why am I afraid?"

"You are afraid because you fear what you will see, of what will come to be. But your fear is misplaced."

"But I am afraid, Thel."

"You are afraid to see yourself in the future."

"Yes."

"You cannot."

"But I can! I can see shapes…"

"Shapes. Have you ever tried to focus on those shapes?"

"No, I withdraw before I do, without even thinking of it or realizing."

"Ambra, no matter how hard you try, even if you overcome your fear, you cannot see the details of your future."

"So, the future can only be seen in general terms?"

"No, that is not what I said. We believe that you will be able to see many details, of many lives, just not your own."

"Why not my own?"

"Few Readers have ever been able to see much about the future. Those who have seen the future always failed to see themselves. We of Xix believe we understand why. You have begun to study physics in earnest. Do you know the Uncertainty Principle?"

"Something about not being able to know where something is and how fast it's going?"

"That is an example. The general principle involves the effect of the experimenter on the measured. You cannot detect something with high detail without putting energy into the system, for example, using electromagnetic waves to visualize slides in a microscope or atoms with X-rays. The more precise you try to be, the more detail you seek, the more you disturb the system just by measuring it. Try to determine where an atom is exactly, and you add energy to it and speed it up. Try to measure its speed, and you lose track of exactly where it is. You can't have all the information in the system. Therefore, you can only know facts at a certain level of uncertainty. Information is blurred. A version of this applies when Readers try to determine their own place in space-time."

"Can *you* see my future then, Thel?"

"I have tried, as have other Readers on the ship. We cannot. Your mind casts such strong distortions into space-time that it is impossible to Read too close to you in the future."

"What does that mean?"

"It means, Ambra, that you have powers even we do not yet fully comprehend."

This triggered something in my mind. The Xix didn't understand everything. More than most, or so I was led to believe (and so I was to see verified in my experience and my past searches). But like other creatures, even they did not understand the Orbs. They used them, but like the rest, used only what seemed to be the overflow of power from those mysterious spheres. I had felt the depth and power in them. Something more than anything I had ever experienced. More and more I was drawn to them or, rather, to what lay within them.

"Thel, what are the Orbs?"

Thel was silent for a moment, its eyestalks dancing around. After a few minutes, I thought that it would not answer me, or that perhaps I had offended. When it spoke, it was deeply serious, almost with tones of awe.

"You have made the right connection in this conversation,

subconsciously, I am sure. The Orbs. They are great wonders that all species have studied, and still study, and yet which remain mysterious even to us. Do you ever wonder why it is that they are found only near planets with life, and mostly intelligent life?"

I had to admit I had not.

"It is much more than curious, Ambra. The Orbs are not natural objects like stars, nebulae, or planets. They are artificial, built several billion years ago for a purpose which lies locked within them."

"Built? By who?"

"This is a great mystery. We do not know. Whatever intelligence made them is beyond anything that we currently know in our galaxy—far, far more developed than anything within the Hegemony, even more than we Xix." I could almost detect a smile again in the tones of the voice.

"We of Xix believe that they were meant as portals. Not for the crude use we make of them, but for something more profound. And we also believe that their presence near sentient worlds is not coincidence but is causal."

I felt a strange feeling deep inside my stomach. "Causal?"

"The Dram consider this a dangerously threatening line of thought, Ambra. It threatens their rule, their power in the galaxy. But we believe that something far older than all of us, as old as the Orbs, and which made them, also was instrumental in the evolution of life, and intelligent life in particular, on all the worlds near an Orb. Most call them the Ancient Ones. We affectionately call them the Gardeners."

"Gardeners? Like we are their plantings?"

"Exactly, Ambra. I'm glad you seem to understand. Yes, we are the young saplings the Gardeners planted as seeds a long time ago in the little incubators we call solar systems."

My head was swimming. “Thel, what does all this mean?”

“It means the galaxy and the Dram are small things in a much greater Universe, and this should give us hope.” Thel paused, and then continued in the smiling tone I had come to recognize. “But you are tired, and have had enough for today. We’ll take this and other things up tomorrow.”

Chapter 21

$$S^n = \left\{ x \in \mathbb{R}^{n+1} : \| x \| = r \right\}$$

Imagination is more important than knowledge.

Albert Einstein

Nothing good ever lasts, someone once said.

I would add that even something that is okay is bound to get snatched away, too. I'm sorry to be such a cynic. I've just seen too much.

My time on the Xixian ship was not pleasant, was not what I wanted, but it was a time to heal, a time during which I learned much, when deep seeds were planted that would soon grow. It also turned out to be a short time, after which decency was once again shattered and evil stamped its ugly print upon everything in its path.

The attack came just as we were preparing for our next hyperjump. I sat in one of the navpods, helmet in place, getting ready to guide the ship as we approached an Orb in orbit around a star system with thirty-three planets, if you can believe that. It was mostly a computer-controlled run through the system of mostly dead worlds, each surrounded by automated mining equipment extracting materials for shipment to systems that supported life. We were maybe ten minutes from close approach to the Orb. I closed my eyes for the moment, resting my mind.

I had been making some progress in my studies the last week. More and more, I was allowing myself to face the visions of the future that lay just in front of my awareness. Mostly, it had been nibbling at the edges, predicting highly controlled events in the context of their measuring devices. But recently I had begun to reach beyond this. Seeing the future has much in common with seeing the past, but the past is not relived. When you see the future of your surroundings, and then watch it play out in front of you, it is at first extremely unsettling. In fact, if you glance just on the edge of the Now, you can recapture the ability to see the world around you, even in blindness. Almost in phase with the Now, it was useful for me. The further from the current moment I glanced, the more out of phase my vision was with what was happening, and yet the future would quickly become the Now. Like beats of sound when the tuning between two strings is just slightly off, my consciousness was battered by the rhythm of events – seen first in my mind, experienced next in my present. It is hard to explain, but it was fun to play with as I got the hang of it.

Just this day I had found myself creeping even farther forward, discovering events several minutes before they happened. I noted it to Thel, wondering if my knowing could lead me to alter the events I'd seen, and then wondering what I would see when I gazed ahead again.

"Paradox is only evident in a simplistic view of time, a

linear view of time. Space-time is decidedly non-linear, recursive in manners your scientists have yet to appreciate. Your visions themselves propagate waves through space-time, Ambra, which themselves alter what you see, like your swimming in the water changes the shape of the water in which you swim."

The memory of it prompted my mind forward again. Part of me was tired from it, like using a muscle unaccustomed to exercise. But I was also a little bit drunk on the wonder of the experience, and this thirst for the experience pushed me past the fatigue. I extended my awareness around us, even outside the ship and forward into the future.

My screams brought several Xix running to me.

"Thel. Where is *Thel*?" I called out, my breathing heavy.

"Ambra, Thel is not in the control center. We may send a message if you wish. What is wrong?"

I could barely speak, the shock of my vision like a blow to the stomach. "Oh God…Danger. Something…coming. The ship…attack! *Thel…*"

"The ship is in danger of attack?" repeated one.

Alarms erupted around the control room, the bright lights of the room went dim as emergency defenses were activated. A Xixian pilot called from one of its stations.

"Dram warship. Armed and closing." The Xix switched to their own alien language for more rapid communication. I still didn't know much about their technology. I assumed that they had some sort of defense shield or the like. But really, as so often in my journey from Earth, I was ignorant and helpless. All I could do was wait.

One of the Xix came up to me. "Ambra, we are trying to make a run for the Orb. Please be ready to make the jump. The Dram ship is firing on us, and we may not make it."

"Firing? I don't feel anything."

"You will not unless our defenses fail. We are absorbing tremendous energy from a determined attack of a fully armed Dram battle cruiser. There is only little hope. Please be ready."

I nodded and slipped the helmet on securely. The ship was dashing madly, flying dangerously through this obstacle course of planets and asteroids, heading directly to the growing presence of the Orb. The String we needed was clearly visible, and it would be easy to guide the ship, even at this speed, into its path. It would only be a few minutes at this rate. I was sure we would make it.

I felt the ship lurch horribly, artificial gravity failing, circuits exploding around us as power surges ran through the system. Our course maintained, however. Only moments to the String.

A Xixian voice spoke through my navpod. "Ambra, it is no use. They have hit the Time Turbines. We have normal mobility, but we cannot make the hyperspace jump."

My heart was stuck in my throat. *The Dram!* What would they do? "Will they destroy us here?"

"No. They hit us there to prevent escape. They could have destroyed us. Now, we are trapped in this system and cannot evade them. They want us alive, Ambra. They will board us."

In my mind the vision of the future I had glimpsed poured through my awareness. "Thel…" *No!* I shut my mind to the terrible visions. I couldn't let them board us. I couldn't let it happen. Thel said I could alter visions by my knowledge. *I would!*

The multifaceted and layered glory of the Orb still approached. I stared at it, drawn by my fascination and my desperation. Thel had said that they were portals, that we used them only in a crude and clumsy way. Portals to be opened how? I probed the layers, focusing all my thought on the Orbs, the layers, the interlocking pieces, tunnels in space-time that mixed and dove and intertwined like some sort of multidimensional maze.

"A labyrinth…"

"What was that Ambra?" the voice asked through the communication system.

"Steer us into the Orb."

"What? Ambra, that is impossible. It is certain death."

"*Please*…trust me. I can see….*doors* in the Orb. There are paths through the labyrinth…"

"Ambra, no one has ever approached an Orb straight on and survived. You have great vision, but this…how can we know?"

"Please! If we don't, many will die! It's the Dram!"

There was a moment of silence. Then Thel's voice spoke over the others. "Ambra, the Dram will have us in minutes. Are you sure about this?"

What could I say? Of course I wasn't sure! I didn't have any idea what I was doing. I only knew I had to do something. I *had* seen *something*—structure in the Orbs, and paths. Only I did not know the end point. Could we be lost in a space-time maze forever?

"Thel – I see through the Orb. I can try to guide us through. Give me control of the ship. Let me try."

"OK, Ambra. Better we die in the Orb than at the hands of the Dram. Or worse. I had hoped for more before death. If only to see Xix a last time."

And then, like understanding a geometry problem for the first time, a light spread from my time-sense image of Thel to me, and from me, to the Orb. The light seemed to set a series of tumble locks in motion, one after the other falling into place. *And I saw!* Clear as a trail in the forest, I saw a way through the maze inside.

Right at that moment, I felt the ship's control pass to me, and with a sudden burst, I plunged us directly into the Orb. The sphere seemed to brighten dramatically, as if some button had been pushed, activating it. And then, like the most insane roller coaster ride you could ever imagine, we hurtled through one space-time wormhole after another, darting through countless dimensions in directions that were impossible, perpendicular to everything, that could not exist in the human mind. Faster and faster, as if the Orb were infinitely deep within its finite spherical enclosure, the ship followed the path I directed, the path illuminated for me through means I did not understand. I could focus on nothing else, I could sense nothing around me, only the diving deeper and deeper into the bowels of light and space, bending around a circle yet finding ourselves somewhere new.

It may have lasted a second or a millennium, I could not tell, but there was a *before* and an *after*. The tunnel of light we followed opened not to another branch point but to a circle of darkness in which were embedded countless bright points of light. The ship erupted from an Orb behind us, the sphere glowing brightly as I have never seen the Orbs glow, and just like that, we were in normal space again. A green star shone before us, and very close, the outlines of a crescent of an orange planet.

I lay back in my navpod, sweat pouring down my face. My breathing was labored. This effort had exhausted me, but I knew I had done something never before believed possible. And I had saved us from the Dram.

"Ambra, are you all right?" The tones were Thel's, not elated, but sober, almost still.

"Yeah. Hey, told you I could do it!"

"Ambra, you did."

"Where are we?"

"You don't know?"

"No…crazy, I brought us here, so I guess I should. But I don't."

"It's Xix, Ambra. My home world. You listened to my last wish. Somehow, you heard it, saw its location. You brought me home."

Chapter 22

$$r_s = \frac{2Gm}{c^2}$$

What is life? It is the flash of a firefly in the night. It is the breath of a buffalo in the wintertime. It is the little shadow that runs across the grass and loses itself in the sunset.

Chief Isapo-Muxika ("Crowfoot")

Thel's words made me smile, and I laughed as I lay back in my navpod. "Hey! How about that? *Home.* That is a good word. Safe at last."

"No, Ambra, not safe."

This caused me to open my eyes and sit up in my seat. "What do you mean?"

Thel sounded tired, almost sad. "We've finally figured out how the Dram found us. They've been tracking you since you left Earth, on the chip they embedded in you. Another blind spot for us Xix, the deviousness of the Dram. The Sortax must have warned them that you had been valued as exceptional on

Earth. They didn't believe it, I guess, but they told the Dram anyway, just in case. The Dram, never ones to lose an opportunity, yet unwilling to waste too much energy on a wild goose chase, did not place a standard branding chip within you. They placed a hyperspace tracker, able to send weak signals along the Strings, allowing them to go undetected yet always remain aware of your position. We have just deciphered the signal, as it resonated with the Dram warships."

This didn't make any sense. "But they let me be sold to those monsters! I could have died there! If they were curious about my value, they wouldn't have risked wasting me like that!"

"You don't understand the Dram yet, Ambra. Yes, they would have risked it. In their philosophy, their extreme religious beliefs, strength rises to the top, is manifest in survival. If you had died, it would have proved, to them, your lack of worth, however myopic that viewpoint clearly is. But as we thought ourselves clever in zigzagging our way through the String Tree, the chip was reporting our every jump, and soon it became apparent to the Dram that something highly unusual was going on. We were telegraphing ourselves as suspicious through our clever methods to remain hidden. Finally, they converged on us."

"But we lost them. We are safe now."

"Initially, I had hoped so. But the chip was able to broadcast even through that series of dimensional portals you led us through. We intercepted communications as soon as we entered Xixian space. Dram warships were signaled and will arrive here by hyperspace any moment."

"Can't Xix protect us?" I asked with a growing desperation.

"Not overtly, Ambra. We dare not risk the Dram destroying our home world. And believe me, they can. They can be *terrible*."

My breath came in gasps. I was so tired from the journey that I could hardly think. It took an effort even to scan the near past or future to see around me. "What do we do?"

Thel again sounded sad. "There is nothing to be done. Our ship is without power. The damage from the Dram attack, and even more so the trip through the Orb, has left us floating in space, life support barely functioning. Before Xixian ships can come to our aid, the Dram will be here, right off the String from the Orb. We cannot fight, and we cannot run. We will have to be more clever than that. We will allow ourselves to be captured."

"Why?"

"Don't think that Xix has not been informed. They now know everything about our journey and will study the recordings of the Orb traversal. They will soon be convinced of your powers, Ambra, which are beyond even what I might have expected. But they will help only indirectly, or directly later when the time is ripe."

"Time? We won't have time! The Dram will kill us!"

"Kill us? Perhaps many of us, but not you, Ambra. They have seen what you have done. They will put together the information from the chip and the activation of an Orb. They likely already know that an Earth Reader, of potentially great power that they were tracking, was aboard a ship that traversed through an Orb. Nothing like this has been accomplished before. The Dram will do all that they can to learn this secret, to have this power. They will not kill you, not yet, not until they believe they have exhausted all avenues to gain this power for themselves. They will preserve you, Ambra, although they will not be kind. But you must survive! A little while, no matter what they do to you. I promise you, Xix will come. Somehow, we will come. You are our hope, and the doom of us all if the Dram control you."

"Control me? How?"

"Don't think of such things. Word is out. Xix will come. You must hang on, Ambra."

A sharp rapping on my navpod window shook me out of thought. A Xix pilot was standing outside, motioning for me to exit. I stepped out and looked around. The ship was dark still except for emergency lighting. The crew was mostly gone. The ship did look wounded, at death's door.

The pilot spoke. "Thel is coming. The rest of us are assembling near the entrances. A Dram warship has locked onto us, and we are being pulled into a docking position. They will be here momentarily."

Just then a door beside the elevator opened, and Thel moved in. Thel and the pilot spoke in the Xixian language, and then the pilot walked off to the elevator and disappeared within it. Thel walked over and crouched beside me.

"They are coming, Ambra. The slaughter is merciless. They are killing all Xix and scanning humans for your chip, killing those who do not match. We don't have much time, and I need to tell you something before they arrive."

My mind was swimming. Why couldn't we run? Hide? Something? Sitting, waiting for them to take us, it made no sense to my panicked mind. And something was forcing itself to my awareness, something ominous, something familiar. It felt as if the room were adopting some shape in my mind, a place I had seen before but had not visited. *Déjà vu.* Part of me knew it must be important, but I could not focus.

"Listen to me, Ambra!" Thel had gripped my shoulders, all its eyes bent toward me. "A last physics lesson to take with you."

Physics lesson? Had it gone insane?

"Sentient thought is a *field*. A *physical* field like an electromagnetic field or a gravitational field. This won't make sense to you, but it is a truth of the Cosmos. Now, grand unification theory marries all the forces of physics. Not as your scientists would have hoped, something far grander, and far more subtle. But a consequence of these two things is that sentient thought is coupled to the space-time matrix. The more sentient thought, the more complex it becomes, the more coupling. Advanced civilizations with many billions of hyper-intelligent beings can so distort space-time that this effect can be measured as small perturbations in the orbits of their planets."

I was shaking my head, not understanding. This was all gibberish.

"Ambra, thought *itself* sends ripples through space and time. We of Xix had always wondered if this could lead to communication through the space-time matrix."

I heard explosions and screams, the sounds of conflict and stamping of feet. I would have retreated to a corner and hid, but Thel's strong grip kept me in place.

"Communication?" I could only stammer out.

"Telepathy, you would call it. But nothing mystical or magical. You sense distortions in the space-time fabric, Ambra. Thought contributes to this matrix, hence, with your great sensitivity, you can sense those thought ripples. You can *read* minds."

I shook my head again. "Thel, no, I can't." The sounds were closer, louder. The elevator signaled that it was heading downward. What had called it?

"You can, and you *did*. Ambra, how did you bring us to Xix?"

"I don't know, Thel. I just saw the way."

"You saw a way through the Orb, but to where? You couldn't have known *yourself* where Xix lay. Yet what was the last thing I said to you before we entered the Orb?"

My mind raced. The elevator had stopped below and had begun its ascent. There was no time left. Something was coming. "I don't know! You said you wanted to go home once more!"

"Yes! Don't you see, Ambra? My thoughts were strong for home, and you picked them up, needing a path through which to aim in the Orb. You *read* my thoughts, Ambra, just as you *read* the past and the future. Both are embedded in the space-time matrix."

"It can't be true…"

"Ambra, listen to me. It is. Don't turn away from this! You must develop it and harness your powers. You will need all of them to survive what comes next. *Believe* in yourself, Ambra. *Survive*. You are what we have been waiting for."

Thel shuddered and flung her arms in several directions, one of them striking me. I was driven to the floor in pain. With a crash and a flash of light, Thel fell to the floor, charred and smoking, eyestalks filmed over and gray. Lifeless.

Behind Thel were several Dram infantry, weapons aimed in my direction. One stepped forward, raising a strange device toward me. I crouched lower, tears streaming down my face as I looked at what was left of Thel—alien, *other*, one of *Them*, yet my teacher, my healer, a force in the cold of space that cared for me. Thel was not indifferent or hostile. Thel was another thinking being that had spent its last moments to help me.

Tears for this death, and also for my failure to prevent it, dropped out of my sightless eyes. Now the vision that had been lurking on the edges of my awareness locked mercilessly into focus with the present. Now I remembered. I *had* seen this before, in my terrible vision of the future—a vision where Thel died beside me, the vision that had driven me to warn the Xix, and to find a way to pass through the Orb. I had seen this death and had opened the portal to prevent it as much or more as to escape the Dram warships.

But it had *not* saved Thel. My actions to prevent the future fit into the chain of events leading directly to it. *Why*? Because I had not looked closely enough. Because I had not examined carefully and considered the details of my vision. It did not console me that there had not been time, that the Dram attack was imminent and forced me to act. But in this it was clear that the future and its complexities were not to be taken lightly. I wept bitterly for my naïveté.

I examined the immediate present. The Dram soldiers put down a scanner and spoke in their hideous clicking language. Two armed soldiers raced beside me and lifted me harshly to my feet and dragged me forward in front of the leader.

"They are property of the Dram. Resist not otherwise they are eliminated," came the clumsy sounds of the Dramian translator.

I went limp and was quickly hustled by the soldiers through the Xixian ship and onto the Dram warcraft. Along the way, I stared helplessly down at the bodies of Xix and humans, side by side, gunned down and left to rot by the Dram army. I felt a terrible anger grow inside of me, like I had never felt before, even after everything that had been done to me.

I vowed as their troops tossed me through the ship that I would find a way to avenge those that died, for what the Dram had done to me, to my world, and to all the worlds beneath their savage rule.

Chapter 23

$$ds^2 = -\left(1 - \frac{2M}{r}\right)dt^2 + \frac{1}{1 - 2M/r}dr^2 + r^2 d\Omega^2$$

He who has a why *to live can endure almost any* how.

Friedrich Nietzsche

It wasn't long before they came to question me.

I had been thrown harshly into some sort of holding cell, which, like the rest of the Dram warship, had been made simply, efficiently, and with such a harsh sense of purpose that it bordered on architectural cruelty. Like the underwater chamber on the Sortax home world, the same strange metals and luminescence embedded inside the materials characterized the construction. Armed guards were posted outside my cell, which was surprisingly open. There were only three walls, the fourth some sort of invisible force field that let in light and air but resisted firmly any attempts to press against it. The harder one pushed, the harder the invisible wall became. I managed to slowly press a few fingertips half an inch or so through the resistance, but that was all I could manage.

The guards never glanced in my direction with their eyestalks. They seemed to have no fears of my escape. I suppose dumb humans don't score very highly in the "escape risk" column. And that pretty much was the reality for me. Soon I gave up and sat down in a corner facing the invisible wall, knees pulled up to my chest and my arms wrapped around them. But I didn't cry. Something else was inside me. So much anger and determination.

A Dram officer appeared from nowhere, clicking to the guards, who deactivated the shield wall. The officer entered with a guard alongside. It was shorter than the guards, dressed in a less militaristic outfit, and it carried no weapons. Its eyestalks were surrounded with small bubbles that seemed to float around the central eyeballs but without touching them. *Hi-tech alien glasses?* I wondered to myself. The insect bent its body nearly in half, the lower abdomen and its legs parallel with the floor, the upper part of its body and "head" at nearly a ninety-degree angle to the rest, the eyestalks and little bubbles pointed toward me.

"They are it, which opened the Orb?" it began as the translator barked the broken English at me.

Thel had admonished me to survive, but I could not bring myself to reply to these killers. The insect head tilted left, then right, seeming to seek a better view of me and my silence.

"They are it, which opened the Orb?" it repeated. Still I said nothing.

Then it began saying what I assumed was the same thing over and over in one Earth language after another. After ten or fifteen of these repetitions, it began to get irritating, and I figured speaking to this thing was better than getting a tour of badly translated Dram in all of Earth's tongues.

"English," I spat out angrily. "I speak English."

The insect was quiet, just staring at me.

"They are it, which opened the Orb?" it rang out again.

"Yes, for God's sake. Now, can we move on beyond this?"

The insect pulled out a small device, horribly reminiscent of the one the Sortax representative on Earth had nearly killed me with. Before it could activate the scanner I shouted out loudly, startling the bug and causing several of its many back feet to retreat slightly. The guard partially raised its weapon.

"Careful! You have to use the *lowest* setting on that thing or you'll kill me, and then I won't be any use to you. I am a powerful Reader, and I am far more sensitive to the space-time matrix than others."

"Applicable is this?" it asked.

"Yes! Try the low setting. You'll see."

The Dram officer adjusted the device and aimed it at me. I tensed, but it was not painful. A bit like having several different-colored laser beams flit over your eyes at very low levels. Compared to the Orbs, such simple, boring patterns.

"They are much highly cannot be measured." The Dram turned off the machine. "Why negative the Sortax explain rather to us?"

"Because they are stupid squid-heads," I added helpfully.

"Yes, they are stupid. To be punished." The officer tapped several things into a small device it removed and then replaced it on a belt around its upper abdomen. The thing then just stared at me, silently, for several moments.

Thel's words came back to me then, those mad words about me reading minds. The Xix had said it was real and that I could not turn away from it, but that I would need all my skills to survive. I decided to trust Thel's final words, to believe in them with all that I had. If they were true, then I would find out now and probe my captors.

I closed my eyes as the Dram creature observed me silently. Being blind, it didn't do that much, but it was long habit from sighted years when trying to focus. Slowly, using all my concentration and the meditative techniques Thel had taught me, I scanned with my unique organ, my sixth sense. Past and future spilled back and forth over me, but I ignored them, seeking for something different, something tied to the creature in front of me.

And then it happened, like seeing an optical illusion play out its different visuals in front of you. A subtle, so subtle and effervescent shimmering of a glow beside me came slowly into focus, and I knew, I could *feel* that it came from the presence of the two Dram in the cell with me. One was simpler, far more angular and hard. *The soldier.* The other was still harsh, as all Dram would turn out to be, but more complex, layered. There was a deeper intelligence and complexity in this one that was not in the other. Its thoughts disturbed the space-time matrix in several dimensions at once.

But also so much fear. *That* I could recognize even in this alien creature. A deep fear that was totally absent from the mind of the guard. This intrigued me and gave me a sense of my own power in this place. This Dram officer sought something from me that was terribly important.

My eyes opened. "Why do you fear me?" I probed, deciding to offer a wild opening gambit.

The insect once again recoiled, taking several steps back, then stopped. "They are an intelligent," it finally responded. It decided to resort to a lie. "The Dram fear nothing! But we are we try to we include, what you to be have made."

"You mean opening the Orb?"

"Yes! How human creatures, a nothing member of Hegemony, is in position so that does make such a thing? Which secrecy did you learn of Holy Orbs?"

Holy Orbs? This was getting weird. Since when did aliens get religion?

"Are you a priest?"

I felt a surge of anger from the consciousness of the creature.

"No! Never! I do not grasp the idiots of those superstitions! I besides the fact that power in the Orbs, it seems I and like me, understand those respect in order to control, seeking those."

Control? Power? A technologist! A scientist, perhaps. This made sense, and many of my readings of its mind now fell into place giving me a much clearer image of the personality and motivations of the creature I was dealing with. Motivations to be exploited, perhaps.

"I can control them. You wish me to give you my secret?"

The insect's feet padded up quickly, bringing its hideous face close to mine.

"When Dram wish, they take," it said ominously. I had to be careful.

"If you make a mistake, and you harm me, you may damage my mind, and you will never learn the secret. Do you dare take that risk now, alone? What will your punishment be if you fail?"

The wash of anxiety from the creature was like a prismatic spray. Again it retreated several steps. "They are a human intelligent, yes. Special. But in Dram is skillful large number very with persuasion. The Emperor thinks, is grasped that we consume this you-power; It orders. Then this word of you has not importance. Until time, enjoy the existence."

The officer clicked toward the guard who escorted the creature through the door and re-engaged the force field, leaving me alone, and for the moment, free from their probes.

But for how long? I could feel the time-tugs of hyperspace jumps—we had made at least four since I was brought onboard. The Dram could not go directly to the destination they wished as I had done by activating the Orbs. They were limited to the off-shooting Strings, and had to follow the indirect routes of the String Tree, heading eventually, I presumed, to their home world. The nexus of the Dram Hegemony, with their Emperor, and all their numbers "very with persuasion." Soon, I would be in their hands, and while I doubted that they could learn how I controlled the Orbs – *I* didn't even know – I knew that they very well might kill me in trying to find out. Or worse. I had to find a way out of this, for so many, not just myself.

Every expansion of my abilities has been centered on life crisis, and it was no different this time. I sat down in the cell, crossing my legs, closing my eyes, and throwing out everything that had been a part of my hiding from the future. I decided to take my potential seriously. I decided to risk anything, even my sanity, to cross over the planes of possibility and look the future square in the face. More than my life might depend on me becoming what I was meant to be, to let the seed finally sprout. If the Xix were right, perhaps the Resistance and freedom for so many in the galaxy rested upon it. Yes, it was megalomaniacal. But you can't let humility get in the way of the truth.

Nothing in my life or training prepared me for what was about to happen. I sank into a deep trance, my awareness focusing inward until I could count each heartbeat, analyze each slow breath as my lungs drew in the air and then forced it out. The universe around me became infinitely distant. But the secret in meditation is finding without seeking, and at this terrible distance, it became microscopically close to me. Slowly, one by one, the obstacles my psychology had placed in the way of my vision were toppled over by the force of my will. Each felt like a rush of panic, screaming to go no further, my soul terrified of what lay on the other side. But now I was filled with purpose greater than my fears, and I knocked them down.

Did you ever put a bottle in the freezer, super-cool it, pull it out hours later unfrozen, then tap it hard? It freezes all at once before your amazed eyes. That's how my sixth sense finally awakened fully within me. That enormous organ, grown to grotesqueness at the hands of my fellow humans, opened its odd eyes from a long slumber. It was like the sledgehammer striking the surface of the dam over and over, until the small cracks became fissures, trickling water, and then, with one fateful blow, the concrete shattered, and the water gushed forth with terrible force. I pushed through my fears and weakness, and the future burst over me so that it could not be stopped; a thousand visions flooded my mind, and continued to do so over the next few days so that I could not hope to even process them all.

I fought a strange battle to stay focused, to hold these visions at bay, to integrate the Now and the coming times. Present, Past, and the enormous Future churned and mixed within me so that one blurred into the other in a confused fashion—future events gave birth to past ones, the Past to both the Future and the Now. Cause and effect became meaningless, and it was as if I stepped out of Time and saw a giant ocean of events, tossing and twisting before me, waves undulating and splashing and morphing. There was no center from which to observe, no arrow of time, only the ever-churning currents of an infinite ocean.

I lost myself in this sea, set adrift never to find a place on which to stand. During this trance, I responded to nothing, even as, I later discovered, Dram medics and scientists tried to revive me. For three weeks of travel through the String Tree, and two more weeks in a hospital on the Dram home world, I lay unmoving, unresponsive in a deep coma. Fed intravenously, my captors, and representatives from several other species, watched with great anxiety my condition.

But I found my way home. The meaning of how it happened, I do not know. Somewhere, as the mists cleared before my eyes over the tempestuous sea, I saw Ricky smiling and laughing in the distance. I followed his voice, swimming against the raging currents, to some place within me where there was only me and the love I had. And there the sound of his laughter was full and loud, spanning my awareness.

I had finally understood what he tried to tell me that day.

Chapter 24

We do not rest satisfied with the present. We anticipate the future as too slow in coming, as if in order to hasten its course; or we recall the past, to stop its too rapid flight. So imprudent are we that we wander in the times which are not ours, and do not think of the only one which belongs to us; and so idle are we that we dream of those times which are no more, and thoughtlessly overlook that which alone exists.

Blaise Pascal

I drifted in space once again.

Space was terribly still. Uncountable patterns of stars lit the darkness around me. Behind, the golden light of the sun pushed forward, and, like a giant sail, I drew speed from the solar wind. Slowly, irresistibly, I accelerated, gaining speed past Mercury. Then past the sulfurous clouds of greenhouse Venus. In front of me, the Moon appeared once more, yet behind it, like a quarter surrounding a dime, the blue, white, and green-brown of Earth captured my vision.

Earth! There she hung in the blackness, in all her glory. After the violet seas of the Sortax home world, the alien structures of the Dram, the orange deserts of Xix, and the countless sterile and horrible things I had seen, even the saint-like Xix that still caused primal discomfort in my simian brain, here before me was that one place in all the expanse of seeming infinity that was right for me. For all human beings. *Home.*

I felt myself crying and smiling broadly at the same time. I rushed like some gleeful child into the arms of her mother, dashing past the lifeless Moon, arms outstretched and encompassing the blue marble as it approached me. *I was finally going home.*

My smile foundered, broke and faded like clouds on a mountainside. A terrible mask of horror replaced it as I watched in near madness as the planet I held in my arms began to dissolve. From pole to pole, sea to land, the sphere shattered like some stained-glass window, the separate fragments blurring and melting in my hands. Frantically, I worked my fingers and palms, trying to reshape the thing as if it were some melting snowball on a warm spring day. But there was nothing to stop the merciless process. Dripping right through my clasped fingers like flowing blue-brown ink, the Earth *melted*, and I cried out in anguish as the liquid poured through, then into the blackness of space, only to dissipate, evaporate into a faint mist and then to nothingness.

My scream echoed through empty space like some wolf's howl in a stone cathedral, reverberating and interfering, wailing for a soul abandoned and trapped forever in the cold of space, unable to perish, unable to escape, and forever unable to find its way home again.

Chapter 25

$$r_{\pm} = \mu \pm (\mu^2 - a^2)^{1/2}$$

No visiting angel, or explorer from another planet could have guessed that this bland orb teemed with vermin, with world-mastering, self-torturing, incipiently angelic beasts.

Olaf Stapledon

The first thing I saw when I awoke was the monstrous form of a Xixian medic. For a moment, I thought I was back on the ship with Thel. A false relief spread over me that the nightmare of the Dram attack and Thel's death, and the nightmare that was a dream of the dying Earth, were both unreal. Then I saw the Dram workers standing around the medic, and the doom and dread of reality struck me solidly in the stomach. Along with it came a resurgence in the grim determination I had developed since becoming a captive of the Dram.

"You are awake," said the Xixian medic. The Dram insects crowded around behind the Xix observing, their many hands and fingers tapping against each other loudly yet not interfering.

"Why does a Xix work with the Dram?" I wondered aloud.

"The Xix serve everywhere within the Hegemony," it chirped. "Especially in the medical sciences, where our talents and technology cannot be perverted so easily to actions that run counter to our being. We often prove quite useful," it said, with some seeming emphasis. I wondered if it meant something more than it seemed to be saying. Thel had said the Xix would know about me, would work to help me. Was this medic communicating this?

There was no time to find out. A Dram military officer stormed into the room, its composite armor clicking nearly as loudly as its many feet and the communication to other Dram in the room. It turned toward the Xixian medic. With several bursts of clicking sounds between them, the Xix bowed and left the room. The Dram officer turned to me.

"Depending upon us the best efforts employed, had in order to maintain human, its life. They must better prove the Emperor their worth."

"And if I don't?" I rebelliously replied.

"Then, they will end." It signaled to other officers who came in and began to wheel my bed out of the room.

"No, wait," I interrupted, pushing myself up and swinging my legs over the side. "I am well enough to walk."

The officer signaled to them to release the bed, and I walked of my own accord. The trance had weakened me, and my muscles had not been used for weeks while I was in the deep coma. But I had not been ill or injured, and I found the walk, while stiff and shaky, very much within my powers. Down several hallways and to an adjoining building filled with prison cells, I finally was stopped in front of a cell similar to the one I had been held in on the Dram warship. The force field was deactivated, and the Dram soldiers pushed me inside, reactivating the screen.

The officer stared across the barrier at me. "This health, it is good therefore to be maintained. That we being expected from directly, makes that trial is begun possible. The tomorrow supporter, the Advocate, is to be allotted. That it cooperates to investigation, is best your, with of everything where you are required is made clear."

Yes, best that I make *everything* clear to them, I'm sure. With that hardly veiled threat, it turned and hustled out of the corridor, leaving me to my thoughts and the silence of the Dram prison ward. I shook my head, wondering what this trial would be like, and what an Advocate could be in this system of justice with the Dram.

I was not left alone for long. Within a few hours, a group of four or five Dram that I now easily identified as members of the Technologists—as I liked to think of them—came tramping into my cell. The guards felt to me less than pleased to allow the entrance, clearly far preferring to obey the military wing in the Dram power structure, whatever it might be.

The Techies positioned themselves in a semicircle around me. Already, I had probed enough of the immediate future to anticipate their first actions, and I spoke to prevent any unpleasant scans of my brain.

"Before you pull out your scanners and fry my brain, please turn them down to the lowest setting. I am very sensitive, and can easily respond to your weakest signals."

The Techies nervously twitched and exchanged glances. Finally, one in the middle of the semi-circle revealed itself to be the leader and spoke.

"You expect our energies well."

I decided just to unload on them early. "I *read* your actions. I saw it in my immediate future."

"You are so much powerful Reader?" it asked.

"I can do this and many more things."

"You have then the open of the Orbs," it said, even the lousy translator somehow getting across in tone the awe behind the question.

"Yes."

"This possible with from Ancient Ones?"

"It comes from me!"

This elicited a lot of excited clicking between them.

"It should they are sharing these informations with us, that we can present to the Emperor!"

"I will not do that."

"It should! They will suffer in the hands of Emperor if there is not! And they will be in the danger of partisans that will seek death before they attend to what is known or can made be. For them, you gestate the Heresy, that contaminating the Holy Orbs. They will not allow in it in order to they will live. Only death given with them. It should there is saving and it say to us how this thing is made!"

Decoding their longer translations was always a headache. "The *partisans*? Oh, I see. The Priests." I didn't care if the term was appropriate; getting tangled in the petty politics of this murderous society was the least of my worries. I had seen too much. I decided not to break the news to this thing gently.

"Let me tell you something, insect. In exactly thirty seconds, an angry group of your priestly friends is going to show up here. You will have a screaming fight with them, and their guards will shout at the guards here, and you will be promptly thrown out on your exo-skeletoned asses. I doubt after that you'll get the chance to be alone with me again. So, there won't be a chance for me to tell you anything." I leaned forward, so angry I nearly spit in his eyestalks. "But even if there were, I wouldn't tell you a thing, you murderous piece of Dram vermin. You have enslaved my species. It is because of you that my parents were gunned down in cold blood and thrown into the sea. Because of your power-hungry rule, the galaxy is in bondage. I've watched Dram soldiers murder the innocent and brave. I will die before giving you the key to more power than you already have. And you might as well calm down. Here are your priest friends."

The anger radiating from the group was so great, I feared that they might harm me. But I had vision they did not, and as I spoke my last sentence, the priestly delegation stormed into the cell area, and the shouting (or clicking) match began. Soon, the guards forcibly removed the Techies to great waves of gloating from the Priests. They exchanged angry clicks all the way down the hallway until they were out of earshot. Finally, for the night, I was offered some peace.

But peace would not come. I began to shift through the visions of the future that had nearly consumed me, and that, at a moment's notice, if I did not hold them back, could flood over me again, blocking out consciousness. To stay within the Now, I had to exert enormous control, letting only small streams of information through, holding back the flood with willpower like a dam. Slowly, I was mapping out the near future, and more and more, what lay beyond. This conscious sifting through the events to come was controlled, logical, progressive, and exhausting.

The parade of visions loomed in my consciousness, so many to consider, too many to count, but I was beginning to separate the meaningless, the inconsequential, from those that were important to my life and to the lives of those I might one day affect. Imagine being blind, and then granted sight, opening your eyes at the top of a high peak, staring down over lower peaks, valleys, rivers, cities with bustling people and, in the distance, the glint of a great sea. Then imagine that you had never processed visual information, so that even the details of a falling leaf or the drops from melting snow could grab your mind's attention for hours if you were not careful to focus. Finally, mix in the fact that, down there below you, people you care for were in danger, and you had to find out where and how. This was something like my problem – so much vision, so little experience, and nearly no time.

Inspiration was found only in the world of dreams. Finally, completely drained, I would find sleep overtaking me, and in dreams I would make imaginative leaps to future events of more significance. And dominating everything, over and over again the next few weeks, was my vision of the melting Earth. It hung in my psyche like some bomb waiting to explode. *What was its meaning?* To know, I could not rely on the imagery of dreams. I would have to find my way to that point in the future consciously, and that would likely require a great effort to forge ahead, skipping careful deliberation, risking the dam breaking over me again.

The time was coming, I knew, when I would have to take this risk. But not tonight! I would have to face a lot tomorrow, and I had to face it sane and controlled. The dream would come.

Yes, I remembered, very soon, it would come.

Chapter 26

$G = (H \otimes I)\, C_N$

The single biggest problem in communication is the illusion that it has taken place.

George Bernard Shaw

A day lasts thirty-six hours on the Dram home world, which throws the human biological clock pretty out of whack. We can reset at different start points on a twenty-four-hour clock, but we don't do very well when the duration moves far beyond twenty-four hours in either direction. Here you remain in a constant state of surreal suspension, your body never able to adjust. Never completely awake, never restful in sleep.

The star in this system is a hideous red. Not the blending and warm red before nightfall of a sunset on Earth, but a constant, powerful red that bled into everything, washed out all other colors of human perception, even in my reconstructed memories of color. A giant star, already having burned through its store of hydrogen, ballooned up upon fusing the heavier helium. The Dram had evolved fairly rapidly from simple organisms that had made little headway in the cold, pre-red giant phase of this solar system. With the expansion of the star, their more distant planet had warmed dramatically, becoming a hothouse jungle for many hundreds of millions of years, and then, slowly, a desert world. The Dram were tough, harsh and unforgiving like the desert, capable of flowering at times, but all too often bringing death to those they encountered.

When the door opened the next morning, it was hard for me to know how long it had truly been since I lay down. In many ways, it didn't matter. I hadn't slept—like some feverish convalescent, I had bobbed up and down the entire night on an ocean of visions. The hard reality of my prison was a bracing contrast.

In walked a small guard of Dram, few in numbers, armored and towering insectoidal forms. I loathed them. Behind them entered a Xix with its absurd elegance. A captain of the guard clicked to the Xix, and its troop strode menacingly out of the room. The Xix paused a moment as the shield was reactivated, then bowed to me politely and seated itself on the ground across from my bed shelf.

I had slowly detached from the vision processing as the guards entered and raised my head slightly as the Xixian creature had entered. Now I pulled myself up and sat on the bed shelf with my feet on the floor, half in a trance still, waiting patiently for the Xix to speak.

"Greetings, Ambra Dawn! I am Waythrel of Xix, your Advocate for the Tribunal."

My *Advocate*. Well, this was exciting and unexpected. A Xix! "I am very honored and pleased to find that you are here on my behalf, Waythrel," I began formally, yet brimming with joy. "I feared one of these hideous bugs would be charged with the half-hearted attempt at defending me."

"The Dram often use Xix in official roles. We are masters of their language and laws, and are constantly updated with new tools from Xix itself. We are granted many privileges for our loyal and useful service. Your tone with the Dram shows that you are reckless and do not fully understand your hosts."

It's warning me. These Xix, always teaching! My mind raced, remembering the riddle games I played with Thel. "Updated from Xix" – it knows about me like Thel said! "Privileges for loyalty" – its position as my Advocate will be compromised if becomes clear to the Dram that the Xix are in a conspiracy to help me. "Reckless and not understanding"....what did it matter what I said? Unless here confidentiality meant nothing. Yes, that was it. The Dram were listening to everything! We had to be very careful.

"My teacher was Thel of Xix before my journey here," I began, hoping to convey that I was still a student and would do my best to learn. "I am ignorant of many things. Please be patient with me."

Waythrel removed strange devices from pockets in its robe. As these were activated, several opened to project visual information in discrete planes in the room, as if invisible screens had been lowered from the ceiling. Others opened like semicircular keyboards, one for each upper arm, with hundreds of keys for their many digits, and Waythrel began to type at what seemed like the speed of light.

"Good, then we may begin. You have much to learn before the Tribunal, and now only two Dramian days, or four of your Earth days, to prepare. Your very life is at stake, Ambra. I hope everything I have learned of you is true, because you will need all of your talents before the Tribunal."

Was it saying that I would need to forecast? As a Xix, it must know that I could not see myself clearly in any future.

"Not for points of law and theology – I will handle those myself, as much as that is allowed. But for your own questioning, you will need to understand the context in which you are being examined, Ambra. I will need to communicate this and much more with you, and you will need to understand me very thoroughly." It paused. "Sometimes, I think that these translators we make, however powerful, are almost useless. If only there were more direct ways to communicate these difficult things without the errors of language conversion."

Telepathy. It was telling me to use telepathy! Of course! How else to talk openly about important yet dangerous topics when the Dram were listening in? Somehow Thel had communicated this power to Xix. And somehow, I had to make this work. I had now read minds and feelings on several occasions, but had never tried to read details or send information. Could that be done? Or would I have to speak in this coded way Waythrel did? Could I do that without revealing to the Dram what I was doing? I doubted *that* very much.

"Yes, Waythrel, I think I understand what you mean. I am only an Earth creature, please, put these concepts to me simply, strongly, focusing on the key elements so that I might understand." If this was going to work, Waythrel would have to concentrate on the ideas intensely, and not in a complicated Xixian way, so that hopefully I could grasp them. I closed my eyes and focused inwardly again, breathing deeply. Slowly, sensing the glow of its awareness in front of me, I reached out to the mind of my Advocate.

I momentarily recoiled from the complexity. The mind of

a Xix made the Dram seem so simplistic. Like crystalline spider webs, its maze of thought dangled all around me, as I peered deeply and gravitated toward a brighter glow within. There were ideas I could sense but not understand. Others were accessible to me, and my mind clothed them in images, short memories playing in front of me like a video.

Amazed, I watched as Waythrel opened a memory to me and strangely did so through the eyes of another Xix as it exited a hidden chamber in the ship that I had piloted through the Orb. The Dram warriors had left the craft taking me back to their warship. This Xixian crew member had run to the bridge and found Thel just after the attack. The Xixian had bent down and touched the fibrous material between what had once been Thel's animated eyestalks. When their membranes met, images poured from Thel's dying mind, now only a faint light but still with a last contribution to make. Visions of the final few weeks on the ship, up through the activation of the Orb and the final conversation with Thel, entered the mind of this Xix. It was like a life download. Now this Waythrel had acquired the memories.

You see, part of Thel is within me now, Ambra. With all the Xix. And I know much of what you are and have done. Many in Xix do. We have distributed these memories.

I heard these thoughts! How would I reach back?

"I'm calmer now, Waythrel," I said out loud, "and ready to learn what you have to teach me. I feel that a part of Thel is with me in you."

I knew I had reached my mark by the long pause that followed. When it spoke next, I realized that our conversation today would be unlike any I had ever had.

"In what I say about the Dram law and custom, Ambra, you must listen at two levels," Waythrel began, "doing your best to understand each. I'll need you to let me know from time to time that you have understood all meanings in this complicated discussion."

The Xix's words echoed in my mind. *I mean hearing me here as well, Ambra. Please answer affirmative and nod your head three times if you do.*

"Yes, I understand," I said, following the instructions.

"Good. To begin, you must understand that historically, there has been a balance between the religious caste and the naturalistic caste here on Dram. This division has caused many conflicts, at times creating deadly wars, but it has been preserved through the ancient times of pre-technological civilization throughout the establishment of the Hegemony."

It is in this division of faith and reason that the Dram are at their most superficially powerful, but in truth at their weakest. In the long term, such an artificial separation of the undivided light of revelation is a sickness of the mind and soul, only too obvious in the myopia and brutality of the Hegemony. Societies that cannot believe are sterile. Societies that cannot doubt are arrogant fools driving over a cliff. The Dram sway between them in violence, tearing apart what must be united.

My mind was spinning. It was like hearing a conversation in one ear and a commentary in the other. I concentrated and tried to integrate these two streams of information.

"The Holy Orbs are at a nexus in this conflict. To the religious caste, the Believers, they represent a revelation in a spiritual dimension and must be approached in a purified and humble state before the Creator of the universe. The scientific caste, the Naturalists, sees them as primarily physical manifestations and seek to harness their power. Such actions are viewed as sacrilege by the Believers, who consider profiteering from the Holy Orbs to be a sin against God. Several millennia ago, when the Dram first encountered the Holy Orbs, and earlier Naturalists spoke of making use of the Strings, the dispute erupted into a civil war that exterminated nearly one-fourth of the Dram population."

Remember, Ambra, any species that can so viciously turn on its own kind will, with much less deliberation, become murderous toward those very different from them.

Part of me squirmed thinking about the actions of my own species, of Earth's numerous descents into slaughter. Were we any better than the Dram?

We must focus on the Orbs, Ambra. The Tribunal will make a decision about your life, and the manner of your death, based on how they view your manipulation of the Orbs. We of Xix feel that there is no safe judgment for you. If the Believers prevail, it will be torture and execution for heresy and sacrilege. If the Naturalists win the day, it will be mental enslavement to harness your power. We are convinced of your worth to the Resistance. Therefore, we are planning a terrible risk, to intervene on your behalf and subject ourselves to the wrath of the Dram. Please nod three times that you have heard these last thoughts and understand them.

Even though I was very shaken by what Waythrel said, stunned to hear that an entire species would risk themselves for a single alien creature, I managed to nod my head and to even respond with words.

"Such extermination in the Dram wars is something I would never wish to see, Waythrel."

The Xixian Advocate bowed slightly toward me. "In all such sacrifice, there is the belief that a higher purpose is being served. In this motivation, you may understand many choices, many actions."

I cannot yet tell you what we will do. We are placed in numerous positions of power across Dram and can therefore manipulate much to our designs. But this must be planned thoroughly, because for so many reasons, we cannot fail.

"At the Tribunal, you will be questioned by Advocates from both castes, who will then debate your fate before the High Inquisitor."

"Who is this?"

"The Inquisitor holds an office created many thousands of years ago to aid in mediation between the castes. The position, second in power only to the Emperor, is entrusted to an individual who must balance law and Dram culture between the Believers and Naturalists. This individual must come from one of the Isolation Zones, neutral ground in which the teachings of both castes are withheld until the Dram pass the age of maturity—roughly thirty Earth years. This is to ensure no bias in judgments."

And therefore this position is one of the most corrupt in the system. Enormous bribes are the norm, and those that climb to this position of power too often are hungry for such benefits. Beware the High Inquisitor!

"Tomorrow, you will be brought before the Inquisitor for an assessment in advance of the Tribunal. Here, you may receive offers of clemency should you acquiesce to the Emperor's will."

So much information! Information that I should be internalizing and thinking about. But I couldn't. I was still reeling from the offer of the Xix to risk so much to save me. I knew they were going to do this because they hoped I might provide a way out of the bondage to the Dram. But I also knew that it would mean certain death for the Xix, whether or not I was what they hoped. In my mind, I wouldn't be a hero, I'd be a murderer, responsible for the destruction of an entire species, the brightest and kindest and wisest I had encountered. I didn't know what to do. Something inside me rebelled against it. It couldn't be right. And my mind dashed forward in spacetime like some mad thing, heedless of getting caught in those infinitely complex folds that had nearly killed me the last time. I *had* to see enough of the right possible future to know what to do!

Ambra, we of Xix will risk much. All. We need you to promise us that you will do all within your *power to follow our plan when it is developed. Soon, I will come back with instructions. I need you to tell me now that you understand, and commit to this to us and our plan.*

What could I do? I could not lie, not to the Xix, not in this situation. But I could not let them do this. I steeled myself. What I *could* do was go along with their plan until I developed a better one. I had at least seventy-two hours until the Tribunal. I had to find a way out of this nightmare, just like I did with the Orb. Only this time I would look closely enough not to jump from one trap into another. This time, there would be no mistakes.

Ambra? Did you hear me? Please respond.

I was so full of emotion, that what happened next was over before I realized it had begun, and yet it opened the final door to the destiny that awaited me.

Before I could formulate a response in words, I felt myself emotionally reach out and answer Waythrel. In that instant, I watched it recoil slightly, its mental web showing some disorganization, and I sensed anxiety, surprise, and then awe as the webs reassembled into new and delicate patterns.

Ambra Dawn, what have you done?

What *had* I done? I didn't know how to answer. Its reaction – had I caused it? How? I looked in confusion over toward the alien creature.

You have entered my mind. Your thoughts were impressed in my consciousness. There was another pause. *We never expected this. Even Thel underestimated your potential.*

"Waythrel, please. I am not sure I have understood everything that you have told me today."

"You have understood much, I am sure. And we will speak more tomorrow."

Its thoughts continued to sound in my consciousness. *What has just happened is as important as your power with the Orbs, Ambra. I must report this immediately and seek advice. It makes you far more dangerous, even to us, than anyone could have imagined.* Waythrel paused in thought, concentrating on me with its alien senses that displayed odd and confusing images in my mind. Its next thoughts shocked me.

It means you not only Read, Ambra, you also do something few have even dared suggest might someday be possible. You touched my mind, its thoughts—my consciousness. This goes far beyond merely altering my mind, because of what it means to do that. Remember your lessons with Thel! To alter my mind means that you can modify space-time itself. This is unprecedented. It is terrifying. No one knows where such power could lead. Ambra, you are not just a Reader. You are a Writer. *The* first *Writer.*

"Until tomorrow, Ambra Dawn. Think about what I have told you."

Waythrel signaled to the guards, who disarmed the shield, and let the lanky Xixian past. I curled up once more on my bed, exhausted from today's efforts and now stunned by this recent exchange. *A Writer?*

Things were moving too fast.

Chapter 27

$$S(\Psi) = \frac{1}{2}\langle \Psi | Y(i)Y(-i)Q_B | \Psi \rangle + \frac{1}{3}\langle \Psi | Y(i)Y(-i) | \Psi * \Psi \rangle$$

Nothing is more despicable than respect based on fear.

Albert Camus

The red starlight waxed and waned, forcing its relentless way through my room across the small force field–buttressed window on the far wall. But I was becoming increasingly abstracted, diving into future memories and sifting, beginning to see the patterns of possible futures, of paths through them toward the goals I sought—escape, freedom, and ways of preserving the lives of the innocent who sought to help me. Waythrel returned several times over the next day and, noticing my withdrawal, questioned me. But while my ability to penetrate minds and use telepathy increased at a frightening rate, my focus was elsewhere, and, as yet, I dared not explain why to my Advocate. I absorbed the lessons to some degree, but, increasingly, as I worked my way through the future's maze, it became less important. Many of the details around my future self I could not see, and those that I could, many I ignored to find my way to a path that led home with the least suffering for all.

I did learn that my alterations of Waythrel's mind, the imprint of my own thoughts in its own, hadn't done any damage. The Xixian medics had performed scans of the brain-like organ in Waythrel's chest and had seen nothing unusual. Apparently, this telepathic communication I used was something like an external stimulus. But Waythrel was uneasy, voicing concerns that it need not be that way. And with the ability to modify space-time itself, all the Xix were very concerned about how my powers would develop.

All that mattered to me was that I got us all out of this. I had seen enough to know that, in the paths where I did nothing, where others took the lead, even the Xix, there would be untold carnage and chaos. Genocidal fires would smolder across many worlds in a galactic war.

Not that way. I began to see another future in the jungle of time. A safer path. *Safe for many*. A great tragedy loomed over the time horizon in my consciousness, but it was spatially distant and not dependent on what I could do. At that time it was bigger than my own abilities. I would face it as I had to.

As I struggled to find an answer, the hour arrived for me to be brought before the High Inquisitor. An unusually large and formally attired troop of Dram escorted Waythrel and me through the detention zone, via ground transports to another building, and finally into the chambers of the Inquisitor.

The office was held by a surprisingly unimposing Dram. One might call it a runt if it weren't still over six feet tall. From what I had learned of these creatures, it was old, its slow movements the best giveaway – at least to an alien life-form like me who had trouble distinguishing the signs of aging in other species. The Inquisitor was perched more than ten feet above us behind a green and gold counter, like some too-tall judge's bench. It looked down on us—no doubt literally and figuratively—from above during this short but very informative *assessment.*

Waythrel and I were marched in front of the bench, allowed a small but still claustrophobic space by the Dram guard. Everything was taller than me – the seven-foot-high Dram guards, the elevated Inquisitor, and even my Advocate. What did it matter? I had my own strengths.

Waythrel and the Inquisitor clicked back and forth for at least ten minutes. The Xix had told me that it would try to have the Tribunal abolished but had little faith that this could be achieved. There was clear documentation of my manipulation of the Orbs, and this made me a center of questions for power and religion in the Hegemony. After the discussion swayed back and forth between them, the High Inquisitor waved off Waythrel and addressed me.

"You have been informed of the charges?" The translator was of Xixian manufacture, an unusual choice for the Dram who were so suspicious of foreign devices that they most often chose to use their own, far inferior machines. Unless they were dying and needed Xixian medics, of course. Or, in this case, when a member was less intimidated. Waythrel had told me this mentally early on in the assessment.

Whatever it pretends to be, this one is a Naturalist. Only one very comfortable with technology would wear one of our translators. He will seek to make a deal with you to reveal your powers over the Orbs.

"Yes," I responded to the Dram above me.

"Would you repeat them for the Inquisitor."

"I am charged with High Sacrilege in the contamination of the Holy Orbs by an impure species."

"And do you know the penalty for such a crime."

"Purification, and then death." Meaning torture and then death if the torture didn't kill me first.

"There are other ways, human."

Ambra, here comes the offer. Please hear my thoughts on this before you answer.

The giant insect pressed a button, and lights dimmed as a cone of energy came around the three of us, leaving the guards and others outside of it.

A cloaking shield, Ambra. No one can overhear or record what happens inside. The Inquisitor is protecting itself from what it is about to say.

"The Emperor is very keen that the Hegemony possess the power you have revealed. I and the Emperor share a more enlightened view of your deeds than others on our world. While they may prevail in the Tribunal, we would have it otherwise. And if you will agree to the Emperor's terms, the Holy Office of the Emperor has the authority to annul the Tribunal."

"And if I refuse?"

Ambra! Wait, I said!

"Then you will find yourself at the mercy of the Tribunal," said the insect, an anger radiating from its consciousness. "And should the Naturalists prevail, you will find less kindness in your service to them."

The stupid fool. Already I could sense all the lies in it. I would suffer no matter what they said or promised. They would enslave me and recoil from no indecency to my person in attempting to extract the knowledge they desired.

Ambra, this is an important political turning point. If we can bypass the Tribunal, it will buy us considerable time and likely the momentary facade of better treatment. I suggest that you accept its offer. Let me express this to the Dram.

No! I shouted into its mind, and I saw my Advocate momentarily disoriented from the impact of my thoughts. I stepped forward and spoke angrily to the Inquisitor.

"Should I accept your offer, so that you will place me in better conditions for a time before ripping my mind apart? Turning me into an experimental subject on which you will work and likely fail to extract the secret you desire? No! I will risk a better death in torture before that! I will not work with the galaxy's fiends and murderers! Tell your Emperor that a lowly creature from Earth spits in his face!"

Waythrel had recovered by that point, and I sensed the overwhelming shock and panic in its mind. The anxious Xix thought the High Inquisitor would have me executed on the spot for this. That was nearly right, so much anger boiled out of the Inquisitor from my outburst. But I had seen the bright path to safety, and it did not end here. Poor Waythrel, it would be so hard to explain. *Soon, Waythrel, soon you'll understand.*

The High Inquisitor clicked angrily and soon the guards were ushering us back to my cell. Even as it spoke those commands, I had begun to withdraw. Seeing the bright path, I understood more and more what was required. Waythrel was speaking animatedly to me on the return trip. Little of it entered my consciousness, and surprising even myself, I began speaking out loud in the relative safety of the noisy ground car, a stream of consciousness as my mind's eye stopped seeing things around me but glimpsed the coming futures.

"They will fight over me, Waythrel, and the Naturalists will prevail."

"Ambra, what are you talking about?" it asked incredulously.

"Not even religious dogma can win over the chance for new power. I see them, conniving, backbiting fools. Scheming and drunk on power. But it will only be a prelude to a greater movement; and then, a crescendo of joy and sadness."

"Ambra, please, what…"

I turned my face toward my Advocate, tears trickling softly down my face. I didn't see the alien next to me. My mind was overflowing with the vast horror before my unique sense in time. "I can't *look*, Waythrel, I can't let myself look at the sadness, even though I know what I will see!"

We sat in silence for the rest of the trip to my cell. Just as well—I was somewhere else anyway.

Chapter 28

$$S = \frac{1}{2}\langle e^{-\Phi}Q_B e^{\Phi} \mid e^{-\Phi}\eta_0 e^{\Phi}\rangle - \frac{1}{2}\int_0^1 dt \langle e^{-\hat{\Phi}}\partial_t e^{\hat{\Phi}} \mid \{e^{-\hat{\Phi}}Q_B e^{\hat{\Phi}}, e^{-\hat{\Phi}}\eta_0 e^{\hat{\Phi}}\}\rangle$$

In this playhouse of infinite forms I have had my play, and here have I caught sight of him that is formless.

Rabindranath Tagore

When Waythrel next visited, it was a while before I could be roused. I lay on my bed shelf with open eyes and a slack-jawed expression. At first Waythrel misunderstood, as the tender skin where the laser had sealed the surgical incision had leaked some blood, staining my clothes quite visibly from the outside.

"Ambra, wake up! What have they done to you? Are you drugged? Have they tampered with your mind? Ambra, answer me!" The distressed Xix shook me with its smaller arms, eyestalks darting about in a panic. Some detached part of my mind watched it speak into a communicator, and within what seemed like seconds, although it was much longer, Xixian medics were surrounding me.

"She is not drugged currently," I understood one to say, but whether through a translator or through my telepathy, I don't know. "Remnants of a human chemistry narcotic are present, but at such low levels, they cannot be affecting her now. Furthermore, there is no intervention anywhere else except the abdomen. Her brain is untouched."

"Why is she like this then? She has to be at the Tribunal in four hours!"

"The visions," I whispered hoarsely, "they have never opened up to me like this before, Waythrel." I swallowed, my throat dry, my words croaking out. "Infinite layers and webs inside of membranes….I must learn to better control my exploration; it is too easy to be lost in it."

"Ambra, what are you talking about? What have they done to you?"

I felt more tears in my eyes. For myself, for the others I had seen, for the history and future of pain and injustices that cannot possibly seem to be balanced even by all the love in the universe.

"My eggs, Waythrel," I said, turning my head toward them. "You didn't think that they would risk losing me if things go badly at the Tribunal or afterwards."

"Your eggs." A statement. I could *sense* the wheels turning in its mind.

"Last night, they came, threw me on a table, cut me open, and took them. My possible children, taken from me before they could ever be." I felt a few sobs spasm through me. I had never thought that much about having children, especially with my deformity. I mean, really, what man would have this? But I had never thought I would be invaded and robbed like this. With this act, something primal in me had been violated by these monsters, and my soul cried out. My soul cried out to the heavens, wondering what else would be taken from me.

The Xixian medics scanned the areas where my ovaries were and confirmed the results.

"I am sorry, Ambra," Waythrel began. "We did not anticipate this. Once again, we have been overly naïve in imagining what the Dram might conspire to. It is obvious upon reflection. They wanted more genetic material to breed out your powers again. They could not clone you – human chromosomal instability has yet to be solved by the Dram. But your eggs – they could inseminate them with diverse sperm from males similar to your father. They have been plotting far ahead." Waythrel paused and only repeated, "I am very sorry."

"Waythrel, there was nothing we could have done to stop it," I moaned, trying to sit up comfortably. "Not now, not when larger things must be done."

"What larger things, Ambra?"

"It's all becoming clear to me now, Waythrel. A straight path home." I laughed bitterly, almost a cry, really. "No! Oh, *God*, no. Not home. Never home. But escape."

"Have you seen this? The Xixian Council is formulating a final escape plan. We suspect the worst for us, and are evacuating many of our kind as secretly as possible. But if you have seen our future, Ambra, you must tell us!"

I smiled toward the lanky alien. "It's okay, Waythrel. It will be okay. I'm seeing to it."

"You're seeing to it? Ambra, please, these stakes are too high for such riddles!"

I was beginning to fade again. "Don't rush me, Waythrel. Just a few loose strands left to tie up now, and the path is sure. Can't…rush like …. before. Must see…..*all* the paths." I floated in and out of a trance for the next few hours with Waythrel and the other Xix anxiously flitting about me.

Time marched slowly in my cell, yet danced maniacally before my consciousness as events rushed past me. I don't know how it happened, but finally, at a single point, these two different melodies of time met, and out of the myriad strings of the *perhaps* emerged a single thread of *destiny*. I know it sounds absurd, but that is the best way I can describe it. I opened my eyes, seeing the future and my present, superimposed like counterpoint, just as the Dram guard entered. We were silently marched to the Holy Tribunal.

Along the way, I continued speaking in stream-of-consciousness manner. I'm sure it sounded like nonsense to Waythrel, and the poor Xix likely thought I had gone mad at the most inopportune time, minutes before trial, hours before the Xixian plan that might lead to their destruction was set in motion, both of us trapped on a hostile and ugly world at the center of the Hegemony.

"It will never be the same," I spoke as the blasted landscape, cooked as if in a red furnace, devoid of greens, or blues, or even yellows, blurred by us in the ground vehicle. "A fetus as a single grain of sand; twenty billion souls burned, ruptured in a moment of time; all gravity; it was so simple; only *gravity*; space-time that bends thoughts, and kills; eons only it sat there, one long orbit after another; a stupid planet wannabe; but it would slay an entire world. These bastards, Waythrel—they will debate their creed while slitting a baby's throat."

Waythrel tried to have the Tribunal postponed, but the Dram would hear nothing of it. Of course, my mental state was not really of interest in these proceedings. It wasn't about truth or fairness to me. It was about their power struggle, laws, and creeds. There would hardly be a part for me to play in the entire farce besides showing up. My poor Advocate would be reduced to listening to the blowhards debate.

"I'm ready, Waythrel. This toy Tribunal is a proud gasp in the face of the infinite. The only thing I dread is the awful waste of time it all is. I wish that I could replace one piece of time with another..."

Waythrel simply stared in my direction with its many eyes. I was too engrossed in thought to bother even trying to sense its state of mind. I'm sure it was pretty bad.

Chapter 29

$$S(\Psi) = \hbar \sum_{g \geq 0} (\hbar g_c)^{g-1} \sum_{n \geq 0} \frac{1}{n!} \{\Psi^n\}_g$$

Men never do evil so completely and cheerfully as when they do it from religious conviction.

Blaise Pascal

The audience in front of the High Inquisitor was impressive, but nothing prepared me for the Tribunal itself. Even as we pulled up outside the giant dome in which the trial would occur, it was obvious this would be something that had Galactic Empire written all over it.

The dome was incredible. Easily the size of a small city on Earth, it had been covered with that disturbing metallic marble-like substance the Dram loved to build with, yet it was polished in what must have been a million facets, each focused slightly differently so that they reflected the red light of the star upward and outward from the center of the sphere, radially like a giant incandescent bulb. I suppose this was to give it the appearance of power radiating from within, but I found it hideous and tacky, astounding me only in the force with which these aliens pressed upon all things that they encountered.

We were led through an enormous corridor on levitation flats, small rectangular devices with guardrails that traveled a few feet above the ground back and forth between the entrance and the inner chamber of the dome. Of course, these were designed for the Dram, and even a normal human would have trouble holding onto the rails. At my height of five foot two, there was really only a post to secure myself to, although the devices were almost completely bump-free. Still, they moved pretty fast, and instinct made me hold on tightly.

Soon, the cylindrical tunnel opened up into a mini-dome within the main dome, yet still the size of a football field. It was completely absurd. In the center was an elevated platform, perhaps two hundred feet in the air, on which Waythrel and I would stand for the entire ordeal. Hovering from above, several hundred feet in length, was an enormous platform for the seats of the Tribunal members, arrayed in a semicircle around a second platform opposite the entrance. The far walls were hardly lit, and light was focused down on the smaller platform, leaving most of the Tribunal in dim illumination. The only exceptions were the seat of the High Inquisitor, and next to that, towering above him, the grand throne on which the Dram Emperor sat.

It was all created to have an effect on the accused, and to bolster the Dram inherent sense of their own superiority, I guess. It had the opposite effect on me. It was in some ways the final sign of how mad these aliens were. At that point I lost whatever hope I had that there could be any way besides my plan to escape this situation. Even more, it had the effect of increasing my confidence. These Dram were so unbalanced, it would not be hard to defeat them now. This room was the proof. They sacrificed anything of practical value for show. The scale of the thing was so large that it was impossible to see the members of the Tribunal from the platform, and therefore they could not see us. So, they had rigged giant suspended holograms to display things, like monitors in Times Square or something. I nearly laughed at the ridiculousness of the entire farce. I suppose that I should have been more respectful. They were smarter than me, much more powerful than any other species, and, of course, very willing to do terrible things. But it wasn't me that was blind now. I had sight in a world where the rest were blind.

The Emperor dangled ten feet in front of me, blown up to ten times its already large size in the projection, its form and clothing familiar from my vision on Earth, from a time in my life that seemed a thousand years ago. It clicked out sounds as Waythrel and I settled onto the platform, bathed in light. The clicks rocked against my ears, amplified by Dram technology. The Tribunal was in session.

It lasted nearly four hours, and I will spare you the details. Most of it was taken up with a constant religious and legal back-and-forth between the High Inquisitor and appointed Advocates of the Naturalists and Believers. The Believers presented their case, showing evidence recorded by Dram sensors of my manipulation of the Orbs, the original notes from Earth about my abilities, and a brief questioning of Waythrel and me about whether or not I had indeed done these things. Honestly, it seemed that many in the Believer camp had a lot of trouble *believing* that a lowly human could have power over the "Holy Orbs." They spent a lot of time arguing the impossibility of an impure creature having such power, focusing on my deformity. "This human is even a monster among its own kind!" one particularly empathetic Believer Advocate exclaimed at one point.

Their case was pretty easy to understand – I was an instrument of evil, a vile creature empowered by dark forces to sacrilege. Seriously, how could an impure, lowly and deformed piece of humanity have any legitimate power over the Holy Orbs? There could be no cooperation with me, nothing good to come from my actions. I should be purified of the evil that possessed me and sent to death for my sins in punishment, and to prevent any further desecration of the Orbs.

The Naturalists then took up their position. They countered immediately the words of my deformity by casting it in a positive light, saying that the Creator had no doubt endowed me with special gifts, a new organ of vision. They played up a false respect for the Believers' faith. Who was to say whom God had chosen as the instrument of revelation? Did not the scriptures claim that even the lowest would see God? Had I not opened a Portal? How could evil ever have done so? How could God have allowed it? They argued for a break from what they called barbaric interpretations of the Believers and a more progressive, modern view. They argued that I was sent from God, and must have been put in their presence for a purpose. The Dram should make use of this instrument of God and discover that purpose.

On and on it went, back and forth, until I frankly stopped caring and finalized in my mind what would be done in the next few days. The dancing futures in my mind – these were real, while the bickering insects around me, their power struggles and ancient superstitions, were the true dream. Deep in thought, ignored during the long debates, I lost track of the time around me until Waythrel shook me back into the present. Apparently, they were nearing an end. The Advocates had been ordered to sit. The High Inquisitor stood before us, its face hovering in space.

"Finally. Let him spit it out at last," I muttered to Waythrel. Through the Xixian translator I wore, the Dram clicks morphed into English in my ears.

"The Emperor has signaled closure. The debate has ended. All hail the Judge and receive Judgment!"

The High Inquisitor sat down, and the projection flicked to the form of the Emperor. Even I could tell the Emperor was old. The bent legs, the poor posture, the discolorations in the exoskeleton, and the aids to vision that surrounded the three eyestalks – this was a creature that had been worn down by many years. Yet there was a sharpness in its words, even through translation. Sharp in essence, but not in effect. I sighed; I had heard them so many times already.

"The evidence and arguments have been presented. But there is still too much mystery. A primitive creature is said to have power over the Holy Orbs and yet shows no sign of the faith, no knowledge of the Ancient Ones. How can such power have come to such a lowly creature? How can we know it was this Earth creature that opened the Portal, and not another force that lays the blame on it to divert attention?"

I felt Waythrel stiffen beside me. The Xix had not anticipated this paranoia in the Dram. To blame the Xix because of their superior technology – it was classic Dram. But deadly serious.

"We need further proof!" Soft clicking could be heard around the chamber. "I command that this creature provide the core Tribunal with a demonstration! In four days we mark the end of the Sun Spot Cycle. It is a Holy omen. We will travel to the Dram Sacred Orb, and this creature will show us the truth of its power, or perish in torment for its heresy!"

Several in the Believer camp broke out in some kind of protest, while I felt the Naturalists smile with pleasure inwardly. The Emperor was clever. It would test that I did hold this power, and at the same time establish a use of it by the Dram. It would make its task easier to insist upon my exploitation to the Believer caste.

"Silence!" the Emperor thundered, pounding a clawed hand upon the throne. "I am empowered by the Holy Powers and rule with their authority! I *command* it. In four days, this creature will be brought before the Holy Orb! Take them away!"

And then it was over. The guards entered, hurried us out of the chamber and out of the absurd dome toward the ground transports. I saw Waythrel shield its many eyes from the outdoor light, bright and searing after our hours in the dome. The noise of the Dram city filled the spaces around us. I leaned over towards the very exhausted-looking Xix and whispered, "Now that we've endured their hot air, we have plans to set in motion."

"Plans?" Waythrel asked.

"Yes, Waythrel." I smiled and sighed at the same time. It was good to finally open up about this.

"Soon, we will escape, and there is a lot we need to arrange. We must make sure it is as I have fore-planned."

"Ambra, you will tell me now what you have seen?"

"Oh, Waythrel, that would take more than our lifetimes. But a local corner of it all, yes, I'll tell you. These arrogant bugs, they are going to lead us right to the exit."

Chapter 30

$$r_c = \frac{\operatorname{arccosh}(3)}{\sqrt{2}\omega}$$

It is incomprehensible that God should exist, and it is incomprehensible that He should not exist; that the soul should be joined to the body, and that we should have no soul; that the world should be created, and that it should not be created.

Blaise Pascal

The path through the labyrinth was clear now. Like some luminescent highway in my mind, composed of a thousand different threads of time from possible futures woven together, it dominated my visions. In my present, I helped lay each new thread, and knew those that must be stitched in the near future. It all was within what I could do. Only by choice now would I not be able to follow the bright road. But only through that path could we escape, could the Xix survive, and could I finally return to where my journey had begun. It was the right path for so many, even as I could hardly face what waited for me at its end.

I told Waythrel that we needed a chance to speak more openly together, without the Dram overhearing. While the sounds and movements outside between the Tribunal and my cell masked our conversation, there was not enough time to explain what the Xix had to know. I told Waythrel to ready all of the Xix on Dram, and all of those that could exchange information and service with their home world, to prepare for what I would ask of them. I felt the resignation within Waythrel. The Xix assumed I would ask something similar to their own plan to endanger themselves. Deferring to my visions, Waythrel felt a growing helplessness as I took over the planning of our escape.

The next day, Waythrel and several Xixian medics entered my cell. Pretending to examine me, one injected something into my arm. It wasn't painful and barely left a mark. I made no sound and waited until they left the room. Waythrel spoke.

"We have implanted in your skin a small device that will mask our conversation from the Dram. I have a similar device in me. The device will mimic malfunctioning Dram eavesdropping equipment, which will give us a short time to speak openly. The device is organic, and will dissolve and be absorbed within your tissues in thirty minutes – undetectable. Speak quickly, all that must be said."

I closed my eyes, the bright path in my consciousness.

"When they bring me to the Orb, the Emperor will ask me to activate it, planning for me to guide the ship to Earth. A measure of the cruelty of the Dram," I said without further clarification. "But this will not happen. The Resistance will swing into Dram space and hit the escort ships. They have been moving into near jump space the last few days."

"Ambra, I have no word of such plans, what are you

saying? Why would the Emperor demand that you bring them to Earth?"

I ignored its words and continued. "At that time, a delegation of Xixian scientists will be revealed to be Xixian defenders, and will begin to immobilize Dram soldiers."

"Ambra, please…"

"Listen to me, Waythrel. " I shook my head. There wasn't time to explain it all. The alien would have to trust my visions. "The Dram have too many numbers, and such terrible weapons, the Xix cannot stop them all." I smiled, thinking of my gentle friends. "These others I will stop."

"*You* will stop? How, Ambra?"

There was only one way to convince the Xix of this. I concentrated on the pulsing waves of thought that emanated from Waythrel. Such complex lines, such beautiful webs within webs. So much more refined and deep than my thoughts, and yet even the Xix were blind where I could see. Only I could see these thoughts. And only I could touch them. I reached out, kindly but firmly, and plucked the web.

Waythrel recoiled as if struck. The elegant web of thought became scrambled for a moment, and it used its many arms to balance along the walls of my cell. The eyestalks rotated wildly around the room, unhinged, disoriented. Slowly, the web reformed, and the long alien body relaxed, the eyestalks calming and turning slowly toward me. I lowered my head.

"I'm sorry, Waythrel. You would not have believed me otherwise."

"You frighten me, Ambra."

"I know. It's too much power for an Earth mind. I *feel* that inside. Seeing our history, I *know* it—we are not wise enough. But this power *is* mine, good or bad. Perhaps both." I raised my head and leveled my sightless eyes toward my Advocate.

"And I was gentle, Waythrel. I don't have to be so gentle." I could feel Waythrel recoil instinctively from the implication of my words. "The Dram will be helpless, at least the number around us on the ship. I can handle that number. They will not understand what is happening and will not target me before I have incapacitated them all."

I shook my head in disbelief at where things had brought me. "I have seen it all, Waythrel. You must trust me. Report my words back to the Resistance. The Dram will want Xixian scientists there to try to explain and capture the mystery of my power over the Orbs. Irony—they need you even as they don't trust you! Fill their ranks with fighters. Tell the human who plans with you what I have said."

"The human?" Waythrel asked with astonishment. "How do you know?"

"I can *see* him, Waythrel. I can see him in my future, and I can see him as a distortion in the matrices of space-time. Thel's little seeds are sprouting so quickly, I can't even keep track of them as they grow within me. Soon, we will go to him and to the heart of the Resistance. I will meet him before the end."

"The end?"

"The end of many things. The beginning of the end of the Dram."

"If these things are true, then my heart will rejoice."

"Stop being silly, Waythrel," I smiled. "You don't even have a heart! Your translators are too poetic."

"The sentiment is the same."

"Yes, but it will be mixed with grief. Terrible grief. Tomorrow we head for Earth, but we will not find it."

Chapter 31

$$\zeta(s) = \sum_{n=1}^{\infty} \frac{1}{n^s} = \frac{1}{1^s} + \frac{1}{2^s} + \frac{1}{3^s} + \cdots$$

We must admit with humility that, while number is purely a product of our minds, space has a reality outside our minds, so that we cannot completely prescribe its properties a priori.

Carl Friedrich Gauss

The trip into space was far grander than anything I had known or would know again. After the Sortax introduction to space, followed by the nightmare in the smugglers death holds, and most recently the detention cell in the Dram warship, the Emperor's ship was majestic. It was the largest spacecraft I had ever been on, easily twenty times the size of the Sortax training craft. The energy needed to bring that thing out of the Dram world gravity must have been colossal. It was also finely crafted, at least for the Dram, and certainly compared to the warship they used to kidnap me. Inside it seemed that no effort had been spared in creating a luxury ship for the ruler of the galaxy. Spacious corridors of plush fabrics led to high ceilings in rooms that housed the most complex technology and the finest materials and decorations. Dram-style art hung from the walls, typically their favored weavings of desert plants into carpet-like hangings and floor coverings painted with images from their histories and mythologies. They meant little to me, and often were hard to even decipher. I suppose human images would be equal nonsense to alien life.

We weren't given long to observe. The guards firmly escorted us to the bridge where the Emperor and its entourage awaited us. By the time we reached it, the ship had already ascended into space, using some sort of artificial gravity, I suppose, to keep things from being pushed vertically during liftoff, and keeping everything normal now that we were technically in zero-g. When we entered the enormous command center, I was struck by the panoramic windows built into the walls, now showing nothing but the blackness of space interspersed with the pinpricks of white starlight. I marveled at the engineering, the materials science that allowed windows to be placed there under the incredible pressure from inside pushing against the vacuum of space. Whatever the material was, it was tough or perhaps was aided by some sort of energy field that lessened the outward forces on the windows. It sure made for a spectacular sight, almost like floating out in front of the ship in the darkness.

The windows dimmed dramatically as the system's star swung into view, its oppressive red now confined by the blackness of space around us. Its light was still intense, in fact, more intense now that the atmosphere didn't absorb the radiation, and there was an automatic filtering of the light by the windows to protect those within the ship. The starship continued its arced course, and the red sun moved across the viewing area, as shadows shifted sharply from one side to the other around me.

Waythrel and I were brought forward to a small raised platform at the foot of the Emperor's throne. I suppose this was where those granted audience with the Emperor were placed. I looked around and noticed the fifteen or so Xixian scientists hunched over various pieces of equipment. I hoped these were not true scientists but a Xixian team trained for combat. I glanced toward Waythrel and probed its mind. Waythrel seemed to understand my concern and clearly formed the answers to my question.

The forces are in place as you have requested, Ambra. So are the Dram troops, as you have noticed. There are at least forty of their elite guard. I hope you are up to this.

I impressed upon its mind that I was.

The Resistance will be here upon my signal through the Dram Orb string, after which they will make the jump to this system. We will have only minutes to escape from this ship and board a Resistance freighter. At any moment we could be destroyed by a Dram warship. It will be perilous. And finally, what of the Emperor? We dare not risk injury to the Emperor. It could mean terrible retaliation.

I smiled, and spoke out loud. "Don't worry, Waythrel. It won't be pretty, but we'll be okay."

Waythrel acknowledged me only by bending several eyestalks in my direction. Alien sarcasm! Well, I couldn't blame the poor Xix. I was the one-eyed woman leading the blind.

I sensed it before anyone else in the room stirred. There is nothing in the galaxy like an Orb. Not even the complexities of the Xixian mind matched the convoluted and intricate maze of space-time that churned just beneath the surface of those spheres. My sensitivities let me feel the local space-time distortions from the Orb acutely. The Orbs reached out and touched so much in the star system. I had noticed it off-handedly before, but now it was so much more clear. It was as if the extruding and receding tendrils of power from the Orb had a purpose: tending, *gardening*, the majority of their efforts reaching out to the Dram home planet. Thel had spoken of it. *Gardeners*. Could it be true? I felt the energies reach through my body, and a tremor ran through me. What were those tendrils *doing*?

Waythrel sensed my reaction. "What is it, Ambra?"

"We are close," I managed to get out through a dry throat.

Several Dram officers clicked to the Emperor, and soon the Orb became visible to all through the viewing windows. In the visual realm, how boring the sphere seemed! But whatever effect the Orbs had on the sight of those around me, I could sense within their minds the stirring of awe. Some religious, some exclusively scientific, but all knew the power in what we approached. The portals through time and space planted around the galaxy by the mysterious Ancient Ones, left for billions of years to be discovered by species too primitive to understand how they even functioned, or why.

My translator echoed the Emperor's tones. "We have reached the Sacred Orb of the Dram! It is now time for the heretic to prove its truth and worth, to open the Orb and reveal the power of the divine, or to fail and expose itself to be a fraud of the Evil Force."

How I hated these dramatic moments of voodoo, made worse by the fact that the Emperor was a hypocrite who sided with the Naturalists anyway. Sanctimonious hypocrisy mixed with extreme power – nothing was worse, especially when the authorities could soon be deciding exactly how to torture you.

The Emperor turned to Waythrel. "Your client is ordered to open the portal."

"Ambra, obey the Emperor's command."

I sighed and inhaled deeply, closing my eyes. *Okay, buddy, get ready, 'cause here it comes!*

I went deep inside myself, to that place where my unique sense opened up to me and occupied all my consciousness. To my sixth sense, the Orb flared like a supernova. I felt its energies as nearly overpowering. I held steady, focused, and reached toward it.

This time it was more straightforward. The pressures are far weaker without a Dram warship chasing you through space. And my powers had grown in so many ways even in the short time since I had opened the last Orb. Add to that my confidence that I could do it, and that in my bright path I had seen it happen. All I had to do was dance with destiny.

I felt the equivalent of gasps from those surrounding me, even from Waythrel, as I unlocked the Orb. Visually, it was quite a light show. The dark surface rippled into a multidimensional maze of lasers, a many-layered tunnel in space erupting before us, seeming ready to swallow the ship whole. *As indeed it was.* It took some concentration to configure the Orb to remain open without drawing the ship inside, and even so, I think everyone on board felt the space-time tugs. A subtle anxiety seemed to sit deep within all.

I opened my eyes and glared at the ugly cockroach on the throne. "There, *your majesty*," I spat out. "Is that what you were looking for?"

The Emperor and other Dram were too transfixed to hear me. Even the guards were staring up at the heavenly-hell of the endless and structured light of the Orb. I noticed with satisfaction, however, that the Xixian team was not. I spoke mentally to Waythrel to send the signal. It nodded, pressed a device on the translator and breathing device around its neck, and transmitted both to the Resistance forces and the Xixian team below.

And that's when everything went nuts.

Chapter 32

$$|\Psi\rangle = \int d^{26}p\left(T(p)c_1e^{ip\cdot X}|0\rangle + A_\mu(p)\partial X^\mu c_1e^{ip\cdot X}|0\rangle + \chi(p)c_0e^{ip\cdot X}|0\rangle + \ldots\right)$$

Battle not with monsters, lest you become a monster, and if you gaze into the abyss, the abyss gazes also into you.

Friedrich Nietzsche

It was a few seconds before the Dram realized what was happening.

The Xixian scientists immediately began to immobilize, but not kill, Dram warriors with special devices they had concealed. As the giant insects began dropping to the ground, a cry went up from crew monitoring space. I'm not sure whether they had detected Waythrel's signal or were responding to the small fleet of Resistance ships materializing from the Orb String and opening fire on surrounding Dram warships escorting the Emperor's vessel. Whatever the reason, I had to act quickly, before they turned the firepower of the ship on the emerging craft. The Resistance had been instructed not to fire on the Emperor's ship. How could they? I was onboard, and I was the only reason that they were here. They had to get me off this ship and safely away.

I spun and faced the rows of ship technicians, pilots, and weapons staff. Their intense thoughts in the midst of combat struck my awareness harshly. How quickly they revealed their presence to my mind! *If they only knew.* One by one, I struck them. Focusing thoughts tightly, it was a mental slap the likes of which these creatures had never known. A second or two for each, and then the next, and the next, on and on like dominoes I dropped them. When I had incapacitated those at the consoles, I took on the soldiers, who were now in a deadly fight with the Xixian team. The Xix had done well, and piles of soldiers lay in front of them. But the insects were like ants from a nest, pouring in through the many doors along the walls of the room. The Xix were being overwhelmed: two had already fallen to Dram weapons, lying charred and twitching in a growing wreckage caused by the Drams' less elegant weapons.

I found myself improvising, and in a giant mental sweep, like summoning a wave from a quiescent sea, I sent a burst of mental distortion across the hordes of Dram soldiers. I was in some strange hyperkinetic state, and the power I let forth caused scores to drop instantly, some, I am sure, permanently. Seeing another horde coming through the main entrance, I recalibrated and released another burst, sending all but a handful down on their faces. Those remaining looked stunned, unable to function, and they wandered aimlessly around the room for several minutes before falling down, staring vacantly, and doing nothing. I don't know if these were permanently brain damaged.

I felt a powerful swell of anger and realization rise behind me, and a venomous urge strike toward me. *The Emperor*. I read its mind all too easily. The monster who had directed the pain of so many aliens and humans filled my consciousness, and I sensed its thrusting of a deadly weapon in my direction. *It knew.* It would seek no Tribunal to decide my fate. Funny, I had not seen this in the visions! Too close to my person, I suppose.

Waythrel screamed, "Ambra! Behind you!"

Poor Waythrel, so worried! By the time I turned to face the Emperor, Waythrel sent out thoughts of shock and awe, and stared at the Dram ruler. The beast stood still, its upraised claw clutching a weapon aimed in my direction. The creature gasped for air, yet could not move, trembling in a tremendous effort to break free of the invisible bonds holding it in place.

I walked slowly up to the insect, staring into its many eyes.

"Emperor of all Dram!" I shouted at it. "Now you will hear *me*." And then, I let thunder in its mind: *One way or the other!*

The Emperor tensed as my anger slapped at its consciousness, and fear flowed toward me like a cold river.

"You are right to be afraid," I said. "You have a debt to pay for all the souls you have tortured, murdered; the light you have extinguished."

I could not help myself, I felt my thoughts squeezing, tightening in their fury. The Dram began to make wheezing sounds, pitiful throaty wails of an alien physiology, yet no less desperate than a human being strangled.

I slapped its mind hard. *I know what you have done.* I felt desperate cries of pain and fear from the creature, but in response I gave no pity or mercy, but played out in its mind the scenes of my visions. The Dram Emperor recoiled in shock at my knowledge, and my power, seeing now that its executioner was near.

"Ambra," Waythrel whispered near me, but the Xix was

only a butterfly near the hurricane of my vengeance.

"See them scream, Emperor? See the billions boil and burn? I've seen them. Day after day, night after night, I have seen them, and I know you decreed their deaths."

Tighter and tighter I squeezed. The creature could no longer stand on its own power and began to sag to the ground.

"You gave your victims in your dungeons no rest! Up with you!" I felt myself invade its mind further, and, overpowering the normal biology, I diverted energy from other vital life processes and strengthened the signal to the legs, forcing the Dram to stand, turning its eyes that flailed vainly for help or escape, turning them toward me. I filled its mind with my image, my anger, and its imminent demise.

"Ambra, you must stop!" Waythrel cried more strongly.

"Know now the helplessness of those you have tormented and murdered. Feel their histories drown you." I opened the valve of vision and directed the terrible currents through my mind into that of the Dram Emperor. I watched as the captive consciousness was battered in the visions of other lives, other worlds, other dreams and hopes that could not be processed. The insect began a terrible trembling across its body, the legs, even under my tyrannical control, losing strength, the creature's body near the breaking point.

"Ambra, don't become a monster!" a voice pleaded with me. "Release it! Don't let your own power consume you!"

There was a pause, a breath in Time. Only my awareness was mobile. In that moment, somehow, some part of me heard the plea. Some part of me looked and saw the mad she-god I had become, summoning a deathly storm of power around me.

I stepped back from the edge of my own damnation. I can't analyze how it happened or why, but like waking from a dream, I shook off the crazed mood and released the Dram Emperor. It fell unconscious to the floor. Alive, yet forever wounded, always to remember and experience the suffering it had created.

Waythrel grabbed my shoulders with its spidery arms. "Down to the airlock. A ship is docked."

We raced through the Dram ship, the surviving members of the Xixian team loping like crazed ballet-dancing spiders, incapacitating the stray Dram that got in our way. We reached the airlock, entered the chamber, and transferred to the connected ship of the Resistance.

Within seconds, our ship and the remaining Resistance craft that had not been blown out of the sky converged near the Orb. Crew members screamed that an armada of Dram death boats was headed our way and would be within firing range in minutes.

"Ambra, please, get us out of here."

I looked over at Waythrel, not even sure I was really sane yet—from what I had seen, and done, to what I would see, and do. It all blurred together. Time—it was churning through past, present, and future. It was hard to know which way was forward.

"Sure, Waythrel. Got an express ticket."

"To where?" it asked.

"Home, and nowhere, Waythrel." I shook my head. "You can never go home, they say."

I fixed my mind on the destination and flexed my thought to open the Orb. And it opened, filling my mind with radiance, filling the eyes of all around with a different light. We dashed through a million dimensions of nowhere and everywhere, leaving behind the red of Dram, filling the windows of our ship with the golden rays of Sol.

Chapter 33

$$z_{n+1} = z_n^2 + c$$

Nothing we can do outrages Nature directly. Our acts of destruction give her new vigour and feed her energy, but none of our wreckings can weaken her power.

Marquis de Sade

Without willing it consciously, my mind darted back in time, deep into the recesses of the past.

For nearly three billion years this cratered rock had waited for its day. Circling endlessly, cold, silent, an outcast from the warmer rock huddled around a blue star, the largest of millions, yet failed. Orbit after orbit, the stars whirled across the rocky horizon, and yet it did not lose patience. It did not count the eons. Without promise, without hope, without thought, it held pregnant within its core a fate unguessed. And then, in the wink of an eye to this ancient entity, moving at the rapid pace of life, hundreds of small metallic gnats buzzed around it. Each nudged softly, surely, augmenting each other, until a crescendo built, and the old path was discarded. It latched upon the seemingly infinite energies of the tendril of an Orb, slingshot toward another star system, guided by malevolence, erupting from hyperspace with a swarm of demons blackening its outline. Inward toward the bright golden light it rushed, gathering frightening speed, aimed like an arrow with terrible purpose. Gravity. *Only gravity*. Slight alterations in gravity, then an exploitation of ancient and mysterious powers, leading to terrible accelerations and flight toward its final fate.

The cool morning breeze blew through a young woman's auburn hair. A vivid blue sky welcomed a new spring day, and she watched the children run across the concrete playground in London. Other mothers sat nearby, or walked shepherding their young. All familiar to her, many known well. She squinted into the bright sunlight and made out the form of her three-year-old stumbling forward and pointing to the sky.

"Look, Mummy, there's a falling star up in the sky!"

She followed her daughter's finger into the cloudless day. A bright speck, as if it really were a small star, shone brightly in the west.

"Yes, darling, it must be a falling star. I've never seen one in the daytime before." She smiled as the toddler grinned upward.

"Mummy, mummy, I'll make my wish! I'll make my wish!"

"Make it a good one!"

The little girl closed her eyes tightly, frowning in concentration. With a squeal she opened them again and hopped into the air.

"Mummy, I can't tell you. It's a *secret*, or it won't come true!"

The young woman smiled and glanced up into the sky once again. Her smile froze a moment, then faded as several lines formed on her forehead.

"Look at it. It's so bright."

High in the atmosphere of Earth, where each day thirty tons of material the size of sand grains enter and burn up in the atmosphere, something horribly larger ignited. One thousand miles away from London, a deep shadow darkened the capital of Iceland. Vendors on the street looked upward, people in office buildings glanced out of their windows, and frantic calls on military and national security lines screamed in urgency at the completely unexpected calamity set to befall. The Sun was blotted out, yet a second star now shone, moving like some crazed thing across the sky, erupting into a brilliance so terrible it could not be viewed by the creatures on the ground without causing blindness.

The atmosphere of Earth exploded over Canada. The energy of one hundred trillion megatons of TNT from the rushing object began its conversion into diverse forms of energy on the Earth. A fireball nearly two hundred times as bright as the Sun was born, igniting everything within its growing radius. As the Earth's surface absorbed the impact, the thin outer layer of crust was peeled off in a growing wave from the center of impact, like the skin off an apple, thrown with tremendous power high into the atmosphere. On this skin were the world's oceans, its land masses, every town, city, and state. Every living form on Earth. Underneath, and also ejected high into the now burning air was an ocean of magma. For all of human history, hidden from view by the cooled crust except for rare volcanic eruptions, enormous volumes now were poured over the Earth's surface and into its skies. In front of the growing impact crater that spread like some yawning maw across the planet, a hypersonic pressure wave of compressed atmosphere rushed away from the impact, carrying the equivalent of winds blowing at over eight thousand miles per hour. Everything in its path was flattened and then set aflame by the fireball that followed. Earthquakes of magnitude fourteen on the Richter scale threw down anything else that somehow remained standing.

Within hours, the playground in London had been lifted off the Earth's surface and thrown into space. Along with all the remaining crust ejected, it would then fall back to Earth as fiery meteors to rain destruction on the rest of a dying planet. There was no chance for any reaction, no ability of the small creatures dotting the planet to take any course of action that could protect them in any way. Those within several thousand miles of the impact were vaporized almost immediately. Ten billion souls cried out into the blackness of space, and then were silent.

Within a day, the entire surface of the Earth was a raging inferno, where the oceans boiled to nothing, all vegetation was reduced to ash, and every sign of life was wiped clean from the molten landscape. The once blue and white marble in the solar system became utterly black, lifeless, and still. The third planet from the star was now sterilized.

The Emperor's will had been done.

Chapter 34

$$H(X) = -\sum_{x \in \mathcal{X}} p(x) \log_b p(x)$$

The choice before human beings, is not, as a rule, between good and evil but between two evils.

George Orwell

From the infinite maze of light, the starship plunged into the blackness of space. The glowing Orb behind us burned brightly for several moments, and then, as if a switch had been thrown, went dark. The Sun radiated at the center of mass of the small system of nine worlds and asteroids, its disk large in the field of vision near the third planet from the star. The Xix at the controls on the bridge exchanged rapid conversation. I could sense them three floors up.

Waythrel rushed down the corridor to my room. It signaled outside the door, and I pressed a panel to allow entrance. The door slid open, and a very frazzled-looking Xix stepped inside—if you can ever really describe a disturbing alien life form with such a human term. I looked up from the overlarge chair I was sitting in and waited for it to tell me what I already knew.

"Ambra," the Xix began hesitantly. "We have come upon the coordinates of Earth."

The weight of the unspoken was heavy in the air. I simply nodded and waited. My emotions were both drained and repressed. I had cried inside one thousand times for the future that had become my present.

"There is something wrong. We need you on the bridge."

Again, I nodded. I stood slowly, feeling no weakness or fatigue in my limbs. Only a terrible stillness deep inside.

I followed the alien through the ship and up to the bridge. The Xixian pilots and crew were silent, almost still before their instruments. I had chosen a black robe from the clothes provided to me. Xixian make, overly large and oddly proportioned for my human dimensions, it lay draped around me like an odd funeral garment. The robe was fashioned of some strange material never imagined on Earth, and it seemed to drink the light and then somehow subtly reflect it in hints of iridescence in the midst of darkness. On my head was Ricky's Red Sox hat. Ricky, murdered in another age of my mind, cremated only hours ago.

Waythrel spoke. "Ambra, the coordinates are correct. There is a rocky satellite of a mass and distance as specified. The planet must be Earth. But…"

Tears streamed down my face as I finally spoke, the words unlocking something deep within me. "It burns before us still, my alien friends. My home world, where my roots would have found soil again to end the withering of my soul. Spirits like dust are riding on the solar wind, blowing over our ship's shields. I hear their voices, *billions* of them crying out. I've heard them again and again. Can you feel the wind of their *souls*?"

I walked forward to the view screen and stared at the blackened sphere, rivers of magma a dull red like bloodshot eyes crisscrossing the surface. Across nearly the entire Northern Hemisphere, an enormous orange pool of lava, boiling like some eye of the Devil.

"The Dram have left by now; their work is finished."

"Why?" Waythrel whispered. I felt a terrible shudder from it and the other Xix. Alien, all of them, and yet they all cared. More than so many humans I had known. If any creatures carried the torch of divine love in our galaxy, it was the Xix.

I looked across the control room. "They have my eggs and many human captives for sperm. They believe I can be recreated. They desire a monopoly on my power." It was all so logical, so coldly calculated. "The gene pool of Earth, waiting to produce more Ambra Dawns, and who knows what else of Reader power, was a threat to their Hegemony. So they removed the threat. And so Earth has been put to death."

"Ambra, I don't have words for you," Waythrel began and then paused. "You have known this?"

"Since my arrival at Dram."

There was a stunned silence. "Ambra, why? Why didn't you tell us? We could have stopped it!"

"No, Waythrel!" I cried out, the alien's words cutting deep inside me. "I have seen all the threads. The possible futures, Waythrel, there are not infinitely many, not in the short term. There was only one path out of the Dram home world, one possible hope for me to survive." My tears came heavily now, and it took all I could to stop myself from sobbing beyond the ability to speak.

I stared out at my blackened home, where my bare feet

would never touch the soil again. Where so many innocent lives had been extinguished. "I chose the most horrible choice. That the lives of many should be sacrificed for the life of one. Because others had foretold and foreseen hope for many more worlds than Earth. A hope in me."

Waythrel and the other Xix were silent and still as stones. I could feel their churning emotions at my words. I turned to Waythrel. "I chose to let my world die, so that we might save so many more, now, and for the years to come." Wiping tears from my eyes I choked out words at all these monstrous forms around me. "I hope we will not make their sacrifice a vain one."

And I turned away from them, my form the most monstrous of them all, the greatest mass murderer of all time fleeing in her dark robes like Death into the bowels of Hell.

Chapter 35

$$\int_{\mathcal{R}} d\omega = \int_{\partial\mathcal{R}} \omega$$

The Tao that can be expressed is not the eternal Tao;
The name that is spoken is not the unchanging name.
That without name is the beginning of heaven and earth.

老子 Lǎozǐ (Lao Tzu)

We landed on the Moon three hours later.

The Resistance had established a base there years before, on the dark side, tunneled into the lunar rock several miles to shield it from Dram scans. It was, of course, one of many such secret bases throughout the inhabited worlds, but being close to Earth, the Earth that was, had a special significance. Earth had been the source of all Readers of importance, and the greatest supply of Readers in general. Now only the Dram in their human stockyards would breed more of us, as slaves, programmed to do their bidding.

We passed over the barren lunar landscape, pocket-marked

with impact craters – the longtime evidence of celestial violence never erased on a body that had no wind, or rain, or tectonic plate movements of any kind. The Xixian ship descended into one of the larger craters, and a channel appeared in the rock. We entered this tunnel that dove straight toward the heart of the Moon, the light from above quickly dimming, and only the ship's navigation beams eerily illuminating the sharp edges of the drilled rock.

Soon a dim glow arose from underneath us, and grew in intensity until it seemed bright after the relative darkness of the tunnel shaft. The passageway opened into a large chamber in which numerous ships were docked. We taxied to a free space, and the large vessel came to a stop on a landing pad hewn out of the lunar rock. Once we had Earth and gazed to the lifeless Moon. Now life stirred only on the moon, as Earth smoldered a quarter-million miles away.

A small group was there to greet us, both Xix and humans somber, the members of my species pale and burdened. A young man with a blond beard led them forward and stopped before Waythrel.

"We received your transmission, and your codes match those smuggled to us yesterday," he said gravely. His eyes darted towards me. "*She* is with you?"

Waythrel gestured in my direction. "Michael, let me introduce to you Ambra Dawn. She led us through the Orbs and defeated the Dram Emperor herself. She is our great hope."

This Michael eyed me cautiously. "Hope," he muttered. "There is not much of that left. We are left in darkness after yesterday." He glanced at me again, looking over my dark and loose-fitting robes, baseball hat, my absurd skull. "She will be brought before Richard. He will continue to guide us, and tell us what value this girl may have now."

"Then, he still lives?" Waythrel asked.

Michael bristled at the question, a fire in his eyes hidden only poorly by his attempts to control his anger. "Yes, although the medics cannot say for how much longer. The cursed Dram poisons continue to degrade his tissues, but he has lost none of his powers!"

Waythrel spoke softly. "Of course, Michael, we expected nothing less. Please forgive me if my question seemed insensitive. You know we of Xix are doing all we can to preserve his life."

The man lowered his gaze. "Yes, and we are thankful. You know as well as I that his Visions have made the Resistance possible." At his last words, he glanced once more in my direction and then turned to the rest of the party that had accompanied him.

"See that they are housed and attended to. Afterward," he added, turning to Waythrel, "we may arrange a meeting between these two Readers. Richard has waited long for this day."

With that, he turned and strode out of the docking chamber, leaving us alone with the remainder of our hosts. I questioned Waythrel with my mind.

"A complicated politics, Ambra. Michael is loyal and attached to his leader, who lies dying after his torture at the hands of the Dram. You come here with the rumor of greatness, beyond even Richard's powers. Michael resents this, and you will need to walk carefully in the beginning. Don't worry for now, there is much to learn. With your powers, I have no doubt you will know all there is to know soon."

We exited the docking chamber and entered an elevator that sped us even deeper into the Moon. The last stage of my journey had begun.

Point γ

First the Cosmos, then the gods.
So, who can say from where the creation arose?
Perhaps, it created itself.
Perhaps, it did not.
The Being, the first Origin of Creation
Who looks down on it:
Only He knows.
Or perhaps, He does not.

Rig Veda, Creation Hymn

Chapter 36

$r = \cos(k\theta)$

The flower which is single need not envy the thorns that are numerous.

Rabindranath Tagore

We were quickly led to our quarters within the hidden Moon base. Waythrel and I insisted that we be housed together. There was too much of great importance happening, and we both wished to have the time to discuss matters when needed. It was strange to be in chambers designed by humans, even if the Xix had aided their efforts. The personality of a species can be felt even in its architecture, and just that small piece of humanity comforted me.

The base was still not completely made for humans, however, and many concessions had been made for the Xix that also lived there. The humans probably outnumbered the Xix twenty to one, a ratio only to be found in the Resistance base so close to Earth. Waythrel spent half an hour in an ultrasound Xixian chamber in the room, a strange device that bombards the occupant with high-frequency sound waves. The Xix find this soothing in a way humans cannot understand and certainly cannot experience. I took the human equivalent, a long, hot shower, hoping the steam and temperature would somehow burn away all the horror of my life. Of course, I stepped out merely numbed for the moment and had hardly finished dressing when we were pinged by a messenger outside our door.

It turned out to be an aide of the leader they called Michael, and he asked us to accompany him to meet with Michael and be taken to their great Reader. Waythrel insisted on accompanying me, even though the aide was firm that the initial meeting with Richard would be private, only with me. With that understood, we marched through the tunnel-like corridors of the Moon base, descending several more levels in the process on elevators, which opened into a large medical ward.

Waiting for us there was Michael. With my mind somewhat recovered from the shock of seeing the dead Earth of my nightmares, I was able to study him more closely. Of average height and stocky build, he looked like he could have played football for some Midwest college team. Yet there was a crispness to his blue eyes, a trimness to his beard and hair that spoke of great discipline and scholarship. Whoever he was, he appeared formidable as a leader.

At his side was a white-coated woman, Asian features, long midnight hair tied up in a bun. She was likely an attending physician. It was clear that Richard was a dying man.

"Waythrel will need to wait outside," he began. "Richard

insisted on meeting Ambra alone this first time. He wishes to commune with her as a Reader. Human to human."

"It is understood," answered Waythrel, although its translator conveyed an annoyed tone.

The doctor interrupted. "I'm Emily Chan," she began, "I am the ranking human physician in the medical wing and have been overseeing care of Richard Cross. We apologize for this inconvenience," she said, gazing between Michael and Waythrel. "In the medical unit, we are only too aware of the aid the Xix have given in all our efforts."

Michael glanced with some annoyance toward the doctor but then motioned for me to follow. I walked behind them, down the hallway, nearly to the end of the medical wing, where we stopped in front of a set of double automatic doors. He turned to me and looked me gravely.

"Behind those doors you will meet the most powerful Reader in the Resistance. He has guided our strategies, risked his life, his health, his very sanity to serve our cause. Don't underestimate his vision."

Dr. Chan twitched uncomfortably at my side. "Michael, stop antagonizing her! This is *Ambra Dawn*. She unlocked an *Orb*, faced down the Dram, and has been brought to us by the Xix. She has the potential to surpass anything any Reader has yet done, if she has not done so already. We *need* her!"

Michael set his jaw, his anger plainly visible on his face. "Whatever rumors you have heard of this girl, until she has served the Resistance as Richard has served, she is nothing more than another lost Reader who has been found."

"So, why is she here? Why has Richard desired to see her?"

"The Council believed in her potential."

"Which means you don't, I suppose."

"What I believe is not of consequence."

This back-and-forth about which freak would win in a throw down reminded me too much of what was juvenile in our species, arguing about our heroes, superheroes, our gods. All I could think about was that behind these doors was someone who could finally understand me, someone who maybe had enough of my experiences to have some clue about what life was like inside my head. Maybe, in this seemingly indifferent universe, I might not be completely alone.

My frustrations boiled over. "We don't have time for this! I've come a long and horrible way under knife and death and madness. Now I stand near the blackened Earth to listen to your bickering?" I nearly shouted. "Richard has asked to see me, and I *will* see him before he passes." I held up my hand as Michael began to protest. "Yes, he will pass. And it will be soon. I can see it even in the distortions of space-time he causes. Just like I can feel your anger at this future you do not wish to accept."

"I don't care who you are!" shouted Michael. "I won't have you speak like this!"

He took a step toward me, but before he could follow through or the doctor stop him, I sent a hard thought into his mind. Not enough to hurt him, but enough to stun him momentarily and shake his anger out in surprise. Plenty of surprise, as well as a little fear.

I will meet with your Richard. I have hoped to meet him for some time. I will not let you stop me. I have too much I need to learn and share with him.

Michael stepped backward, his eyes swimming, an awed look on his face.

"Michael, what is it? Are you okay?" Dr. Chan asked as she glanced with concern at the paleness spreading over his face.

“I’m fine, Emily,” he said hoarsely. “Just…just let her through.”

Both stepped aside, opening the space between me and the doors. I took a deep breath and walked forward. The sensors detected my presence and set the machinery in motion.

The doors opened.

Chapter 37

$$\int_{-\infty}^{\infty} e^{-x^2}\, dx = \sqrt{\pi}$$

While God waits for his temple to be built of love, men bring stones.

Rabindranath Tagore

I walked into a dark room. The lights were off except for a few that dimly illuminated a countertop directly across from me. Between me and the counter was a hospital bed surrounded by numerous instruments of human and Xixian design. Many wires and tubes from these machines led towards the bed, and converged on a prone figure: Richard. As I drew nearer, I could see that his back had been opened up, revealing his spinal column, into which numerous tubes and wires entered. These invaders of his flesh were surrounded by an odd plastic, likely of Xixian manufacture, coating everything and sealing it off from exposure. Likewise, a number of tubes and wires also entered into his skull, giving him a look of some nightmarish dreadlocked singer. His lungs breathed regularly, too much so, so that it was clear that they were aided by machinery as well. I felt a great sense of pity swell in me. Here was another who had paid a great price for his talents and his choices.

Out of some indefinable respect for this price, I withheld any probing of his mind. Slowly, I made my way around the machine to a chair that had been placed at the front of the bed, likely used by those who wished to speak with him. As I approached, his features became more clear. A black man, tall and thin, perhaps once of athletic shape now shriveled to near-skeletal form. His eyes were closed, and yet still I did not probe to see if he still had conscious thoughts. I sat quietly and waited. After a few moments, his eyes fluttered open, and he spoke.

"I knew you were here before you even landed on this barren rock," he croaked out. "It's amazing. You distort the very space you move within."

I smiled. "So they tell me."

"I apologize. I cannot give you a better welcome. I can hardly look you in the eye. But then again, you see so much, and not with your eyes, am I right?"

"You are right. I am blind."

"And yet not blind," he continued, and a short coughing fit took him. "Ah, that hurts. The Xix have been so helpful. I know it looks horrific, but all this, it keeps my mind as free from the Dram poisons as possible, while also maintaining my life functions. Without all this," he gestured with his eyebrows and a slight motion of his head, "I would have been in the throes of dementia and death months ago."

"The Dram have little mercy."

"No doubt, you know too well. You have seen it, I suppose, my capture, my torment, and escape from their dungeons."

"Yes," I said, feeling a tear in my eye. "In dreams long ago, and in visions more recently. The Xix were never suspected in your escape, although many humans died."

"Yes, our greatest burden, Ambra. That so many would die, that we might live."

I could say nothing. My pain was too great.

"And yet I did not see it coming. This greatest of calamities. I have waited to speak to you for so long, while fate kept us apart. I had so much to tell you, to inform you, of this universe, of Earth occupied, of our long plans to set it free. Now, after what has happened, I don't know what to tell you. I have no more words of wisdom. Only the question of why this terrible thing never revealed itself to me."

He began coughing again and motioning to his throat, indicated that he could no longer speak.

That will not keep us apart, Richard.

His eyes widened, and then closed, and I allowed myself to fully enter his mind.

This is more than I could have imagined, his thoughts relayed. *You have grown powerful beyond the dreams of even the Dram.*

It is a power that is limited, as you can see. Earth is reduced to ashes despite all I can do.

Why, Ambra? You had foreseen it. Why didn't you stop it?

I can't explain, Richard. But I could show you. Do you have the strength?

I don't know. But I would rather die knowing and also experiencing even a small piece of your vision, than live a few more hours in ignorance.

So be it. I focused my thoughts, stripping away all that was not necessary. I had to show him the bright path through the maze of destruction, so that he could understand. Whether he could accept humanity's sacrifice for the rest of the galaxy, I did not know.

I reached out as gently as I could, and joined our minds,

letting the flow of visions enter his. His strength was barely up to the task, and the machines blinked and beeped in consternation as his vital signs approached dangerous levels. His body shook, trembling softly as the shock roiled through him.

And then it was over. I withdrew from his mind to give him time to recover, keeping a tendril of contact to know when he was voicing his thoughts again.

I am sorry this had to be placed on you, Ambra. So much you have had to endure and carry. So alone. At least I can tell you, I can feel more than anyone the toxins you have swallowed.

I felt tears well up in my eyes. I reached out with my hand and touched his head. "And I know yours, Richard, in seeing your broken body and in communing with your mind," I spoke aloud. *I only wish our parting would not come so soon. I don't wish to be so alone again.*

Yes, soon. Even my visions are fading, which means the poison has finally reached my central neurons. I am fortunate that the Xixian treatments have slowed the progress so much, that the rest of my body is nearly destroyed and will fail before I go completely mad. But it grows dim, even dark at times. And yet, I believe I still can see something you cannot.

Tell me.

I can't see you, Ambra, because you twist all space-time around you. But I can see your form, like a glacier crushing everything in its path, carving out a new landscape by your power. Your form is constantly being made and unmade. But now I understand why I did not see Earth's destruction. In my mind, Earth still exists in our future, even though it does not now. How can this be?

His thoughts faded as the machines began complaining again. His body was truly dying now.

Richard? Please, are you there?

I reached deep into the recesses of his blurring mind. His consciousness was now fluid, trapped at sea, bobbing above and below, knowing thoughts only in those moments of breaking through to the air and taking a breath before plunging downward into near oblivion.

Fading…Ambra…You are turbulence in the path…Blinded me…

Dr. Chan came springing into the room, followed closely by Michael. She glanced at the monitors and called a code to other nurses in the medical wing. I closed out their efforts. Time was short. I focused on his dying thoughts.

Ambra…events are fluid…like the sea…turbulence…can't see into it…but I can see—after. A miracle. So much light…the voices of heaven singing…

I didn't know if he was sane any longer. True visions? Or hallucinations of his dying mind?

Fingers of Divinity, Ambra….through you they will speak…you only need to touch it, and the course of everything is new.

There was a team of Xix and human medics standing around him now. Waythrel turned toward me.

"Ambra! You must stop! The strain is too much for him! He's dying!"

Don't listen to them, Ambra…better I die now than live empty and only for suffering. Goodbye, Reader. It has been my privilege to know you…so much light…

His thoughts became silent, lost in a more primitive boiling of mental functions, and I didn't know if he had lost all consciousness. I glanced up at Waythrel.

"It is his wish to share with me before he dies."

Michael looked over at me in horror and back to his leader with pain etched on his face.

"I'm sorry," was all I could offer him.

Ambra…. The thoughts came as if from far way, deep within the cave of his mind. *Ambra, change the course…they will help you…you…must…change…its course.*

His mind went completely dark, and the machinery became ominously silent. The frantic activity around me stalled, and for a moment, everything was as still as empty space.

"He's dead," said Dr. Chan. "There's nothing we can do."

I heard Michael weeping as he knelt beside his leader, burying his head next to his fallen friend. I also felt a palpable sadness in the Xixian minds. They mourned the passing of a friend and a powerful force in their fight against the Dram.

Even so, I felt their hopes reorient and turn toward me, however unsure and directionless in their uncertainty of my abilities to take up that role. The hopes of entire species, and the remains of a massacred human race, all became set on Ambra Dawn. It felt like the weight of a star.

Even that was secondary as I stared off into space. I had lost the only person who could remotely understand me, someone with whom I could relate fully as a Reader and as a human being. Richard had left his last thoughts with me, urgent thoughts that conveyed something he had seen that I could not, something about me that he had strained to convey as his mind died.

And I had absolutely no idea what he was trying to tell me.

Chapter 38

$$\sigma_x \sigma_p \geq \frac{\hbar}{2}$$

I don't think of all the misery, but of the beauty that still remains.

Anne Frank

I sat still in the guest room with Waythrel, partially nauseous from the low gravity on the satellite. The Moon base had been hastily constructed in great secrecy even as the agents of the Dram herded our clueless kind on nearby Earth. There had been no time to be sophisticated, no time for gravitational enhancements or even a crude rotating design to increase average gravity. I had refused lunch, sick from the odd gravity, sick from watching Richard Cross die, sick from watching Earth die one hundred times in my visions, and sick from a long and empty conversation with Waythrel about a dying man's thoughts.

"I am sorry, Ambra," it spoke after a long silence. "For all we know, those words were spoken in a decaying brain state and perhaps have no meaning. He may have been speaking nonsense."

"I don't believe it," I whispered softly. "I could feel him fighting to maintain focus, to convey to me something he finally understood. If so, it's important, and I need to find the answer. If it's nonsense, then it doesn't matter."

"Except that it will drain your energies from other tasks."

I felt like screaming. "What other tasks, Waythrel? I may have found the strength to do what I did, but I am wounded to the core. Would you feel any differently had Xix been destroyed? How can any creature ever thrive without their home world, even if it is just the knowledge that it is there to return to? We are like limbs cut off from the tree, and we will wither."

"Ambra! You must not! Or else this sacrifice will be in vain! You are now our best hope for defeating the Dram. You must find strength in that!"

I sighed heavily. "Waythrel, I will try. And that is why I hope to find the meaning of Richard's last words. I felt a hope in them, a hope specific for my kind. I wish he could have told me more. But that hope is what keeps me going now."

"Then may it not be a false hope."

"Take my mind somewhere else, Waythrel. I am too exhausted to seek answers. What has happened since our escape? What do the other worlds know of Earth?"

"The Dram have reverted to full militaristic mode. Their aggression has increased a thousand-fold, and all are harshly reminded once again of how terrible they can be. Information from Dram is censored, but of course we of Xix are able to elude their crude technology and transmit. The Emperor is in critical care. His mind is wrecked by your actions. He babbles nonsense and cries out for protection from humans. The High Inquisitor has followed succession rights and assumed interim control of the Empire until a new Emperor is chosen – an archaic and barbaric ritual of the noble houses that I will save for another time. In the meantime, the military has orders to violently suppress even the hint of any insurrection in the Hegemony. Many innocents are paying with their lives."

"Yes, I had seen this. So much pain. Even in hope for victory, so much pain."

"Word of Earth has spread throughout the Hegemony. I am sad to say not so much in concern for Earthlings, but much more for the implications. Firstly, reminders that the Dram are more than willing to slaughter entire worlds, as if this could have been forgotten. Secondly, that the greatest well of Readers to supply the galaxy has been destroyed. I am sorry to make it so clear what worth humans have been to the Hegemony, but this is the hard truth. You have been a resource, a necessary resource, and a great fear is sweeping through the galaxy that this resources has been destroyed."

"It's okay, Waythrel. My experiences have made this clear to me, in ways far more painful than your words."

"Yes. I can't doubt that. Now, all worlds see that the Dram hold whatever humans may be left, that they fully control all aspects of a scarce resource, without which interstellar travel will cease. The Dram tighten their control of all space with this slaughter."

Waythrel stood up and began the strange Xixian tap dance as it paced back and forth across the room.

"But one thing the Dram did not suspect – that word of you and your actions would escape. We of Xix have secretly seen to that. Word of one who has opened the Orbs now grows and takes shape. Word that this human also escaped the clutches of the Dram Emperor. Like a spark dropped in a parched land, a fire has kindled and is spreading wildly from world to world. I have never seen anything like it. The Dram strike out mercilessly to stop the blaze, only to find their actions testify to its veracity – they feed the fire in their clumsy efforts to snuff it out."

Waythrel stopped pacing. "Ambra, you are fast becoming legend."

I just shook my head. I hardly had the spirit to laugh at this absurdity I had also foreseen. "From slave-freak to legend in a blink of an eye. Waythrel, all I have done is watch passively as my home world was charred black. Do you know if I close my eyes, I hear their screams? Billions of them." I began trembling as the voices passed over my consciousness again. I fought them back and pushed the vision aside.

"Ambra, legends seldom earn their status, even if you are a heroine in your own way."

"No."

"I will not argue with you over your sacrifice, or theirs," it gestured upward, indicating Earth. "What I mean to say is that legends serve a purpose for those who nurture them and spread them to willing ears. They need hope, Ambra. This oppressed galaxy crushed under the tyranny of the Dram has lost the capacity to believe in victory. Only something larger than themselves, that they can believe is larger than the Dram, can give it back to them. Your feelings in this matter are irrelevant. Your legend grows because they need it, Ambra."

"Then I will need to find a way to live up to it."

"You have said it. So I can only believe it will be."

We didn't speak anymore that night. I was exhausted, even

if Waythrel required nothing resembling sleep. I had to rest. I prepared for bed, told my alien roommate goodnight, and collapsed on my mattress, falling instantly to sleep.

Some legend.

Chapter 39

$$\left[M\frac{\partial}{\partial M}+\beta(g)\frac{\partial}{\partial g}+n\gamma\right]G^{(n)}(x_1,x_2,\ldots,x_n;M,g)=0$$

We cannot define these things without obscuring them, while we speak of them with all assurance. ...our doubts cannot take away all the clearness, nor our own natural lights chase away all the darkness.

Blaise Pascal

And the dream came.

I flew through the heavens, launched by my father's arms. I saw the cold indifference of the distant stars and sensed the evil that lay hidden among them. I passed through my past and sat at my family's kitchen table to see the demon-man. I ran through the high corn to feel the blow of his henchmen, who dragged me off to be butchered and altered.

But in the darkness, as I lay on my back, staring up the high stalks to the green of the ears of corn, then to the blue canvas of the sky, the sunlight blocked out by the shadow of evil standing over me, as the light faded and blackness closed about me, I did not wake up screaming. Not this time. Not like all the other times.

This time, I floated in the blank emptiness, without light, without sound, without smell. Madness lurked in this sensationless null, yet it sharpened my awareness as I approached the abyss of sanity. I reached desperately out into the nothingness for contact.

Then came a disturbance. So soft at first, I could not tell which sense was being engaged – was it sight, a soft light growing in front of me? Or touch, a cool breeze, a ripple of air like a whisper over my skin? Or did it stir faint memories of cold winters in the plains, when one could barely discern the hint of a smell, that taste of wood smoke from a fire that resonated with ancestral memories of safety in the ice?

None of these. As the sensation grew, it was as if a thousand voices came to be recognized, as some celestial choir, a melody growing in the darkness around me. But this sound was more than sound, it came from the force of personality of the chanters, not from their mouths but from another place deep within. A place I knew more than any human who had ever lived. Their song painted the emptiness around me in a beautiful light, a light I knew, a light I could touch. And as I reached out to this light, it became not just a song I might listen to but a water I could swim within. A clay I could shape.

And then *I knew. I understood,* and the voices around me seemed to laugh with joy. From all directions, their energies came to me. I had only to reach out and embrace them.

Then—cold, hard, irregular. I felt it before I saw it. Turning around in this directionless place, seeking, I found a new disturbance. Slowly, a shape unblurred before me. And like a net with infinite dimensions, the light around me bent and surrounded it, enveloped it, and waited.

Everything was still, all the energies potential, like the taut string of a bow with the arrow notched.

I needed only to aim and release the shot.

Chapter 40

3:2

δῶς μοι πᾶ στῶ καὶ τὰν γᾶν κινάσω:
Give me the place to stand, and I shall move the earth.

Archimedes of Syracuse

I don't understand," Waythrel said again, as we raced up the corridor to meet with the Xixian physicists.

"Waythrel, I don't have the words, the understanding. I don't even know if you and the Xix do, so how can I hope to explain rightly?" I gasped out in frustration, as we approached the Xixian wing of the Moon base. "I only have intuition. Like Thel once told me, before I was blind, I didn't understand the physics of seeing, and yet *I saw*. I don't know how this can be, or what it means, or how to say it. I only know I believe it and can do it. But I will need *help*."

Waythrel was silent until reached the doors to the makeshift laboratory. "Then we will try to explain to our scientists. Of course we don't have the best of them here, or even the best representation of the areas that you need. Only a handful of Xixian technologists spared from other needed activities, sent to this Resistance base to serve multiple functions, mostly as engineers. I hope this will serve."

The doors opened, and we walked inside. Several Xixian scientists were waiting for us at Waythrel's request. I could sense the curiosity, expectation, even as I was unable to venture into the complexity of the Xixian thoughts.

"Go ahead, Ambra. It's your show." Waythrel stepped slightly to the side, and I was left in front of about five other Xix.

I took a deep breath. I might as well just get to it. They were the experts. They would have to figure out what I meant.

"Thel once told me that space-time is like a gel, an ever-changing fluid where events of past, present, and future depended on the shape of the gel itself."

One of the scientists spoke up. "A crude description, even in your simple language."

"Yes, okay," I said, not wanting to lose their trust in me. "Humans can understand simple causality— events now creating future states. The gel is squeezed one way, and reshaped in future dimensions."

They were silent, waiting, likely demoralized at my conceptualization of it all. But I had to try. "So, why isn't it possible for the future to reshape the past?"

There was some exchange of conversation between the alien creatures, and I felt an intense concentration from Waythrel. The one that had spoken to me stepped slightly forward, in shape slightly larger than Waythrel, its coloration a greenish-blue with iridescent stripes, contrasting sharply with Waythrel's deep-purple spots.

"You distinguish falsely between past, present, and future, so that it is difficult to communicate with you on this topic without distortion. Within these constraints, however, it is something considered long possible, but which has been untried."

"Why untried?" I asked.

"Because we have lacked an understanding of how to proceed technically, and because it has been considered unwise to enter recursive space."

"Recursive space?"

"It is difficult to explain in this limited language. Should you alter the events of the past from the future, you also alter the future, perhaps impacting even your actions to reach into the past. A circular chain of events, which, simplistically, appears to lead to paradox."

"Like killing your mother before you were born, so that you would never have been born to kill her."

"In general terms, yes. These are effects within effects, like procedures in a computer program that call on themselves, potentially looping infinitely in causality. Such loops cannot be followed until they resolve."

"What does that mean?" I wondered out loud.

"That we cannot predict the consequences of such actions. Why do you ask us this?"

I looked at Waythrel. I had to come clean, tell them my hopes. I knew I couldn't do it without them.

"Because I think I can save Earth."

"Save Earth," asked Waythrel incredulously. "You mean by altering the past?"

"Yes."

"How, Ambra? Even we of Xix cannot do this."

"I don't know exactly how, but I know enough of what I

can do that I am hoping with your help I can succeed." I walked around, almost aimlessly, as I tried to explain the vision, tried to put into words what were insights beyond any words I had. "There is power, Waythrel, enormous power beyond anything you have ever imagined in the millions of latent Readers of Earth. *Earth Before*. Readers that were, but who are no more."

"I don't understand, Ambra."

"They are also *Writers*. Blind Writers, but with latent Writer potential. Some more, some less. I can shape space-time, you know this. So can they, but they cannot direct it. Their prescient organ is too undeveloped. But they can be channeled, Waythrel! Their power refocused!"

"To what end?"

"I can *read* the past. I can *write* in the present. You must see the next step."

One of the scientists spoke up, excitement radiating from her thoughts. "You believe you can alter the space-time of the past."

"Yes!" I nearly shouted. "But there are at least two problems that I can see. And probably more I can't. First—it needs too much energy. Much more than I'll ever have. To reach backward in time and pull the strings of space-time as we need is beyond me. I know this. That is why I need them."

"The Earth Readers of the past?"

"Yes! Together we have the strength. Our energies can be combined, guided by me, like a chorus singing together. Tens of thousands. So much more powerful than one voice."

"What is the second obstacle you mentioned?" Waythrel asked.

"The second—I'll need a lens to focus this power. Even if I can direct it, the power is still too weak, dispersed like a mist or fog. It must be focused like the light of a star through a child's glass, a bright spot that sets a piece of paper on fire!"

"What kind of lens? How do you focus such power?" asked another of the scientists.

"You can't guess? What is the most powerful distorter of space-time known to us in the galaxy?"

I felt the dawning of understanding in the Xixian group, a sense of the audacity of my ideas. Waythrel whispered out. "The Orbs."

"Yes," I nodded. "And I know them and how to travel through them. We have thought of them only as tunnels between different spatial points in the Now. But they are… *more.* I have seen infinite doors in the Orbs, opening one behind the other. Not only in space, but also in time."

One of the Xixian scientists spoke up with agitation. "But each Orb leads to another, either indirectly on the Strings, or, as you have shown, directly, when the Orbs are opened. How can you direct through time what is forced through space? How do the Orbs connect to each other through time?"

This was the part I didn't know if I understood myself. *And yet I saw.* Maybe I didn't need to understand. These alien geniuses could figure it out. I would speak simply of what I could see.

"The Orbs do not connect to each other."

"Ambra," began Waythrel as I hesitated, "of course they do."

"No, it seems so, but you cannot *see.* Your instruments cannot probe. They don't *connect.* I don't know how it can be, but I have seen it. All those Orbs *do not exist,* not as you believe. There are not many Orbs: there is only *one.*"

"Only one?" whispered Waythrel.

"Yes, only one, and it is in all these places at the same time, an infinite door opening to infinite spaces, infinite times. Spaces far beyond those of the String Tree, the worlds you have discovered the Strings to connect. A door opening to spaces so much farther than we can imagine, galaxies half a universe away…."

Astonished thoughts passed through the group around me. "Not only distant spaces, but also *times*, near and far. The Orb here, the opening of the door in this space, will do as well as any to focus the power of Readers past."

"And where will you focus this power, Ambra Dawn?"

I looked over to the Xixian scientist who asked the question, awe and fear in his voice as he contemplated the possibilities of my words.

"On that which murdered my people," I said calmly, firmly. "Richard Cross asked me to change its course. So I will."

Chapter 41

$$m\Psi - i\gamma^a e_a^\mu D_\mu \Psi = 0$$

Where there is sorrow there is holy ground.

Oscar Wilde

Months of research followed this conversation. Soon, the best of Xixian minds had transported to the Moon base, and I was introduced to the intellectual stars of their species, minds even many Xix could not fathom.

It didn't matter to me. I was a simple rodent to these developed creatures, but a rat with a power and insight they did not have, who had stimulated a cascade of ideas in their science never seen before. And I gave them a "humanitarian" reason to pursue these ideas—a chance to save an entire planet and perhaps its dominant species, with all the Reader potential held within it.

So they imported minds and equipment, and experiment after experiment was performed. How they did this without discovery by the Dram amazed me. For several weeks, I spoke to Xixian scientific delegations. They listened to my words and questioned me again and again, and developed their theories for making this bold attempt succeed.

Then, for an entire month, I was left alone, as they pursued the implications of my ideas independently. Only Waythrel would keep me updated, telling me of successes and failures, using the simple terms my poor human mind could work with. In the meantime, I fought off the terrible chill that was creeping over me.

You who read this are sitting somewhere on beautiful Earth, surrounded by an ocean of life—humans, other animals, insects, even the bacteria in your gut and on every surface of your body. In some ways you are a small cell in a giant living body scientists called the biosphere—that tiny shell of air and sea and life, paper-thin floating on a lake of magma.

But that lake will be set loose. It has poured over field and stream, peak and valley, sea and city. Burning. Burning them all to ash. You cannot feel what it is like when the great organism of Earth has died, and you, a single, small cell, are cast into the cold of space. Cut off. *Dying*.

That is the feeling I had, the feeling I sensed from the other humans around me. We were dying some kind of death never before cataloged. A death of having the planet to which we belonged murdered. So different from traveling away from it. Traveling, you are cut off as well, but there is some kind of psychic link, some connection, that is like an umbilical cord keeping you alive, feeding you, calming you, until you make your return. Now, Mother Earth was truly, utterly dead. And for those of us who were left, it was getting terribly cold in space.

Expeditions went regularly to that horror around which we

revolved each month. Some even ventured to the surface, searching places where the fires had been less fierce, where perhaps some life might still remain. But nothing. Even near the deep-sea vents, where bacteria had thrived near geothermal springs at temperatures near boiling, there was only cooling lava.

And all of it was so pointless. Even if some form of life survived, the biosphere could not be re-created, not in a million years, not in one hundred million. It had taken several hundred million years the first time, and four billion for life intelligent enough to think about itself to evolve. As far as humans or animals or plants were concerned, our planet was gone. The charred cinder we still called Earth might start over, with perhaps something evolving to consider the universe again in another five billion years. By this time, our sun would die, would blow up to a red giant like the one in the Dram system, cooking the Earth beyond salvage. Cheering thoughts.

Only once did I join the surveyors and travel to Earth. We left the Moon base on a Xixian spacecraft, circling around from the dark side of the Moon until we witnessed Earthrise. Not the Earthrise from NASA images, those stirring photographs of a crescent blue-white marble hanging in the blackness of space. Instead, a cinder-shrouded ash heap decorated with rivers and lakes of lava peered like some monster's eye over the lunar horizon.

Within hours the powerful ship had put us in orbit around Earth, from which we then descended to examine the landscape. Our home was unrecognizable. It was impossible to see very much through the clouds of smoke and ash and the constant yet diminishing plunge of debris from space back to the planet. Things were extremely hazardous as well, and Waythrel and others had strongly protested my traveling. But at different wavelengths the Xixian instruments could cut through the smoke and reveal the ravaged landscape beneath. Without the oceans, the continents were difficult to discern. No polar caps, and it became easy to lose orientation of north and south. And nowhere could be spotted even a single reminder that we had ever been there. Even space had been swept clean of our satellites and space junk by the material hurled into orbit, much of it still waiting to return to Earth and bring more fire in its fall.

A few hours were enough, more than I could bear, and nearly shaking with horror we returned to the equally desolate surface of the Moon. *Equally lifeless*. But Earth was more desolate for what it had once been, for what had been lost and burned or buried in that cataclysm.

Afterward, sitting in my room trying to purge my mind of those images, I remembered visions from my travels into human history. Germany, 1940. The slaughter of millions. Ashes sent into the skies. The word they used years later, that ended up in the history books, came to me. A two-part word, from the ancient Greek: *holos*, "completely" and *kaustos*, "burnt." *Completely burnt.* The word haunted my mind.

Holocaust.

Chapter 42

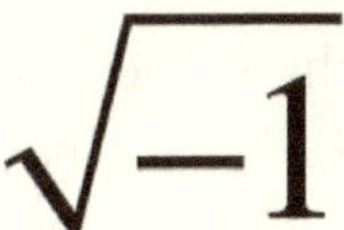

All great truths begin as blasphemies.

George Bernard Shaw

In the meantime, the experiments continued. Even as I fought off the terrible chill threatening to freeze my soul and render me helpless, there was that one small seed of hope trying to germinate as the Xix found their way through the maze of science and technology. After a series of experiments performed without my input, they began to include me in the process. At first it was simple things, reaching into the recent past to modify space-time in small ways that they could detect and quantify. Nothing related to the big task at hand, no manipulation of forces through the Orbs or channeling of other Readers to a common task. I guess they wanted to get a sense that I could do even these simple things, and how well I could do them, before they moved on to more difficult, and more dangerous, experiments.

The second phase was working with other Readers. There was, of course, a high proportion of Readers among the humans on the Moon base, and many of them eagerly agreed to work on the project once they had been briefed about our hopes. A few of the most powerful Xixian Readers also participated to flesh out the chorus of power at our disposal. In all, I would estimate that in these secondary experiments, several hundred human and Xixian Readers were employed.

At first, our success was limited. While I could sense the Reader Fields, it was almost impossible to develop any sort of method to organize the energies, to channel the forces in a productive way. Their latent Writer potential was so diffuse, so weak, that it was like trying to pick up a radio signal from Earth in the Andromeda Galaxy, and to focus those radio waves into a laser beam to burn through a sheet of steel. Of course, the final plan was to focus these weak and diffuse manipulations of space-time through the Orbs, but some kind of initial lens was needed. One not so powerful, but that could take a much more diffuse signal and compact it to send to the greater lens. It was like building some kind of telepathic telescope.

It took a long time to solve this problem, months until it was realized that I could not be this lens, that my own power could not solve this problem. While I could focus my thoughts, I could not focus those of the other Readers. Only *they* could do this, but there seemed to be no way to teach them how. The Xix tried as they had trained me, but all efforts failed. Perhaps because my abilities were so great to begin with, the Xixian training was productive. But not here. Not with the average human Reader. We were stalled and getting nowhere.

. . .

I had begun to despair when the monk came.

He was an old man, Tibetan, white eyebrows and a bald head perched atop a crimson and orange robe that draped to the ground. The monk stood at the door Waythrel had opened to our chamber, looking neither toward me nor the Xix beside him. His eyes seemed distant, a soft smile always on the edge of his expression. I sensed hesitancy in my Xixian friend.

"Ask him in, Waythrel," I said, and it invited him inside.

The monk bowed and entered. He walked up to me and knelt, taking the hem of my black robes. I was getting used to this, my gradual deification in the eyes of my species. For whatever reason, they did not brand me with the guilt of my choices, and my abilities appeared almost magical to them. I suppose my strange appearance only added to the mystique. After Waythrel's words about my becoming a legend, I realized there was little I could do, even if it seemed ridiculous to me. So, I let him prostrate himself.

"I am Chodak, Daughter of Time," he began.

I gasped. "Where did you hear that name?"

Visions of that terrible dream returned, as did the last words I spoke with Richard. Outside of my visions, I had only heard one other person use that title: the scientist who had helped make me the abomination I was.

"Forgive me, Sighted One," he said, bowing further, his face nearly touching the ground, his strong accent garbling the words. "It was spoken to me in a dream."

I took his hands and raised him up. "Please, sit with me. Tell me about your vision." He nodded solemnly and I thanked him. "And call me Ambra. No titles, please."

The old monk limped over to the couch in the chamber. We sat side by side as he spoke intensely, the entire time never releasing my hand. His constant smile was blissful.

"It was in my meditations, Ambra Dawn. Always, I see most clearly when in the deepest meditation."

Waythrel danced over and stood across from us. I sensed a deep concentration in the alien, but could not focus on its thoughts.

"Always, I seek to find you, to find how your Light will deliver us and save us from this darkness. But you are too hard to see, and the light is too bright." He shook his head, smiling. "Until last night. Then I found my mind *inside* the mind of another. It was difficult to understand how this could happen, but I traveled across the entire galaxy in a single moment and entered. Then I saw you with his eyes."

Waythrel interrupted. "You entered the consciousness of another?"

The monk shook his head in the negative. "No, truly only his brain. A flesh in which his mind abided. Or so it felt."

I didn't know what to think of this. "And what did you see?" I asked.

The old man closed his eyes and was silent for a moment. "A lifetime's worth of experience in the time of a butterfly's breath."

"And did these experiences show you how Ambra prevails?" asked Waythrel.

"No," he said, opening his eyes, the smile still there. "It was of a different time, a different place. One that made little sense to my small soul."

I squeezed his hands tightly. "Then why are you here, Chodak? There are many visions. Many futures and many pasts."

"Because he loved you, Ambra Dawn," he said simply, his eyes shining. When I did not speak for several moments, he continued. "Not only as we love the One who has become our

Light in this dark time. This and more. He loved you also as a man loves a woman in the flesh, and he attended to your every movement. And through his eyes, I saw this. I saw the deepest meditation of a lover for whom all time stops as his beloved simply turns her head to the side or takes a step. Focus and concentration on each detail, each hair strand, each breath. And always filled with adoration. Through his eyes, I also saw *your* eyes. Deep, blind green eyes of sadness, but with the joy of him in them. You were to be married."

I could hardly breathe. Was this vision a metaphor? Or had this monk seen into a future where some human man might dare care for me? As I have told you, the reality of my deformity, my blindness, the monstrosity of my actions had shut down most normal human thoughts. And there had been no time, no chance to examine the idea of my womanhood. Not a single moment to exist in that human dimension. To shine this light onto it was disorienting. It hurt.

I couldn't help myself, my thoughts leapt over to his mind, and breaking a privacy I always try to respect, I looked and saw that it was true. He spoke the truth of his vision. In his mind I could witness the adoration of a lover from a time yet to be. My own face stared back at me through the memories of the eyes of a possible future.

The monk smiled and patted my hand several times. "He loves and serves, and he awaits you. I came to tell you this, to tell you so that you would know that in a future I found, you will be loved in this way."

The universe is cruel. More than anyone, I know that there will be no single future, and that even what has been could *unbe*. Was it better to know that there existed the possibility of such love, even knowing it was unlikely to be realized? Or better to never have known, never have felt the imaginative stirrings of affection in a dying life? How could I sit there infatuated with the cyst-inspired hallucinations of an old Buddhist monk?

Waythrel interrupted my thoughts. "Chodak, you said that you see more clearly in your deepest meditations."

The monk nodded. "It is so."

"We of Xix understand the focus of consciousness, the stepping out of it and becoming more even as you become less. We trained Ambra in our ways as best we could an alien mind. But you are human," it said, in a tone I had come to imagine as it smirking, "and a professional."

"Devotion is not a trade for us."

"I understand," it said, continuing to probe. "How did you find this man's mind in your dream?"

The monk glanced upward and to his left. "I searched for Ambra Dawn and could not see for the light. But there was a tunnel, a path that seemed to lead toward her. One that I might follow without becoming blinded by the light. I turned toward this path, and it took me to him."

"You *chose* this path? You *directed* your Read?"

And suddenly, I understood. My emotions leapt over toward Waythrel. *Yes, Ambra. Here, we may find our answer.*

"Yes," he nodded. "But only with a great stillness."

Chapter 43

$$E_k = m_0(\gamma - 1)c^2 = \frac{m_0c^2}{\sqrt{1-\frac{v^2}{c^2}}} - m_0c^2$$

It is by logic that we prove, but by intuition that we discover. To know how to criticize is good, to know how to create is better.

Henri Poincaré

And so we stumbled on the process of prayer.

Yes, you heard me right. *Prayer*: An idea from a Buddhist monk who was part of our Reader cohort. You may not know it, but before Earth died, there was a good bit of scientific research that showed that meditation, prayer, whatever you want to call it, has a remarkable ability to alter brain states, focus consciousness, even improve health. Jesus said: "Pray, and it will be as you believe." Yeah, I know that's not quite like the Bible has it. But I heard it from the Rabbi's mouth, so trust me on this one. And he had a good-sized cyst, in case you were wondering.

What seemed to be passed down from generations, and what science seemed to be measuring, was that *prayer* affected the *mind* and the world around the mind. Given the human Writer potential, it should have been obvious what was really going on. Prayer focused and stilled the mind, cut it off from the five senses of the world around it, and allowed our sixth sense the stillness and quiet, the resources it needed to function optimally. And that's where the magic of humanity is born. "Be still and know that I am God." In some strange way, we've always known the truth.

Our monk had delivered to us an answer to the misdirected energies of our Readers. Waythrel saw the answer before we could ever have hoped to on our own, and that very night we began an intense training in the thousand-year-old practice of Tibetan meditation.

Chodak and I worked together to direct this giant, prophetic prayer group. I had discovered an alien form of meditation with the Xix, but he taught the Earthlings among us a more *human* way. It was far, far more effective, even for me, than the Xixian training. We performed basic meditation practices throughout the day at first over several weeks. But the results were so immediately measurable that we were motivated to continue the arduous hours of stillness for months. I could see the energies brightening. Instead of the diffuse fog around me from this Reader chorus, now there were little will-o'-the-wisp shimmers dancing around each of them.

It felt crazy even to me, despite all the miracles and madness I had seen, but it worked. Intense sessions of meditation and feedback snowballed, and I was soon able to drive the space-time distortions of the Readers into a much more organized and malleable form. You have to understand, individually, each of them was so much weaker than me. They could affect little in the space-time fields. Even groups of ten or twenty had little power. But these focused *prayers* of hundreds of Readers actually registered as a blip on the instruments and became like some congealing blob in a lava lamp to my vision, a clay that I could reach out and touch, tug – *shape*. Saints we weren't, but we sure began to spike the detectors of the Xix.

Now we were getting close. We had a means to bring together and integrate the power of many Readers in a way that I could channel and control. But still, that wasn't enough. Not *near* enough, even should the Xix and I succeed in using the Orb to focus the energies one thousand times. It was the combination of moving through time and space that made it so difficult. It wasn't like adding the difficulties of one to the other. To reach back into the past and alter space-time in a major way was like multiplying the energies involved – thousands, tens of thousands of Readers would be needed. There were not enough left in the galaxy for such a deed, or if there were, gathering them all together would be impossible under the eyes of the Dram and the needs of interstellar travel.

But the numbers *were* there. Waiting, if I could reach them. And so, when the Xix finally came to me and said that they believed they could use the Orb to channel the energies (with my help, of course), all that remained was the little task of getting those tens of thousands onboard with the plan. Tens of thousands who lived decades, hundreds of years ago, on an Earth that no longer existed, in times and cultures diverse and distant. I had to find a way to reach them and convince them all to *pray* for our deliverance.

Thank God, I had an idea. Unfortunately, we first had to deal with an unfriendly visit from our insectoidal hunters.

Chapter 44

$$|\delta\mathbf{Z}(t)| \approx e^{\lambda t} |\delta\mathbf{Z}_0|$$

You need chaos in your soul to give birth to a dancing star.

Friedrich Nietzsche

Michael came bursting into our room without knocking. Waythrel and I stood unmoving, deep in telepathic communication over our recent progress with the Reader groups, and had to shake ourselves out of the trance. To help us along, the entire base was plunged into red emergency power lighting as alarms began to sound.

"Dram warships," he gasped, nearly out of breath. "Five of them surfing off the Orb String."

"*Five?*" I had seen the damage one of them could do.

"They know we're here," he continued. "I don't know how they discovered, but that doesn't matter. We were too optimistic. It was bound to happen."

Waythrel danced around in that impossible Xixian fashion.

"Ambra, we have to get you off this moon! Michael, what ships are available?"

"No time! They set this up perfectly and were detected only minutes ago. They came off the Orb Tree at a tremendous velocity, aimed right at us. Already their longer-range weapons have disabled our sensor ships, and we can only track them from Moon systems. The Xix team has taken over, redirected all power to defenses, but it won't last long."

I sensed a deep anxiety within Waythrel that was only partially focused on me. "We had no advanced warning, even through our Time Tree relays. This can only mean one thing."

Michael nodded. "Word came in shortly after the ships appeared. There has been a mass purging of Xix on Dram, and spreading to Dram-controlled worlds."

"And Xix itself?" I could feel the creature nearly dissolving. Its mental patterns were much simpler now, less complex, primitive emotional-like states dominating the structure.

"No word of any attack. Yet. Maybe, they don't have the evidence to suspect that much. Maybe, they are just purging Dram in case."

Waythrel moved quickly. "Michael, there must be a ship we can use to try an escape!"

"You'll be blown out of the skies in seconds. You know nothing will get by."

I couldn't stand it anymore. "Or should we just sit here until they liquefy the base? Is that better?"

He shouted. "I don't have a plan! We're helpless!"

My mind raced. I began to feel the first tremors of explosions, likely the initial impacts of Dram weapons on the lunar surface. At that distance, with the generators we had, it would likely be a few minutes before they could effectively target the base. But only a few minutes.

"Michael, assemble the Readers in the meditation chamber." He stood there quietly, perplexed. I shouted. "Michael! Get all the Readers down there, now!"

I felt a dawning awareness spread across Waythrel's mental web. "Ambra, no, it is much too dangerous."

"What is too dangerous? Why do we need the Readers?" His face was completely blank.

I pushed past him, beginning to sprint down the hallway, a blind woman dashing through narrow corridors, feeling with my hands along the walls, feeling with my mind along the Strings. "Waythrel, gather the Xix techs and fire the damn machines up. We've only got minutes!"

By the time we had critical numbers, we were starting to take damage. The entire base was rocking with the explosions and impacts. *Five warships!* It was probably enough firepower to destroy an entire metropolis ten times over. They wouldn't even have to kill us directly—just knock out the life support on this airless and frigid rock. Of course, the Dram would make sure and boil the base away as well.

Waythrel and the Xixian scientists had already powered up the amplifiers or whatever they were that would aid in channeling our space-time manipulations. They performed coolly under pressure, much better than my human brethren.

"Everyone!" I shouted over the din of war and human panic. "Listen to me!"

But it was no use. People were shouting, running around, clutching each other. My voice could not penetrate the cacophony. So I closed my eyes and resorted to more brutal means.

It was a brief burst, but harsh. There were several cries as everyone in the room simultaneously grabbed their skulls, shutting their eyes tightly in pain. Several fell to the floor and slowly stood up again. One did not rise and remained motionless on the floor. They looked at me in dawning understanding. Some looked betrayed.

"I'm sorry!" I screamed, as much to stop my own thoughts of what I had done as to focus their attention. "Listen to me! The Dram will destroy this base in minutes! We can't beat them in a fight. We can't stop or repel their weapons." The room was utterly quiet except for the rumbling from above. I swallowed and pressed on. "We have *one* chance to stop them. When the Orbs are opened, there is a terrible distortion of space-time around them. Unless tightly controlled, there is so much curvature, the Orbs will draw into themselves anything nearby. Even warships."

I heard Waythrel in my mind. *Ambra, hurry! Time is running out!*

"I can open the Orbs, but I can only do it if I'm close to them. And I don't know if I can control them from this distance. Not without your help! This is the time to use all that we have been practicing for. Right now, I need you to quiet yourselves and harmonize, and reach out with me. Together, maybe we can open the Orb and draw the Dram warships into it!"

"What if you can't open it from here, even with our help?" a woman called out.

"Then we die as we surely will anyway," cried Waythrel.

The monk stepped forward, his smile only a weak shadow. "And if you cannot control the Orb?"

I looked at Waythrel and its thoughts echoed my own. "I don't know. I think it could consume the entire system."

There was a second or two of buzzing, but a strong earthquake shook the room, and dust rained down on us. Waythrel cried out, "Unless you survive, your star system is already dead! The only risk is delay. Take your positions! Calm yourselves. Find your focus and direct it to Ambra!"

They listened. The Readers crouched and sat. As a group they frantically tried to reach a Zen-like calm. Have you ever tried to reach a Zen-like calm frantically? The ultimate irony: in order to save our lives, we were forced in panic to reach an enlightened state of calmness in which we no longer feared for our lives. It wasn't working.

Sensing the inability to focus, the old monk called out reminders of his teachings, stepping among the Readers calmly, trying to coax them to relinquish their attachments to themselves. To safety. To life itself. To seek a state of detachment where death does not matter in order that we might save our hides. That wasn't working, either.

I became desperate as more explosions rocked the base. Once again, survival drove me to actions I never would have imagined in saner moments. I thought back to my invasion of the other Readers' minds, my mental slap to calm them down. I had stunned them all, possibly damaged the mind of one, in order to get their attention. Was my only option disturbance? If I could cause such damage, couldn't I also heal? I decided that I would try, even if it meant in the end a form of mind control. I sent my thoughts out over the Readers before me, waves of intricate space-time distortions that interacted with their mental fields. At first, everything was out of phase, clashing. As I adapted and sought to know each personality that I touched, one by one, my calming thoughts began to resonate with them. One by one, I drove out the thoughts of fear and panic, and the Readers were freed of them. They could then focus as they had been trained, inwardly seeking to concentrate and redirect their own force fields towards me.

I felt Waythrel's thoughts from across the room as it

deduced what was happening. *I love you, Ambra Dawn, but I fear you. Now you control even the thoughts of others.*

I didn't have the luxury to question the ethics of what I was doing. This was the only way I knew to save our lives. And it was probably not even going to work.

Chapter 45

$$2^{\aleph_\alpha} = \aleph_{\alpha+1}$$

A set is a Many that allows itself to be thought of as a One.

Georg Cantor

I floated midway between the approaching Dram warships and the lunar base.

Like in the dreams of Earth from before, I had no body, no damage suffered from the vacuum of space or the scalding radiation of the sun. I was a disembodied sentient knot of space-time, projected from inside the lunar surface, the product of my own mental structure and efforts and the amplification of hundreds of Readers and Xixian space-time modulators.

I didn't have time to examine how this had happened or what had truly happened to me. Not only to me—but to the entire Reader chorus that strove and connected with me. This projected, multi-dimensional knot of consciousness, the product of the mind-space-time field that Thel had introduced my inadequate human intelligence to, was something new. My consciousness dominated the matrix. I shaped and held it together. But there were hundreds of threads, thousands even, from the thoughts of the other Readers entwined. Not only entwined, but *interwoven* so that we became something more than simply a chorus in harmony. It was almost like the birth of a unified, newborn synergistic mind greater than our individuality. Formed of the combined strength and power of multiple minds, augmented by the advanced technology of the Xix, but like ice melting, transitioning into a new state beyond all that had been known before. *We* had become something *Else*. It was like waking up, except that the being that awoke had just been born.

Some portion of me was still inside, meditating with the others inside Earth's Moon. But what it was of me, of all of us, that was outside, I to this day do not know. The Xix do not know. It was me but only a part of me. A "me" projected and concentrated, but that could dissolve leaving no damage to the rest of us sitting quietly in lotus position in the middle of a dust-choked room entombed on Earth's satellite.

The Dram energy weapons passed through me without effect, and their explosive missiles did not detonate. Nor did they impact the base. Already, I had left sharp warpings of space behind me, between me and the base, so that, as the Dram radiation and solid weaponry followed available paths in space-time, they curved, seemingly repelled by the base itself, and scattered harmlessly around the remaining surface of the Moon. It was an intuitive "shield" I constructed, in my efforts to will their weapons away from the base. It was also draining, but I knew I could keep it up longer than they could.

Their inability to target us only fueled the Dram soldiers to anger, and they unleashed a bombardment the likes of which I had never seen, even in the space battles I had witnessed before in my journey. Five powerful Dram warcraft unloaded on the little lunar base and, like some prismatic spray impacting a wall, exploded in light of a thousand colors casting shadows on the Moon's surface. Part of my mind rejoiced: they were draining their energy supplies dramatically, and when the gravitational vortex came, they would have that much less with which to resist it. I could maintain this shield long enough to debilitate them. I was not in a hurry. In fact, I felt strangely calm.

Ambra, open the Orb!

I discerned the intricate threads of Waythrel's consciousness calling from within.

Ambra, now! There isn't time!

It was hard to feel the same desperation out here. Without the full flood of my body's limbic soup—its adrenaline, cortisol, hormones, oxygen, sugar—I felt a strange form of detached peace. And what was the hurry? The stupid Dram army was just draining its batteries, anyway.

It's okay, Waythrel. I've blocked them. Let them empty their ammunition.

Ambra, please! It's not about them, it's about you! Your body—something is wrong. It is losing temperature. Your heart rate is slowing dangerously. You must return! Open the Orb!

Strange. *My body.* Yes, I could still sense it. Back there, linked weakly by a thread to this new me. I guess I would need my body. If I were to continue my journey, end the Dram war, I would need to survive, would I not? Was this motivating? I wasn't sure that it was. In this new state of being, all my ideas of what was and wasn't important took on new forms. Eons seemed to shrink to ages, parsecs seemed to be only short trips.

Matter and energy and time mixed and spun and transformed in millions of fashions.

So what if my body died? How imprisoned we fleshly creatures were! So blind to the vastness, the openness, the *possibilities* of the universe. Our vision myopic, tunneled by bone and blood and limited mental horizons. What I had become was something very different. I was not unhappy or harmed in this state. To the contrary, I felt empowered, strangely free. I could explore the universe. Perhaps forever.

Ambra! Please, no! We can feel your thoughts. Please, please don't leave us. Ambra, I am only a Xix, but...I...we...we love you.

The Orb fluxed brightly in my mind's eye. It was a pulse of power, a flash, blinding like a detonation, and it had not been part of our plan. I had not reached out to it as yet. This was not my doing. Instead, I felt *it* reaching out, reaching out to *me*. A tendril of radiance sped at greater than light speeds and targeted me like a missile. I could not move or escape its approach. It struck me as a mental blow and enveloped me. I was surrounded, enfolded into an energy field not of cold indifference, not of some mechanical production, but of something that felt much more organic. Something that felt *alive*. Something that felt more than alive and that had a will of its own: *The Orb was conscious.*

And, it spoke to me.

Chapter 46

$$\phi = 1 + (1/\phi) = 1 + (1/(1 + (1/(1 + 1/...))))$$

In love all the contradictions of existence merge themselves and are lost. Only in love, are unity and duality not at variance. Love must be one and two at the same time.

Rabindranath Tagore

Once again, I awoke after a long sleep to stare up at the alien form of a Xixian medic. Detectors were positioned around my body, data collected, vital signs examined by the wonders of Xixian technology. The room was dim, and even so the weak light hurt my blind eyes. The occipital lobe at the back of my oblong head may have been obliterated, but my retina could still very much feel pain.

I felt sore and cold, and I blinked several times. Slowly, an awareness beyond the five senses grew, and the consciousness of many creatures washed over me—human and Xixian. And of *another* in the distance. Now that I had experienced it, I would never again lose the sense of its presence. Powerful.

Quiescent. Alien and yet more human than myself. I knew something was different. Something profound had happened. I just could not remember.

Close at hand, I felt the mind of Waythrel. I reached out to it.

Hello again, my dear Xix.

The room burst into applause. With my prescience, I scanned the immediate past and saw that a crowd was gathered around my hospital bed, cheering and crying, smiles and melting anxiety washing the room like a rainstorm. I couldn't help but also smile.

"Were my thoughts so loud?" I asked through a croaked voice.

There was laughter and more tears. Waythrel touched my forehead with one of its many tendrilled fingers. "We are tightly bound now and sense each other as never before. We nearly lost you, foolish human child."

My sleep had been dreamless, empty, and my memory was a torn patchwork. "What happened, Waythrel? My last memories—they are of you calling for me to open the Orb, and of… something else."

The entire room was silent. Waythrel continued to stroke my forehead. "You are our prophet, Ambra. Your mind was traumatized, and you can't remember right now, but a higher power spoke through you."

"A higher power? What do you mean? What of the Dram? What *happened*?"

"The Dram are gone—where, we don't know. You opened the Orb, or, perhaps as we understand better now, the Orb opened *for* you. The ships were dragged into the wormholes and sent to some distant place. Even a distant time, perhaps. There is no record of them appearing in any system. The base is secure. As soon as you recover fully, we will return to our training. To our plan." I felt it reach out to the others with a fluidity and skill I had never sensed in it before. "I think that you will find our performance will improve dramatically."

I processed this wonderful victory quickly, its other words disturbing me. "What do you mean the Orb opened *for* me?"

"Do you remember nothing, young one? Nothing of the personality that embraced you in the emptiness of space? That brought you back to us because not only our love called out, but because it loved us?"

I sat up straight in the bed and pulled my knees to my chest, wrapping my arms around them. Like some dream reawakening, I felt a golden warmth surround me, a caress of light and gravity penetrating my consciousness. "The Orb," I whispered as the events came streaming back: the detachment as I was projected into space and encountered the Dram, the emotional call of Waythrel and the other Readers for me to return, and the sudden response to that call from…*the Orb*?

"Yes!" said Waythrel, a happiness, nearly giddiness, spilling from its mind. "The Orb! We were all linked together as your body was dying, as you began to detach from your fleshly form—from us. It came when our breaking hearts cried to you, and it answered our prayers. It spoke to you, and you listened. The Orb opened, the ships were scattered. And you returned."

"What did it say to me?" My memories were still blocked.

Waythrel was silent. I sensed the smiles around the room, the hundreds of humans and aliens that in joy knew something that I could not yet recall.

I can't explain it. Not even in the Xixian language. Read, Ambra. Read my mind.

When you first learn a new language, after you have studied for some time the syntax and grammar and begun to spend the necessary days and months immersed in the spoken reality of the tongue, you reach a first important threshold of progress. At this point, you can understand a great deal of what is said to you, sometimes nearly a fluent comprehension. But your speech will lag, flounder, and fail. You will stumble to match the fluency of your understanding with words from your own mind and mouth. So it was here.

Waythrel's thoughts opened up to me, and poured an experience I cannot describe in this shallow book with these empty and clumsy words. I understood it, I understand it, but I cannot express it. I can only say that all the vague prophecies and poems and scriptures in human history that spoke of the divine were made mute by this vision. It was a singular interaction between a cosmic space-time anomaly and my enhanced and projected consciousness. It was a revelation from the Orb to hundreds of Reader minds interwoven like counterpoint with mine. An entity that scores of alien species had crudely manipulated for gain, so far beneath its true purpose, that it was like ants walking across a discarded telescope to bridge a small stream. *The Orb had spoken.* In this revelation were shards of cosmic truths that even in our enhanced state we could not understand, and in our separated individuality we grasped even less. The divine had entered the room, and we could not even comprehend the dust it scattered. We could only stand in awe.

The visions flooded me from Waythrel and stimulated at last the full release of my own memories. It was beautiful. It was terrible. It was so vast in space and time, and simultaneously so localized and intimately personal, that it generated mental vertigo. It's as if you went deep inside yourself to that point of the sharp awareness of existence, and at that dimensionless singularity, from that single point exploded all of universal creation. Trillions of galaxies, their billions of star systems, planets, living forms, civilizations, culture, science, religion blasted like a fire hose through your mind. And at the center of it all, in the middle of a thousand dimensions of complexity was a singularity simple and impenetrable. Eternal. Indestructible. A unified force that bound everything else together, that gave it structure, and that generated the very laws of mathematics and physics underscoring existence.

Of all the words I have in my own language for this thing, there is only one that comes close. It fails badly, it distorts, it lacks—but it is the distant echo of a dream whispered across infinity. It is not God, for the idea of God is too human, too finite. It is not faith or hope, for in the end these fail before the darkness.

The only word I know that I dare use—is Love.

Chapter 47

$$dt_E^2 = \left(1 - \frac{2GM_i}{r_i c^2}\right) dt_c^2 - \left(1 - \frac{2GM_i}{r_i c^2}\right)^{-1} \frac{dx^2 + dy^2 + dz^2}{c^2}$$

The child ever dwells in the mystery of ageless time, unobscured by the dust of history.

Rabindranath Tagore

So, the hunt began for human Readers of the past, and you won't believe where we ended up the first time we launched ourselves backward in time.

Maybe we were all a little cocky now that the group had become some Orb-integrated, psychic, Dram-warship-trashing space-time commando team. Maybe it was because we were just completely new and clueless to this bizarre new occupation of communal-mind time travel. Or maybe we were a sad collection of broken mortals slowly dying off near our grilled home world, and this was just the best we could manage the first time.

Whatever the reason, none of us, not even the Xix, anticipated the wee little problem of my focusing into the past and zeroing in on the strongest Reader signals I could perceive. It was enough trying to move through the Orb Time Tree, navigate its labyrinths with my hundreds of fellow intellects, discern in the space-time fabric the lights and undulations that bore the unmistakable stamp of humanity, and surf the strings to those points in space-time. Our naive logic sent us straight to the brightest collections of these past Readers. Surely, they would be the ones we needed to persuade to spread the message and form the massive trans-chronological prayer group we envisioned.

Our multidimensional knot of consciousness erupted over the beautiful landscape of an older Earth. An Earth before magma had spilled over its surface. An Earth before concrete and human industrial pollutants had tarnished our solar system's gem. An Earth radiating life and potential. It was the more primal Earth of our ancestors, and every human mind that I carried with me nearly swooned to drink in the beauty of our planet once again. The azure skies dotted with puffy white, the breezes stirring smells no longer alien, but of home. Green of leaf, brown of branch and soil. Bird's song. If a disembodied group mind could weep, ours did.

Even the Xix were moved. Sharing our consciousness, they were exposed in an intimate, direct manner to human experiences, memories, and sensations in a way that was only fleeting by the more unconscious space-time telepathy of a standard Reader. Although I could sample the minds of humans and aliens alike by myself, even the most powerful Readers of the Xix were as unconscious in their abilities to Read as any human. But with my mind stitching all the others together, they *saw*. And they felt what it was like to be human. These shared experiences more tightly bound our consciousness.

After a few moments of wonder, we forced ourselves to

attend to the business at hand. There was some surprise that we were in an earlier age of human history. Most of us had assumed that we would encounter the most powerful Reader concentrations in the modern age, which provided the additional benefit of many more numbers and the technology to spread our message widely and quickly. But perhaps it was not so strange. Weren't the faith and devotion of the inhabitants of earlier epochs unique? Maybe their prayers would make up in their intensity for what they lacked in numbers.

I focused our mind more intently. A very strong source of human space-time distortion was near, and I followed the warped pathways through a forest and up a steep slope. There was smoke spilling up to the sky, and the indistinct sounds of voices ahead. With increasing anticipation, our little thought matrix sped upward and broke through the trees and came out into a clearing. It was rocky, the tree line beginning to fail. There was snow and ice covering the ground and a large fire burning in the middle of a rock-lined pit. A loud chanting was underway, rhythmic, accompanied by a strange music.

Banging on animal-hide drums and piping on animal-bone flutes, a group of short men wrapped in wolf hides danced. They were unkempt, bearded, heavily muscled and tanned, even in the cold weather. In the middle, a group of very hardy-looking women presided over some sort of ritual slaughter. A deer lay in the middle of the concentric circles, tied with ropes to the ground, its eyes wide with fear. A woman knelt down beside it and lay a jagged white blade to its neck. She let out a long and sustained howl, and as one, with a final crescendo in the chanting and single powerful drum beat, the music ceased.

Then she slit its throat.

. . .

So, after searching the past for the most powerful groups of Readers we could find, we followed their signal, landing in the middle of the religious rites of our prehistoric ancestors.

Thinking back on it, it should have been obvious that this would happen. The human mutations that led to our sixth sense occurred tens of thousands of years prior to the age I lived in. In fact, I was to discover many years later that the individual mutations and tissue alterations had already begun in our hominid forebearers before *Homo sapiens* had arisen. What singled us out, what gave us the edge over the other hominids, the wild animals, even nature itself, was the rapid development of that organ in the middle of our brains that allowed us to forecast.

Becoming sensitive to the space-time matrix, seeing the future and the dangers and opportunities it presented, even if only in the vague manner of dreams and visions, was to become the one-eyed species in an ecosystem of the blind. Like the other senses that had conferred tremendous survival advantages in a dangerous universe, being able to Read changed everything. Once again, we were to learn that it was not our grand intelligence—as we so often thought of it—that made us king of the hill. Did you know dolphins are actually smarter than us? Well, they are. No, what truly made us special was a pre-cancerous neural growth.

There is nothing like having a sense that a mountain lion is coming around the bend, or that dangerous weather is approaching, or that food can be found *that way*. Nothing like the sense that mating with so and so seems to produce a better future. When we forecast, when we Read the world, we had a power over it no other living thing did. We *chose* from the strands of possible futures.

And nature selected for this trait very strongly. In a

harsher age before we had mastered everything, those who could Read, and Read well, were much less likely to get killed before they passed on their special genes. They were much more likely to survive. Give that several thousand generations, and by the age in which we found ourselves, nearly *every* human present was as strong a Reader as I had ever met from the modern age. Every one of them. No wonder they had produced such a powerful and localized Reader signal. Our technical mastery of the Earth—aided in large part in later ages by the alien races who discovered our Reader abilities—removed that harsh selective pressure. Humans in whom the genes produce no psychic cyst could survive every bit as well as the Readers. Better actually, because the Reader genes extract many prices both physically and psychologically. By the time I was born, Readers were rare. Rare and prized like bluefin tuna, and treated about as well.

Not with the cave folks. They were each bright with it and sensitive. In fact, they even detected our presence. Within seconds of the dying animal's drowning cry, as the blood poured over some ritualistic rock carved with strange symbols, the entire group become distracted. They stood up, one after the other, and *turned toward* us! I could feel their minds reaching out, the tendrils of our thought matrix like a warm fire that their hands approached cautiously and pulled back from, so that they would not be burned. They knew we were there. *They felt us.*

I don't know what they thought we were. Something elemental. Divine. The matriarch stood on a rock and held toward us a strange relic—thorned branches of some bush, pruned and adorned with animal bones and rocks. She cried out to the skies with some new chant, and the other women and men knelt down and prostrated themselves, bowing in our direction. It would have sent chills down my spine if I had one.

But what was there to do? With the purest optimism, we tried to interact with them. It was a disaster. Their minds had never encountered something so strong, so abstract or complex. We could give them images of simple things, sensations and conceptions of a life that they had known and understood. These they could grasp without distress. But there was no hope to explain our errand, our need, or what we hoped they might accomplish. All such attempts led at first to frustration, and then fear and even madness in our contacts.

After several days of trying, the group left the cave terrified, conducting ritual after ritual when exiting, marking off the territory with crafted artifacts and drawings in the dirt. It was like some prehistoric occult protection spell from the demonic forces. After several hours, they were gone, and we had no desire to follow them. The most powerful and concentrated Readers in human history were utterly useless to saving humanity.

So, we withdrew from this Earth history having failed completely. Our first efforts, our powerful cohort of human and alien Readers coming off a high in thwarting the attack of the galaxy's most powerful military, had reached out to the past, to the most powerful Readers in our past, and had nothing to show for it.

Nothing but the distinction of having created a haunted mountain in the depths of humanity's past.

Chapter 48

$$\lim_{x \to \infty} \frac{\pi(x)}{x / \ln(x)} = 1$$

It is very hard to find a black cat in a dark room,
especially when there is no cat.

Proverb

Our next attempts were also failures, and for similar reasons, even if the minds and cultures we encountered were more advanced.

It turns out that most, if not all, of the great advancements in human civilization occurred from a coupling of the randomness of genetic recombination and the arbitrariness of human climate, disease, and resource availability. For the world's great civilizations of India, China, Central and South America, and, finally, the European enlightenments of Greece and Western Europe, prolonged periods of plenty and general lack of disease, along with specific availability of resources (either local or imported), set the foundation. But we also discovered that was not enough.

As we scanned through the past, our community repeatedly discovered that the significant aggregations of Readers were nearly always present at these cultural zeniths. Because mastery of agriculture had reduced the selective pressures for survival, the Reader genes were less significant and could be lost with less impact. Therefore, they became more diffuse in the human population, and only when the genes combined in a lucky fashion to enhance the relative number of Readers did we see the effects.

From my explorations of history in human thought, it had always been somewhat of a mystery why there would be these random epochs of such great cultural and intellectual progress and energy. Historians knew that the resources and stability of the environment had to be there, but that did not explain why some cultures with all they needed went nowhere. Often the explanations were centered on racial theories that had more to do with justifying the superiority of the historian's race than with facts. And that's because the critical facts were missing to all of them.

When the density of Readers was high enough in a closely knit group, their combined sixth sense kindled their awareness, opened their minds and stimulated exploration and creativity. You could maybe imagine it if you thought of the world's peoples as being blind but for a few "Seers" who could perceive a blurred fog of the visual spectrum. Just this different and additional stimulus to the neurological structure of the brain set things moving that wouldn't otherwise have moved. New ideas, new perspectives, faith in a bigger universe beyond simple "sound." I can tell you as someone who has seen so much more than anyone else, you have no idea of how deep, how multilayered, how *different* reality is than you imagine it without a space-time perceiving organ. It is so obvious in retrospect, but these random concentrations of Readers in the right places at the right times were bound to drive human cultural development.

It also explained the equally strange tendency of cultures to lose the "spark," to drift for a few generations, and then for the civilization to become something far less dynamic and creative, or even to fall into decay. Always, there was the sense in these cultures that they could not live up to their forebearers. The reasons were mysterious and usually explained by moralistic historians as being due to lax morals or other aspects of the culture or world events. Sometimes, this was true. Usually, however, it was simply that the Reader genes were bred out, mixed in a way that the individuals with developed organs in their brains became fewer, and critical mass was lost. The culture stagnated.

Of course, the Xix were the first to perceive this and to explain it to us. As alien anthropologists, they dissected the development of our species without the biases that we brought to the process. Once we understood, we became excited. We could almost count on the fact that the locations and times in history where we would find the highest local concentrations of Readers would be in ages where humanity made intellectual and cultural leaps, and, most importantly, where their minds were most open to new ideas. And we had a heck of a message to bring them.

But our enthusiasm was misguided. In tragic encounter after tragic encounter, we dove joyously into these bubbling cultures and sought out the powerful Readers. We communed with them. We explained reality and our terrible plight.

And we flooded them.

What we came to learn after numerous disappointments was that even when open to new ideas, there is only so far the human mind can stretch effectively. In ages where the Earth was the center of the universe, where atoms were unknown, where spirits spoke from stones and souls were reincarnated, our hyper-modern, even alien narrative was composed of too many threads for which their minds were not ready. I say "effectively," because there were individuals who could accept our message, even spread it, but they tended to be viewed as mystics or madmen, and sometimes we indeed drove them mad with the visions we shared. We were even the stimulus for several human religious and philosophical movements. We triggered suicides. We helped spawn persecutions like the Salem witch trials. We walked with Jesus and Buddha.

All of this was amazing, unexpected, and useless to the only task that mattered. No matter how much we tried to convey the important essence of our story, we failed. People were encouraged to pray for the salvation of humanity, but the idea of altering space-time as we needed them to was too abstract. Their prayers were misguided. Finally, after emotionally and physically draining months of engaging the brightest eras in human history, we gave up.

We then turned to the only other option left: what we couldn't achieve with the brilliant few of past ages, we would seek to accomplish with the far more dim, but numerous, populations of the modern era. Mediocrity with multiplication would reign supreme.

The final straw was that the Xix had run the numbers. Even if we had managed to get the brightest Readers of the past to understand what we needed them to do, it wasn't going to be enough. There weren't any other Ambra Dawns, and even the strongest Readers of the past were not present in sufficient numbers to alter history as we needed.

The equations told a simple tale: only in the modern era,

when the world's population soared to unprecedented levels, stabilizing around ten billion, would there be the number of Readers we required. More than enough, actually. But only if we could get them onboard. Only if our message could reach them effectively. Only if enough of them took action.

And that really was the problem. Even in modern times, after Einstein, after quantum mechanics, when science fiction novels and films had introduced millions, perhaps billions to the ideas of relative time, curved space, multi-universes—in an era where such crazy ideas were not necessarily tied to a religion or dogma but could lead to further scientific thoughts about cause and effect—even then, how to convince them that *this story* was real enough to take that vulnerable plunge? In an age of cynicism, of the loss of previous cultural values and meaning, when church and state had become objects of distrust, how do you reach out from the future and convince people that they had to do something so humbling, so silly as to pray to save humanity—without driving them to madness?

Some of us argued for creating a new religion, convinced that only through the devotion of religious certainty could we focus the minds as we would need. Despite misgivings from many, we made several attempts to achieve this very end. All were spectacular failures. Those people open to the idea of *revelation* also were the least inclined to be rigorous in thought, and often creatively modified our visions to suit their own emotional needs. Cults were formed, even scientific religions, but they all distorted the message, often so severely that it would have been a comedy if it weren't so tragic. We were especially good at creating doomsday cults.

The idea of creating new religions had failed, and so we moved on. We explored the manipulation of political movements, nation-states, cultural fads, and philosophy. All had certain attractive features to achieving our goals, but all suffered from one or numerous fatal flaws that quickly became apparent. In the end, after we had moved from the best and brightest Readers to the average in order to get the numbers required, we also abandoned the elevated routes of religion, philosophy, and culture. We decided upon the lowest common denominator, the one commonality across cultures that attracted the largest numbers, the greatest resources, and had the longest staying power: entertainment.

In the modern era, nothing could move people and resources faster than a great story told well. We knew we had a great story, but storytellers we were not. So we looked for them. We sought out poets and playwrights, novelists and musicians. We engaged with those who seemed receptive to initial probes. We sought to help them bring about the telling of their future in a way that would capture hearts and move the narrative across the world. To find Readers. To convince them.

You know how this ends. You are holding the resulting artifact right now. After everything in this long and insane journey, this book is how we have reached you.

Chapter 49

$$C_0 = 1, C_{n+1} = (4n+2)C_n / (n+2)$$

Nothing that is worth knowing can be taught.

Oscar Wilde

On a base dug into the surface of the Moon, you might not expect to find a sequestered garden where light and shade, marble and trees, life and death are so balanced, so respectfully interlaced, that you feel you are in a holy place.

Yet, there it lies still. The designers must have been both human and Xixian. There was too much there from the human heart – the quiet fountains, the overhanging branches, the marbled columns approached by grass-shrouded marbled footpaths – this could not be from the alien souls of the Xix. But the realization of the place, the amazing simulation of Earth's atmosphere-filtered sunlight, the acceleration of growth in the towering beeches that could only have been planted a few years before, the slight increase in gravity that spoke of alien technology used sparingly in this base – these had the fingerprints of the Xix all over them.

It was perhaps the most beautiful synergy of human and alien work that I had ever seen. Soft shadows from a spring morning dappled the green grass in front of me with intertwined patterns from the branches and leaves. I stepped softly on the overgrown marbled path, walking silently, solemnly toward a single raised platform of stone. Resting on top and in the center of a marble slab that capped the polished granite was a golden bowl filled with fragrant oil. Floating on the oil was a wick embedded in a light material, perhaps cork sandwiched between two golden pieces of metal in a circular shape. The wick burned softly and steadily over the sea of hydrocarbons.

I knelt down and bowed my head. Using my second sight, I read the words my blind eyes could not: Richard Cross, 2060-2094, *His Memory is Eternal.* So simple, and all the more powerful for it.

"It's time, Richard." I was whispering. "We're going to try once more today. I've found him. He'll tell our story right."

With the work of the Xixian scientists finished, our new experiences with the Orb stitching us more tightly together, and our clumsy apprenticeship in exploring minds of the past, we were ready. Limited time and danger had focused our efforts. Already we had repelled two more Dram warship attacks. From newly deployed Xixian sentries hidden from the Dram, reports spoke of a third armada being amassed—the largest one yet. They were determined to destroy us on the Moon. Even if they did not know what we plotted, they suspected I was here, and that was enough.

I was not so concerned about the Dram ships and weapons —I knew how to handle those with the power of the Orb. Something more nebulous was eating at my mind. The last attack had been different. I had more trouble altering space-time to block the attacks. There was interference, and I could localize the source to the Dram ships. *Something* was fighting me at this new level, in the arena of space and time. But I had no knowledge of my enemy. Creature or machine? One or many? Destroyed or returning? Right now, I held the upper hand. But would it last? What was this new challenge from the Dram? Would I soon be overwhelmed? I didn't know how much time we had left.

We needed a catalyst, a place where a small initial input of energy into Earth Before would turn into a chain reaction. This was where we would push the first domino, be the butterfly wings in America that cause a typhoon in Australia. If there were an America or Australia left. If there were left even a single, elegant butterfly still in existence.

Even after we settled on finding a few *receptive* minds, we were still so clumsy that we tread very lightly. We remembered the problems of our first attempts. We stumbled around lightly, breaking through barriers of space and time, trying to focus on the minds and energies in the shadows of *before* that flitted past our awareness. Initially, we barely made contact.

But then, *such disasters*. Like a bull in a china shop, we smashed and broke and cut ourselves and others in the process. The dangers to my mind were real, and I spent one week in a coma when our efforts went awry, when I entered too deeply into the wrong mind and was nearly consumed. It took the concerted efforts of the Reader ensemble to call me back again. Slowly, painfully, we increased our mastery. Soon I could visit and enter the past minds, interact with them, and return with my health and sanity intact. *But the minds of those I reached!*

My first serious contacts were still so crude. My skills in this work, and, as importantly, my knowledge and intuition of human psychology, were only very rudimentary. Here I was, a seventeen-year-old girl whose life experiences consisted of the absurd tale you have read, trying to mentally contact minds in the human past that were as different and diverse from her own as could be imagined. As in human antiquity, many believed themselves insane when I spoke to them. Many times my thoughts were twisted and garbled by these minds or rejected as voices, demons, or stray thoughts and never pursued. And some minds shattered with the impact, leaving institutionalized wrecks behind, or human vegetables in place of once-whole persons.

I did this. *I* risked them, wrecked them, and wrecked them again and again in my efforts to find a way. Slowly, I learned. I learned the subtleties of human thought, human internal deliberation, inspirations, belief, and motivation. I learned when to sense the fragility of a mind, to know when it was strong enough to handle what I had to give it and when it was not. In the end as I perfected my skills, I learned how to direct these minds toward the course I desired, and to do so in a way that left them completely unaware that I had been there at all.

Now I must finish what I left unexplained in the beginning of this book. Now I must tie together what I have done and what I am trying to do. Now everything must come together.

The sounds of the fountains floated above the soft whispering of the leaves as an artificial breeze blew through the beeches. Water trickling, trees quietly speaking, everything still before the monument to the Reader who had helped guide the Resistance, who had given up his life for that cause. I felt the grass on either side of me, breathed in deep the fresh air. The echo of Earth through space and time.

Prayerful.

Chapter 50

$\aleph_0, \aleph_1, \aleph_2 \ldots \aleph_\aleph$

The eternal silence of these infinite spaces terrifies me.

Blaise Pascal

The fear of infinity is a form of myopia that destroys the possibility of seeing the actual infinite, even though it in its highest form has created and sustains us, and in its secondary transfinite forms occurs all around us and even inhabits our minds.

Georg Cantor

In the end, it was so iconic, that it almost made me laugh.

I walked down the corridor to the new wing built onto the Moon base by the Xixian crews. An area the size of what was once Brooklyn devoted to the power plants and equipment required for this grand experiment. Waythrel opened the door and I stepped in, looking around in shock. Really, it was almost funny.

Imagine an ancient Greek amphitheater, you know, the ones where there are rows and rows of curved benches ascending. The room was like that, with layers of a strange material rising from a center point, like a great satellite dish. At the focus of the room, maybe one hundred feet carved deeply into the Moon, was a chair. And boy, what a chair!

As if going for the greatest stylistic contrast, the chair, a composite of enormous amounts of instrumentation of Xixian design, wires and circuitry, even organic technology, was pitch-black. This showed up wonderfully against the nearly pure white of the material used to build the amphitheater. I didn't ask why.

I was led down to the focal point and strapped in. It gave me shivers remembering my torture at the hands of the Sortax representative on Earth Before, at a time that seemed centuries ago after all that had happened to me. Initially, I did argue with them about my Red Sox hat. They said it had to come off, as special sensors were to be placed on the giant bald patch, the great ostrich egg-sized protrusion from my tumor in the back of my head. The hat would interfere. Finally, I gave in and let them place the bowl-like device over my head with numerous cords running out of it and into the machinery. My hat I held in my lap.

So, there I was, a seventeen-year-old freak of nature, sitting in an obsidian chair in the center of a giant dish designed to amplify and focus gravitons from and to my tumor. Bowl on head, hat clutched like a teddy bear in hands, my porcelain-white skin shining next to the black chair and black robes I still wore. My flaming red hair, now long and halfway down my back, hung loosely, appearing to extend out from the black bowl and wires, cascading over my shoulders and arms. This is what I had come to—child of nearby charred Earth, growing legend in a galaxy, centered in a seat of strange power of alien design.

I had traveled from my parents' farm, under knife, through space and torture and dungeons and violence. I had seen the universe as no one had ever seen it. I had become blind and deformed. I had opened the Orb. But even as I was to join with hundreds of other Readers and form that strange, communal consciousness that empowered our travel through space and time, in my heart, I still felt alone. So alone that I still clung to the hat of a boy I knew only briefly before he died.

How could I let anyone near? I had no family. My own kind had betrayed me, mutilated me, and then I had eaten them in return to stay alive. Finally, I had sacrificed all of them that I might live, all to save aliens often so hideous I still shuddered when I looked at them. I was the corrupted Messiah. The anti-Christ. The alien human. Always, to the end, the freak of nature.

So, here I sat, at the bottom of this technological marvel of a hole. Group mind notwithstanding, I was its homunculus, its center, and without me it could not be. Bright orange and white me in a black chair. Ready to reach out to the universe through space and time and literally change history. If I could.

But as alone as I felt, I could not do this alone. The final players had yet to make their appearance. Finally, they must take hold of this dream and make it real and play their necessary part. The time had come for them to fully understand. The ranks of our choir to be massively filled.

It is now *your* time, Reader.

Chapter 51

$$\dot{x}_i = \sum_j w_{ij} x_j - x_i \sum_{ij} w_{ij} x_j$$

The future needed service, not pity, not piety; but in the past lay darkness, confusion, waste, and all the cramped primitive minds, bewildered, torturing one another in their stupidity, yet one and all in some unique manner, beautiful.

Olaf Stapledon

I have lived in the mind of this author for a while now. It's taken *forever* to get him to write this story, to listen to me, to stop putting it off, to neglect his other duties and tell this crazy tale. I'm bone-tired of massaging his mind, dealing with his personality quirks, his dreadful insecurity problems. But it is done.

After destroying many minds, and after many minds destroyed my words by taking the threads of my story and spinning them into books and films of shapes glorious or ghastly, yet all distortions, I finally found a mind that could survive my manipulations and tell my story effectively.

Of course, *effectively* is different from *accurately*. Looking over the words here, I am aghast at the absurdities that have crept into the story, the distortions of ideas, events, alien worlds and beings, chronology. But the main message is here, the terrible loss of Earth, the power of Readers, and the plan we have to save our planet—here, for the first time, the story in essence *is true*.

And that is the only point. I could never reach all the Readers of the past one at a time. But if I could find a medium to spread the story so that many Readers over time would come to know it, and if I could use this author of your time to make you believe, then perhaps, *just perhaps*, you might take that final step.

And you must. You *must* remember my story, my pain, my struggle, the terrible place humanity finds itself in, both in your time as slaves, and in mine, as nearly extinct. Please, I have never begged for anything like I am begging you now – *believe in me*.

I know it seems impossible. *Ridiculous*. The author himself does not really believe it at all. But *you* must. Even for a few moments, you must believe and channel that belief into prayer. If you don't like "prayer," then meditate, think deeply, focus – your energies must be channeled, you latent Readers.

I'm sure that you've never had a book beg you to believe its story before, let alone ask you to pray with conviction with all your heart and mind towards the future. *But you must.* Only if enough of you do so can the handful of Readers among you become a large enough number to provide us with the power we need to change history.

What history will we change? This is the object of your prayer, the place you must focus all your thought toward. The Dram altered the course of a large asteroid and sent it plunging to Earth. You must seek to change that event, to push the asteroid off the course the Dram had calculated so that it will fly by and miss Earth. That is all we need from you. A little push, and the belief, the trust, to focus your thoughts toward that reality. Your energies will be channeled to me by the Xix, and I will spin them into a force that will bridge time and space and impact momentum.

It doesn't matter when this happens. You could pray earnestly tonight, next month, three years from now. Others could pray in ten or twenty years. The threads of time do not need to come from the same spool. We only need to collect them and weave them together to create a force to warp the space-time in front of a rushing asteroid and send it harmlessly off course, sparing billions of lives and giving the human species, and all of life on Earth, another chance.

I nearly despair to convince you. I must plead my case through the mind of another person who imperfectly transfers my words to print, who himself has not lived through our time of terrible tragedy. How can I touch your heart so that you will be moved? Had you seen it all, experienced it, and stood before me in this instant, I know many of you would fall on your knees and pray that we may be delivered from this nightmare. Just a single viewing of Earth, the charred and lava-stained mutilation alongside our Moon, would forever change you. But here, in the pages of this sterile book that can be tossed aside with no repercussions to you or your life – *how do I reach you?*

My life, my losses, my pains, my dreams, my hopes—you have walked with me through them to this point. You have shared in the wonder and horror of a universe that exists right outside your ability to see it. *Faith is the confidence in things not seen.* Belief reaches across the finite, limited powers of our senses and minds to cross the chasm between what we can't see and what is *true*.

If your heart has been touched by our pain and our love, then what isn't seen has been made real to you, and we exist within the awareness of your soul. You can *feel* me. If you do, and know within yourself who I am, I now ask you to *believe* me and take this final, crucial step. If you cannot, all will be lost.

The story must spread for there to be any hope. We need you. This is my last attempt. There will be no more minds touched, no more stories or plays or films inspired by my efforts. The cold is creeping over me at last. It is covering all of us. One by one, we are falling into listlessness. Perhaps it is simply an understandable depression. But I feel otherwise. I feel it deep within. *The withering of the branches.* We don't have the heart to continue anymore. Our love binds us together, but together still we are ill. Our end comes.

Don't let us die. Don't let Earth fall into fire and final darkness. We have this grand Xixian machine set to receive. *Send to us, please.*

Can it hurt you to reach out with faith, just this once? The cause is just. Our fate, terrible. Our need, more than desperate.

Reader, *dare to believe*. There is nothing more to say, no story left to tell. Our fate is in your hands.

The final step in this journey—*is yours.*

This is not the end.
It is not even the beginning of the end.
But it is, perhaps, the end of the beginning.

Winston Churchill, 1942

Erec Stebbins is a biomedical researcher who writes political and international thrillers, science fiction, narrated storybooks, and more. He was born in the Midwest, his mother a clinical psychologist and his father a professor of Romance languages at the University of Nebraska in Lincoln. His father's specialty, old Romance languages and their literature, is the source of the unusual spelling of his middle name: "Erec." It is an Old French spelling, taken from an Arthurian romance by Chrétien de Troyes written around 1170: *Érec et Énide*.

He has pursued diverse interests over the course of his life, including science, music, drama, and writing. His academic path focused on science, and he received a degree in physics from Oberlin College in 1992, and a PhD in biochemistry from Cornell University in 1999. He has worked for several decades studying the structure of biological macromolecules involved in disease.

BOOK 2, WRITER

"A WORK OF LITERARY FICTION THAT TRANSCENDS ITS GENRE. READ THIS NOVEL. IMMEDIATELY."
—Portland Book Review

Writer, Daughter Of Time, Book 2

From hatred, *Love***. From many,** *One.* A scifi epic about the tragic destiny of profoundly star-crossed lovers with a galaxy's fate in their hands.

Daughter of Time SCIFI Trilogy

"WORKS THAT NURTURE WONDER AND BREAK HEARTS"

—Foreword Reviews

FOREWORD BOOK OF THE YEAR FINALIST

READER, WRITER, and MAKER: Speculative fiction trilogy with time travel, aliens, metaphysical mysteries, action, adventure, cosmology, cybernetics, religion, and romance!

"VISIONARY" and *"ENTHRALLING"*

—authors *Richard Bunning and Norm Hamilton*

HARD TIME SCIFI Series

Where survival is the meaning of life. A speculative fiction serial of adventure novellas set in a strange and punishing world. In Book 1, **METAL** a woman finds herself in two different worlds, as two different people. In one she is a criminal, sentenced to a new and terrible punishment. In the other, she is a stranger and then a prophet, granted the visions of God.

INTEL 1 Thrillers: Omnibus, Books 1-4

"STEBBINS IS THE MASTER OF THE THINKING READER'S TECHNO-THRILLER."
—Internet Review of Books

Four Action Packed Political Thrillers. Three Armageddon Scenarios. Two Unusual Love Stories. One Secretive Intelligence Branch.

"A MONSTER NEW TALENT IN THE THRILLER GENRE."
—Allan Leverone, author of *Final Vector*

www.ingramcontent.com/pod-product-compliance
Lightning Source LLC
Chambersburg PA
CBHW022019240626
47154CB00007B/2165

* 9 7 8 0 6 1 5 7 6 3 8 5 9 *